IN THE LAND OF THE BLIND

A Novel

Robert Schulman

TO SHERRY DAVIS,
For making me go the distance,
and traveling there with me

PART ONE

OHIO 2012

"Y ou've sent me a message."

"Message? I don't understand," Torman said, truly puzzled. This was just his third session with Karen, a young internist who'd been referred by a colleague.

"Steve, you know what you've done." She looked over at the wastebasket by Torman's bookcase. Torman followed her gaze. He noted her using his given name for the first time.

"Something in the wastebasket?" He began to feel uneasy and needing to focus his attention, as if driving on wet pavement in freezing weather. A discarded envelope sat atop the crumpled papers in the trash.

"The stamp. You wanted me to see the stamp." Torman could see the letters spelling "LOVE" against the stamp's red background.

"You feel there's some meaning to this...something I'm trying to tell you?"

"It seems clear to me. You're telling me you love me."

Now Torman sat up straight. Was she psychotic? How could he have missed that? How should he respond?

"So...you imagine I've put that envelope there so you'd see it."

"I'm not imagining anything. It's right there for me to see."

Torman knew he was floundering. He didn't know how to talk with her in a way that would allow them to explore her feelings without making her sound crazy or feel terribly misunderstood. "I think it's important to look at why you think I'd communicate in this way, by putting that stamp within your view." That was the best he could do. His mouth felt dry. He saw her face cloud over.

"*Did* you put it there so I'd see it?" She waited for his answer. She might as well have asked if he still beat his dog. He didn't feel he could say yes, since that wasn't true and would likely fuel her erotic delusion. And a "no" would be crushing and rejecting. Where was the middle ground? Not in Torman's sight.

"No, I did not. But the stamp is there, and we can look at how this has affected you and learn more about you."

"You're an asshole. And a liar." Karen got up and left, slamming shut his door.

Torman, too agitated to write a note in her chart, replayed the session, wondering how he might have responded differently. Maybe he should have refused to answer her question, instead insisting they explore her experience. He recalled their two previous sessions, searching for clues to explain what happened today. What he knew for certain was that she would not be back.

As Torman ate lunch that day at his desk, he thought more about Karen. He found himself staring at the faded Persian rug stretching from his desk to his analytic couch. Out of nowhere he recalled Philip, the hapless main character in Maugham's "Of Human Bondage," a man who puzzles over the meaning of another character's remark that life's meaning is found in a Persian rug. Eventually, the message in that comment dawns on Philip: there is no meaning to be discovered in all that complexity. That's how Torman experienced so many of his patients, full of details and patterns but ultimately unfathomable, mysterious. At least there was order in much of Torman's life, including his office with its simple oak writing desk and matching file cabinet, its twin bookshelves along one wall, framed art prints of Rothko and Hopper, a framed photograph of Freud standing on a street corner, cigar in hand, face partially shaded, and his medical school diploma. He did not shun color, choosing red for his couch and a vivid royal blue for his desk chair. Clerestory windows along one wall invited natural light into this cloistered retreat.

Torman didn't look like your typical psychoanalyst. Not comfortable in dark suits, he preferred khaki pants and casual shirts, usually with the sleeves rolled up. Nor did he sport a beard, the "exoskeletal defense" (an expression used by one of his supervisors) so popular among psychiatrists. Short and built like a rugby player, he seemed out of his element settled in a comfortable leather armchair attending to the emotional state of his patients. And sitting still proved a challenge for someone who worked out regularly in a gym and jogged daily. A high school knee injury ended his participation in contact sports, but weight lifting provided an outlet for his energy and compensated for the loss of team athletics. Torman had trained himself to skip lunch, using the time to shed inertia as he walked briskly from his office to a nearby park.

What patients noticed in their initial appointment were his eyes. "Paul Newman eyes," his mother always remarked. Maybe that's why he favored blue shirts. He wasn't vain but knew his eyes were striking. Not fussy, he kept his coal-colored, thick hair short and without a part. He liked being able to run his fingers through his hair and being done with it. A horizontal scar on his chin, the result of flipping over his bike's handlebars at age seven, and an eyetooth out of alignment in an otherwise orderly row of teeth, prevented him from being described as flawless. A former girlfriend once referred to his "rugged good looks" in a Valentine card.

All in all, Torman resembled a man more likely to settle conflicts with his brawn than his brains.

Torman and his wife Claire lived in a 1920's Tudor-style house in North Avondale, a Cincinnati neighborhood close to the medical center and home to an embarrassingly large population of psychiatrists. We're a bunch of lemmings, Torman thought, all huddled around our current or former analysts. Torman's analyst, Dr. Saul Perlman, lived one block over, though he rarely caught sight of him. Torman had terminated his treatment around the time of their purchasing the house, not long after the housing market crash in 2008. Strapped for cash, he and Claire, recently married, slowly managed to fill their home with furnishings. Over the course of three years, he painted every room in the house, became acquainted with every creak and moan and clang, caulked and sealed openings, and learned how little he knew about maintaining a home. But he loved its solidness, the steeply pitched roof with its thick slate shingles, the copper gutters, the leaded glass windows, the gleam of its oak floors. Even if he was a lemming, there was something comforting being amidst so many psychiatrists. They spoke a common language, shared the same burden of keeping others' secrets, and experienced exclusion and distrust from the rest of the medical profession. So, these physician pariahs, the lower castes of medicine, created a ghetto for themselves in liberal, integrated North Avondale.

Over the last two years, Torman had listened to his analytic patient, Eric Silver, talk about the condolence letters he wrote and prided himself on. Eric, tall, lanky, in his late twenties, spoke of how he wanted to "touch the heart of the griever." Torman tried exploring why this condolence writing was so important to him.

Trying to contain his impatience, Torman prepared to put pen to notebook as he asked, not for the first time, what Eric hoped for in writing these letters.

"It feels really good when I get a response from someone I've sent a condolence letter. The widow of my high school biology teacher sent me a long letter thanking me and telling me all about her husband's life. There were all kinds of rumors about him, but nobody at my school knew anything certain about his private life. He emigrated from China when he was 14, and there was all this mystery surrounding his life. In her letter, she mentioned becoming his student shortly after coming to Arizona from Japan ten years ago. That would've been 2002, a little after he left my high school to teach at a university there. I've even thought of visiting her. Maybe I just want to peek into his life, meet the woman he married, find out what he was really like. I imagined she would be really short and offer me tea and make little bowing movements and I'd bow back." After a pause, Torman, who'd begun fidgeting and felt an impulse to knock off 50 push-ups, commented that Eric seemed excited talking about visiting her and wondered what the excitement was about. "I guess I felt I'd somehow moved her...that a door was slightly open, inviting me in."

"In for what?" Torman felt himself getting pulled in as he leaned closer to hear Eric's reply.

"For some kind of intimacy. She might share her sadness, tell me how hard it is to bear losing him."

"And you'd feel close to her?"

"Yes...I even...thought we might start a relationship, that we'd write back and forth or speak on the phone."

"Are there others in your life about whom you're curious and want to know more and feel closer to?"

"Well, I'm curious about you. I know analysts keep their lives private from patients, but it's frustrating that this is such a one-sided relationship, with my doing all the talking, lying here and staring up at the ceiling, and you just sitting back there, out of sight, pretty much silent most of the time."

"We can learn a lot by taking a look at your curiosity, at what you imagine about me and want to know about me." After a silence, Torman added the usual closer: "Well, let's stop here." Eric swung his long legs off the couch, hauling his 6 foot frame upright, and glanced back at Torman, whose tree trunk frame remained rooted in place.

"See you tomorrow," said Eric. Torman responded with a slight smile and nod.

❖ ❖ ❖

Torman ruminated about setting the record for taking the most years to graduate from the psychoanalytic institute. At least, he figured, those bastards let him do unsupervised cases, like Eric, now that Torman was in his tenth year. Claire, who'd early on been supportive of his becoming a psychoanalyst, had grown increasingly critical of his career path.

"Why're you putting up with all their bullshit?" she asked. "They're like a bunch of fossils, extinct with absolutely zero awareness of it. Cincinnati's the tar pit of psychoanalysis and you're stuck in it too. You're the only psychiatrist in your class. The others are a couple of social workers and a psychologist. That's got to tell you something."

Torman found it difficult to defend his decision to persist in his analytic training. Yet he remained enamored with the psychoanalytic task of delving deeply into the mind of another person, even though his own analysis had proved less than illuminating (something Claire never failed to mention when criticizing psychoanalysis). He tended to blame himself, rather than the training, for his slow progress and frustrations.

Early on, Torman had described for Claire all the steps required to graduate from the psychoanalytic institute. "As hard as law school was," she said, "at least we were treated like adults. A final exam in each class determined our grades. Period. But you guys have to beg for permission to start new cases, you have to turn in regular progress notes, and you have to see a supervisor weekly on each case. And, tell me, why do they call your supervised cases 'control cases?'"

Torman laughed. "I have no idea. But 'control' is the operant word. They certainly like having control over us candidates."

By the time Torman had finished his psychiatric residency and applied to the psychoanalytic institute, psychoanalysis was well on its way to becoming a footnote in psychiatric training programs. Advances in pharmacologic treatments for mental disorders and the advent of briefer, more affordable forms of psychotherapy contributed to the demise of psychoanalysis. However, in Cincinnati, psychoanalysis still reigned as a significant influence, another example of Mark Twain's observation that Cincinnati was always twenty years behind the times (and hence the place to be when the end of the world came).

In spite of Claire's questioning his motivation (and sanity), the longer Torman spent trying to reach his goal, the harder it was to quit and walk away. He reminded himself of the experiences that led to his desire to become an analyst. During his first year as a psychiatric resident, he attended a weekly case conference in which a patient from an in-patient ward was presented to a senior faculty member who then interviewed the patient in front of the residents. On one occasion, an emeritus professor with a long career as a psychoanalyst ran the conference. Residents liked to pick really psychotic patients for the old analysts still hanging on like ancient relics in the psych department's attic, hoping either to prove how inadequate they were at managing truly sick patients or to marvel at how skillful they were at bringing the patients' inner worlds into clear view. The analyst, wearing a conservative three-piece suit instead of the white lab coat favored by the younger, more biologically oriented faculty, asked about the patient's experiences in an open-ended way that allowed him to begin describing his emotional life. What had been a hostile, paranoid individual transformed into someone with a painful past that the patient had been trying to deny and distance himself from. His haughtiness and hostility, described in detail by his treating psychiatrist before the interview, melted away as the analyst gently explored the experiences that led to his hospital admission. What emerged was overwhelming despair and fear of annihilation of his very self. "The voices became so loud," the patient said, "that I had to hold myself tight to keep myself from disappearing." Not just Torman, but all the residents, even those antagonistic to psychoanalysis, sat stunned and silent. The minute the patient left the room, they broke out in spontaneous applause. Afterwards, Torman confronted Jacob Feldman, a fellow resident especially critical of psychoanalysis. All the residents referred to him as "Dr. Feldman," never by his first name, and joked that he slept in his white lab coat.

"So what did you think of the case conference?" Torman asked.

"Look, Steve, I'll grant you it was quite a performance, but of what use? You could have such conversations with that schizophrenic for the next twenty years and he'd never change one iota without the appropriate medication."

"Perhaps, but how do you gain trust in patients, and a willingness to take medication, if you can't find ways to have meaningful conversations with them, to gain their trust."

"I educate my patients about their disease and the reasons why medication is of paramount importance. I explain possible side effects and my willingness to work with them to deal with such problems. If they want to talk with someone about their emotions and their past, I refer them to a therapist."

"But if *you* were the patient, if you were, say, really depressed and anxious, wouldn't you rather see someone who could not only diagnose and prescribe but also would listen and try to understand you?"

Placing his hand on Torman's shoulder, he said, "Steve, this is the era of neuroscience, the 'decade of the brain,' remember? Don't waste your time and effort trying to find meaning in psychotic nonsense." And with that, Dr. Feldman, lab coat flapping, wheeled around to attend to more important business.

◆ ◆ ◆

So far, Torman had completed all the requirements for graduation with the exception of having a "successful" case. Three years ago he believed he had one, but in his final write-up, he acknowledged that the patient never used the couch, insisting he had to sit up so he could see Torman. In spite of all his efforts to analyze his patient's refusal to lie on the couch, he never succeeded in getting that to happen. His case rejected by the institute, Torman tried imploring the relevant committee members to reconsider their decision but was turned away. Decision final. It didn't matter that his patient started treatment as an inhibited, unemployed young man living in his parents' basement and ended it a married, Ph.D chemist with a young child. Seven years down the drain, and the only reason for the rejection was his patient's refusal to lie down. Candidates were expected to be more Freudian than Freud, to never deviate from the institute's rigid views of orthodox psychoanalytic practice. Every time he thought about it, Torman fumed.

This unexpected setback sent Torman reeling back to his former analyst for another go-around. The only positive result from that experience was Dr. Perlman's advice to seek supervision from someone outside the institute. He never did get Perlman to say why he offered this recommendation, but Torman wanted to believe that Perlman's desire to help him overrode his adherence to the customary analytic practice of not giving advice. This unsolicited suggestion, quite surprising yet appreciated, led Torman to pick Dr. Leonard Gold, an analyst in

Chicago he'd heard speak once at a conference. He could still evoke Dr. Gold's commanding presence at the lectern and his refreshing mix of erudition, common sense and humor. Reflecting on a clinical case presentation by a colleague, Dr. Gold had remarked, "What brings patients to treatment, after all, is the desire to feel better." That straightforward comment stuck with Torman. Blocking out an entire day, he flew from Cincinnati to Chicago for a 45 minute session. After Torman presented Susan Edwards, his control case most likely to terminate successfully, Dr. Gold, surrounded by a jumble of books, papers, journals and half-empty styrofoam coffee cups, offered a suggestion that Torman found very useful in helping Susan feel understood. He and his patient had spent a few weeks looking at her uneasiness about a party she and her husband were hosting for his co-workers and their partners. Torman described for Dr. Gold how she'd become increasingly frustrated with Torman's efforts to understand what the party meant to her. Eventually, she'd lapsed into silence and, for his part, Torman, equally frustrated, lapsed into a silence of his own. Dr. Gold, sounding somewhat exasperated, said, "Steve, haven't you ever given a party? Don't you remember how nervous you got, wondering if people would talk and enjoy themselves, whether the food was good, and so on...you need to acknowledge that first before you can explore any deeper meanings this party may have for her." Torman felt foolish for not seeing that himself, for trying so hard to dive head first into a hasty exploration of her unconscious fears and fantasies. He realized that Perlman never empathized in that way with him and that in case conferences in the institute no one seemed to focus on the importance of first appreciating patients' more immediate experiences.

Grateful for the help, Torman, after two more trips to Chicago, asked if they could do supervision over the phone. After all, the trip to Chicago meant cancelling a whole day of appointments and paying for plane fare to Chicago. Getting "gold from Gold" (as Dr. Gold put it) was becoming a very expensive endeavor. To Torman's relief, Dr. Gold agreed. Torman knew that this supervision, sought without the institute's knowledge, needed to remain secret to avoid censure, even though Dr. Gold, an author of books and scholarly articles, was well regarded in the field. It was not as though Torman was cheating, but his seeking outside help would be seen as undercutting the authority and competence of the local institute. Though he generally disdained being devious, Torman understood the risk of insulting the powers that be.

Torman also realized he could benefit from supervision on Eric's case, but he saw Susan's analysis as his ticket to graduation. And, besides, Eric's treatment was an unsupervised analysis, so no matter how well he progressed, the institute wouldn't consider his analysis as fulfilling any of the requirements for graduation.

Torman thought about why Eric talked so much about his condolence letters. He suspected it was a way of lulling him into a state of boredom, of keeping hidden, from himself as well as from Torman, more threatening feelings. Torman believed he needed to find a way to use his impatience and boredom to understand Eric better, rather than just trying to hide his reaction to Eric's description of his compulsive yet well-intentioned epistolary output. Not an easy task. He yearned for something more immediate, more heartfelt. Hell, he thought, a goddam tear would be welcome.

Eric came to Torman almost three years ago. Besides his lanky frame, Torman noted how Eric's clothing suggested a man unconcerned with fashion. It wasn't that he appeared disheveled; rather, he seemed to wear the same outfit (button down shirt, tie, sport coat, slacks) in different shades of brown and grey. Always neat and clean but designed, consciously or unconsciously, to avoid drawing attention to himself. Torman was not surprised to see Eric arrive one day in the office parking lot in a tan Toyota Camry, a dependable, practical car totally devoid of personality. Torman suspected that beneath this Clark Kent facade lurked a much livelier, more vibrant self: not Superman but someone keeping under wraps his enthusiasms and ambitions. Eric resembled a man likely to accept whatever came his way rather than taking charge of his life and making things happen. The adjective that came to Torman's mind was "malleable."

Eric entered treatment a few months after his parents died in a car accident. Initially, Torman met with Eric twice a week for a few months, focusing on his reaction to the loss. His parents were hit head-on by a drunk driver, who suffered only minor injuries. It was his fourth DUI. Though Eric wished for the death penalty, the driver got 15 years in prison, the maximum sentence. Eric attended every court appearance and recounted in his sessions his fantasies of revenge on the man who never glanced his way and whose admission of remorse sounded rehearsed. "I imagined," Eric said on one occasion, "tying him down and slowly running my car over his legs, then over his stomach, and finally over his head. In my mind he was stone sober and his death agonizing."

Other issues emerged in Eric's treatment: ambivalence towards his controlling, rigid mother and unhappiness with his decision to enter the family business, a scrap metal firm founded by his paternal grandfather. Torman suggested meeting four times a week and lying on the couch. After mulling this over for a few weeks, Eric agreed to convert from twice weekly psychotherapy to psychoanalysis.

In Torman's opinion, Eric was a good candidate for analysis: bright, motivated, introspective, troubled by long-standing conflicts and inhibitions but not suffering from psychosis, and able to afford such an expensive commitment. However, Torman knew it might be difficult for Eric to transition from twice a week therapy to lying on a couch four times a week. Not only would he lose the face to face contact, but Eric was also likely to miss the more supportive and directive elements of his initial treatment, such as Torman's encouraging him to attend all the court hearings of the drunk driver responsible for his parents' deaths and asking Eric to bring in letters of condolence that family and friends had sent him and to read them aloud to Torman. Psychoanalysis relied primarily on interpretations of the patient's inner world, without resorting to advice giving and other supportive measures. Like moving, Torman thought, from a soft living room couch to a hard church pew.

Torman saw Eric as someone he could imagine as a friend if he wasn't his patient. Eric read a lot and thought about life in a way that most men seemed to avoid, preferring instead to talk, if they talked at all, about sports and cars but rarely about their internal world. Torman sensed similarities between them, perhaps especially Eric's feeling stuck in his life, aware of some unhappiness but unable to discern what was missing. Maybe, Torman wondered, he felt a sibling concern for Eric, an older brother's wish to help his younger sibling move ahead in life. After all, Torman was an only child and envied his friends who had siblings. He even entertained fantasies of telling Eric how to find a girlfriend, how to overcome his shyness.

The couch Torman used for analysis was the no-frills kind: no arms or back, just a flat surface with a wedge-like pillow at one end that sported a clean, extra-large Kleenex for the patient's head. (Torman liked the story about one of the senior analysts in town who, when he forgot to place a Kleenex on the pillow, pointed to the tissue box and instructed his befuddled patient to "make your own bed.") The vibrant red color of his couch prompted one patient, a man who, it turned out, had many secrets squirreled away, to label the couch "the hot seat." It was almost universal that analysands starting treatment experienced considerable unease the first time lying on the couch. Susan had felt very self-conscious, fidgeting and occasionally tilting her head back to try to get a glimpse of Torman. Eric recalled Woody Allen on his analyst's couch in "Annie Hall," then fell silent, finally admitting it was really weird staring at the ceiling and wondering what he should say.

When Torman lay on Perlman's couch, he occasionally wished he had a tiny mirror—like the one dentists use to peer into the recesses of one's mouth—to sneak a look at his analyst's face in unguarded moments. Entire sessions ended with his analyst saying nothing more than an occasional "Ummhmm" and "Let's stop here." Just thinking about that made Torman furious. Sometimes Torman imagined his analyst's silence reflected how boring and mundane Torman's ramblings were. And yet even such negative thoughts about himself still led him to the notion that his analyst should have challenged him to go deeper. So that, too, made him angry. Most of all he regretted not questioning his analyst about his extended silences. Instead, Torman was a "good" patient: compliant with the rules (saying whatever came to mind, paying the bill, showing up for appointments) and accepting the sterility of the experience. He never realized there wasn't enough life-supporting oxygen in his analyst's office until it was over.

Early in his treatment, Eric talked about the family business. "My grandfather, as a young man, started Silver Iron and Steel Company, a scrap metal business, and it's been run by our family ever since. I manage the Cincinnati branch while my two cousins run the offices in Hamilton and Middletown. In the summer months, as a teenager, I worked in the yard with Johnny, a very friendly guy who seemed ageless but for all I knew was really old. I ran errands and sorted through scrap metal in search of copper. Johnny called me "Doc" because he knew I'd be heading to college some day. He was careful not to swear too much around me and seemed to enjoy my company. The image I have of him is of his beaming smile and wiry build, always moving, surrounded by piles of rusty pipes, auto parts, appliances, and junk of unknown origin. My dad loved the scrap business. He had fond memories of working beside his father, bidding on scrap, calling on customers, eating lunch at their favorite diner. There was never any question that my dad would enter the family business. I think my father assumed I'd join the company, though he never pressured me to do that. But I had mixed feelings about it. In college, I majored in English because I liked reading novels. I thought about becoming a teacher but couldn't get excited about that. I guess the path of least resistance was joining the family business. I kind of just fell into it. Shortly after graduating college, I sat down with Dad and said I wanted to work with him. I remember how his face lit up. Johnny greeted me my first day with his broad smile and joked about my becoming a 'suit guy.' I acted like I was offended and told him I was going to keep my eye on him. He said, 'You do that, Doc. And come join me when you get sick of sitting on your ass.'"

"I have the impression that after your dad died it became harder for you to remain committed to the business."

"Yeah…It's not the same. Both Dad and I valued our time away from Mom and her scrutiny. The office was our escape. We got really close once I started working there. I've kept Dad's office pretty much as it was. I still have trouble looking at his handwritten post-it notes on his desk and the geezer sweater he kept on his coat rack, one of those LL Bean cardigans. Whenever he wore it, I'd start talking in my Mr. Rogers' voice. Dad never exercised much but he had one of those hand-grip exercisers on his desk. He always stressed how important a strong handshake was in business, and I'd see him in there doing reps with it. In a way, keeping his office intact makes it almost as hard to think of leaving the company as his actually being there did. The thought, though, of buying and selling scrap for the rest of my life…I don't know, it just seems like a gigantic waste."

Jesus, thought Torman, another worthless supervisory session with Dr. Steward, who insisted Torman come every week so he could keep tabs on Susan, the control case he'd supervised for the last 5 years. Like an obese Buddha, barely able to get up from his leather Eames chair, Dr. Steward offered the occasional unhelpful comment. It was never clear how to translate these remarks into ideas Torman could offer to Susan. Torman wanted to know how to talk to her, how to promote deeper introspection. Dr. Steward pointed out her defenses, how she repressed awareness of her feelings and memories. But he remained vague about what to do with such observations, as if it were all too obvious to mention.

Torman recalled one of Steward's former analysands, a nebbishy psychiatrist who confided to Torman that he once complained of a headache while on the couch and Steward, unbidden, got him an aspirin and a glass of water. He claimed that was the most significant moment in his analysis. Torman thought what a sad commentary that was on the whole analytic enterprise and wondered what Steward would say if he told him he'd done the same thing with Susan. The image that came to mind was of Steward's reacting with horror at this act of kindness and criticizing Torman for not interpreting the patient's headache (or for not remaining silent). Torman figured established analysts can get away with that kind of behavior but accuse candidates like Torman with committing acts of gratification, the ultimate sin for an analyst. One senior analyst, in the rare act of presenting one of his own cases to Torman's class, confided he'd sent a gift to his analysand's newborn child. No wonder his patients loved him. A nice guy, a fucking human being, Torman thought. But the candidates were supposed to be interpretive machines, blank slates emitting only the light of their patients' unconscious into the room. Torman knew candidates often hid from supervisors some of the things they said or did with their patients. That wasn't something he could do; he'd always been uncomfortable with deception. Plus, how would he learn if he weren't as truthful as possible?

Perhaps Torman should have quit after the first seminar he attended at the institute. With each new class of candidates, Dr. Randolph Schmidt, rumored to be well north of ninety, gave the introductory lecture, never to be seen again. As Schmidt entered the classroom, Torman could almost smell the mothballs. Wearing a charcoal three-piece suit, the standard uniform of an analyst, he looked the part except for the Elmer Fudd shoes, most likely prescribed by a podiatrist.

Eyes uplifted to the ceiling, as if conversing with God or Freud (really, one and the same), Schmidt's first words after introducing himself were, "The three hallmarks of psychoanalysis..." A long pause followed, during which the candidate on Torman's left, Stan Sarno, wrote in his notebook, for Torman's benefit, "Here comes the Father, the Son, and the Holy Spirit." Schmidt slowly pivoted around to write on the blackboard, in large, shakily printed letters, "Consistency, Regularity, Predictability."

At that moment, Torman whispered to Stan, "Sounds like a fucking laxative." The two of them spent the rest of the lecture struggling to stifle their laughter. Grateful for the seminar concluding, Torman imagined Schmidt returning to a hermetically sealed chamber to preserve him for another year and another lecture. Looking back, Torman sometimes wondered what his professional life would have looked like had he quit the institute after Schmidt's introductory seminar. He suspected he'd have experienced a lot more freedom and a lot less frustration.

As if frustration with his analytic training wasn't enough to deal with, Torman worried about his dwindling caseload. Some days he had enough open time to go to the gym, work out, shower, and return to the office with time to spare. The social worker in his office suite saw patients all day long, staying till 7 at night and working Saturdays. Torman couldn't get himself to ask people to send him work and disdained the shrinks who bragged about how busy they were and what great work they did. He didn't believe most of them. The training analysts, atop the food chain, managed to stay busy analyzing wannabe analysts like Torman and former patients returning for more treatment.

Every time a patient quit treatment, Torman's mood tanked, and self-doubt tormented him. Some patients simply left a voice message saying they weren't returning. Others announced their unhappiness with treatment, complaining about Torman's lack of direction or lack of caring. He would try to look closely at these complaints, clearly taking them seriously, yet the outcome was almost always the same. They quit. Occasionally he was relieved, as in the case of Karen, the woman convinced he loved her. But most often these drop-outs left Torman feeling like a failure.

Of course, there were patients who felt like a good fit with Torman. That was certainly true with Eric, in spite of his sleep-inducing accounts of condolence letters. Eric didn't question Torman's ability to help him, didn't require reassurances like some of his patients. Absent the demands for quicker results and given Eric's belief of being in good hands, Torman could relax and focus on understanding his patient.

In medical school, it was the psychiatrists, many of whom were psychoanalysts, who inspired him. More than once, he described to Claire how moved he felt watching one of them sit down with a really crazy person brought over from the psychiatric ward, someone he'd never met before, and, in front of 100 medical students, engage the patient in a revealing, often very moving, dialogue. In short order, this bizarre, delusional person talked about how lonely and hopeless he felt. They'd learned how to do this because they'd trained before the era of big pharma and had to rely on talking to make contact with patients. That's what grabbed Torman. He imagined engaging patients in similar conversations, eventually helping them turn their lives around. Naive, perhaps, but the inspiration carried him through the stress of his psychiatric and psychoanalytic training and counterbalanced his frustration with the limits of his own abilities to connect with his patients and his disappointment in his own analysis.

He remembered his mother's dismay upon hearing his decision to become a psychiatrist. Her older brother, Torman's

Uncle Jack, was a surgeon and, in her eyes, could do no wrong. It seemed that everyone in her family looked up to Jack, a man who, in Torman's mind, took for granted the world's admiration of him. Torman had grown up aware of his mother's ambitions for him. Pleasing her brought him satisfaction. His father, by contrast, seemed removed from Torman's life, neither approving nor disapproving. From a young age, Torman learned to seek out his mother's support and encouragement. Torman's becoming a physician clearly pleased her. He recalled overhearing her on the phone, boasting to her sister about his acceptance to medical school. The pride in her voice thrilled him. But his eventual announcement that he planned on becoming a psychiatrist elicited a puzzled, "Why would you choose psychiatry out of all the areas in medicine?" The look on her face was unmistakable, a combination of dismay and incredulity. He tried explaining how inspiring the psychiatrists were on his clinical rotation. She said, "I just don't see how you could throw away all you've learned and sit with people and listen to their emotional problems." That's where the discussion ended. He hid his hurt. Over the years, his mother feigned interest in his career, but Torman knew she felt he'd wasted his medical degree.

Lying with his forearm over his forehead, Eric started his session haltingly, saying Johnny collapsed and died that morning at work. Torman sensed Eric was trying to remain in control of his feelings, and, in a voice he hoped conveyed his concern, asked how he was holding up. Eric noted he was still in shock, describing how a worker from the yard ran to the office and yelled for someone to call 911, Johnny had fallen and wasn't conscious. Eric ran out to find him lying on his back, staring blankly at the sky. The paramedics arrived quickly, performing CPR while they loaded Johnny on a stretcher, and taking off with him in an ambulance, which Eric followed. At the hospital ER, he was pronounced dead.

"I felt totally helpless kneeling by Johnny waiting for the paramedics to arrive. One of the guys tried to do mouth-to-mouth resuscitation, while I pushed down on his chest. But I'd never taken any CPR training. I was afraid I'd do more harm than good. Johnny just seemed so...lifeless, and our efforts pointless..." For a while Eric remained silent, then added how Johnny was second only to his father as a vital connection to the business.

Torman thought how Eric didn't need another death to deal with. He listened as Eric went on to tell stories about Johnny, some of which he'd told before. Torman's favorite was the time Johnny asked him to get a sky hook and sent him into the yard to get one from the men working the cranes. Eric was just 16 at the time, eager to please and inexperienced. Each guy he asked told him, straight-faced, he wasn't sure where it was and sent him to ask another guy. Someone finally sent him to a local hardware store where a salesman informed him someone was pulling his leg. To his credit, Eric informed Johnny that he'd gone to Ace Hardware and placed an order for a sky hook.

Torman hoped that talking about Johnny's death would allow the two of them to delve deeper into his feelings about loss. At the same time, he knew there would be another condolence letter written to Johnny's next of kin, two sons who, as teenagers, had worked in the yard during summer break, just as Eric had. Torman hoped to find some way to move beyond Eric's prose and into his psyche.

On the same day Eric informed Torman of Johnny's death, Susan, the analysand Torman presented to Steward and who he was counting on to be his successful analytic case, told him that her husband had been promoted at P & G and assigned to Germany. They'd be leaving in 6 months. Torman's anxiety over a premature termination of treatment made listening to her almost impossible. How would Steward react to this news? Would this sink his hopes of finally having a "successful" case?

And what, really, constituted a successful case? In analysis, the goal was not symptom removal, at least not entirely. The more lofty goals of analysis remained fuzzy in Torman's mind. "Where Id was, there ego shall be" was a line often quoted from Freud. Patients were expected to gain insight into their unconscious life and thereby develop increased mastery of their instinctual impulses. Higher level defense mechanisms would replace more primitive defenses. And so on. At the same time, analytic patients often returned for more treatment after completing their analyses. What Torman did know was that Steward's opinion would carry a lot of weight in the institute's decision. None of his other control cases were even close to terminating. If this one didn't count, he was looking at maybe five more years as a boot-licking candidate. An unendurable thought.

Claire got home late from work that night. Dropping her purse and briefcase on the floor by the door, she headed straight for the kitchen. Torman followed her, waiting for the right moment to tell her what happened that day. "Hungry?" he asked.

"Starving to death." Not making eye contact with him, she pulled out some leftovers. "I haven't the energy to cook. You're on your own for dinner."

"Rough day?"

"I really don't want to talk about it. I've had it. Not a moment to breathe all day. There's a frozen pizza you can microwave if you want." Too weary to bother microwaving the previous night's leftovers, she piled the cold remains on a plate and plopped down on a stool at the kitchen counter. Not waiting for Torman, she clicked on the nearby small TV and began eating.

Impatience overwhelming his plan to wait for a good opening, Torman said, "You won't believe what happened with my control case, the one I'm hoping will count as a successful case…her husband got promoted at P & G and will be moving the two of them to Germany in six months." He paused, waiting to see how Claire would respond. She kept eating, keeping an eye on the TV. "This really fucks things up for me."

"Steve, there's always some crisis. I'm sure it'll work out."

Torman sighed. Any hope for sympathy sailed away like an untethered kite on a windy day. So did his appetite. "I think I'll just have cheese and crackers." He rummaged in the fridge, extracting some brie and a soda, then grabbed a box of Triscuits.

"Steve, for God's sake, use a plate. You're just like a little kid, making a mess." As Torman got up to get a plate, he wondered, ever the shrink, if he'd unconsciously neglected to get it in the first place as a way to piss Claire off for showing so little concern for his anxiety about work. What he knew for certain was that he was angry, yet hesitant to say anything to her, knowing she'd had a bad day herself. They ate in silence.

Later, lying next to each other in bed, each with a book, Torman put his on the nightstand and shifted on his side to face Claire. "Enjoying the latest Grisham novel?"

Laughing, Claire said, "I can't believe I'm reading a novel about lawyers, but Grisham nails how creepy and devious lawyers and law firms are." She set her book aside, adding, "I've got to get to sleep. I've got a deposition tomorrow morning and need to be sharp." Turning off the light, she twisted toward Torman, kissed him lightly on his cheek, then turned her back to him, leaving no doubt in Torman's mind that any gesture toward sex on his part would not be welcomed.

Waiting for her breathing to slow, Torman quietly masturbated, something he'd been doing increasingly of late. He told himself it was a harmless way of dealing with his feelings of anxiety and frustration and resisted looking more deeply at what was going on between himself and Claire.

As he tried to settle himself so he could fall asleep, he thought about the upcoming supervision with Gold, reassuring himself that he'd help him figure out a way to address Steward's concerns about "insufficient working through" of Susan's transference. "Working through," as Steward needlessly reminded Torman in numerous supervisory sessions, referred to the interpretation of the patient's transference, not once but repeatedly, and not only in relation to the analyst but in other areas and relationships in the patient's life. "The patient," Steward would recite, as if reading a Biblical passage from the pulpit, "has to be persuaded to remember the past rather than simply repeating it without insight." Unlike Steward, Gold avoided jargon when discussing Torman's case. He focused his attention on Susan's more immediate experience on the couch and helped Torman empathize with her. The last waking thought Torman had was telling himself he'd be getting gold from Gold.

❖ ❖ ❖

Torman sensed Claire's remoteness, yet felt impelled to go into a lot of detail about his worries. Registering her lack of attention, he usually chose to ignore his disappointment in her. He knew she was absorbed in her own struggles as an associate in a law firm where she hoped to become partner. There were obvious parallels in their career paths: both sought admittance to a powerful group that controlled their fates and often treated them with disdain. Decisions about their advancement occurred behind closed doors, with no recourse for appeal. Their absorption in their individual struggles often blinded them to the other's struggle.

Sometimes Torman wondered what their lives would be like with children. Claire had been adamant from day one that she wasn't interested in being a mother. Don, her only sibling, was born with brain damage, creating an on-going burden for her parents, who refused to put him in a group home. A psychiatrist working at a community mental health center treated Don with Trazodone, a very sedating antidepressant, and Risperdal, an antipsychotic medication. While he no longer yelled and threw things, Don slept a lot and seemed listless most of the time. Torman avoided second-guessing Don's treatment, urging Claire's parents to talk to Don's psychiatrist about their concerns. While he understood Claire's fears of having such a severely disabled child, he sometimes wished she'd change her mind before it was too late. But he'd married her knowing how she felt and, at that time, had shared her lack of interest in having children.

❖ ❖ ❖

Torman listened as Eric described Johnny's funeral.

"One thing that struck me," Eric recalled, "was the all-women choir, dressed in long white robes, off to the side of the pulpit. They sang at different times during the service, then closed with the song "I'll See You Again." Even the toughest guys from work were moved."

"You're moved now."

"Yeah. Johnny once told me that when he died the angels in heaven would sing for him. Listening to the women in the choir made me think about that. Johnny was right. Those were his heavenly angels." After a silence, Eric said he was thinking about the condolence letter he'd write to Johnny's two sons and about including that image of the choir. Torman wondered aloud if there was something comforting in thinking about writing.

"I'm not sure that's the right word. The first condolence letter I wrote was to my father, after Grandpa Silver died. I was nine, and I'd never seen my father cry before. I wanted to make him feel better and wrote him a note on a piece of notebook paper from school. He read the note and then really cried, but this time his tears seemed mixed with pleasure. I felt good when he hugged me really hard and whispered 'Thank you' in my ear."

"So these condolence letters express your wish to recapture that moment of closeness you felt with your father, as well as the pleasure in securing his approval."

Eric agreed that it felt good having that experience with his father, then recalled another memory from around sixth grade. "I'd written a short story for English class, got an 'A,' and showed it to my dad. It had an O. Henry surprise twist at the end, which Dad really liked, and he carried that story to work and showed it to his friends and business associates."

"That must've felt really good."

"It did." Eric started laughing. "I just thought about my conversation with Johnny's two sons after the service. One's a policeman, the other's a high school teacher. As teenagers they'd worked in the summers alongside their dad, just as I had. Turns out he'd sent each of them in search of that elusive sky hook."

❖ ❖ ❖

Dr. Steward's office occupied the ground floor of a small brick house nestled among a mash-up of conventional two-story office buildings and older homes. While close to the medical center and the psychoanalytic institute, where most of the analysts practiced, the office set Dr. Steward apart from his colleagues. Torman imagined he couldn't get along with his fellow analysts, but he'd never asked Dr. Steward how he ended up all by himself. A more charitable explanation, he realized, was the privacy and lack of exposure to others that this location offered patients. The nondescript waiting room, lacking comfortable chairs and reading material, gave the message this was not a place to linger or make oneself at home. The inner sanctum, referred to by analysts as the "consultation room," was spacious, filled with natural light, and dominated by a massive wood desk fit for a CEO of a Fortune 500 company. Steward angled his Eames chair at one end of a black backless leather couch which sported a small oriental rug over the far end and inclined upward at a 45 degree angle at the other end. Lest one failed to scrutinize the diplomas arrayed on the wall, a black captain's chair with cherry arms and top rail displaying Yale's seal stood guard by the consulting room's exit door.

Torman dreaded hearing Steward's response to the news about Susan's moving to Germany. Not surprisingly, he balked at the idea that Torman could successfully wrap up the case over the next six months. He emphasized how she needed to "work through her transference neurosis," by which he meant she had to gain insight into her reliving with Torman her childhood oedipal conflicts. Steward even suggested that she had encouraged her husband to take the P & G promotion as a way to defend against further exploration of her erotic impulses towards her analyst. After offering that gem, Steward, clearly pleased with himself and totally unconcerned with Torman's mounting anxiety, settled more deeply into his Eames chair, placed his hands steeple-shaped beneath his chins, and urged Torman to go on with his account of the session.

Torman felt his temples throb. He complained of a headache, just to see if he could rouse the self-satisfied Buddha to haul his fat ass out of his comfortable chair in order to get him an aspirin. When that failed, he spent the rest of the time imagining ways of getting revenge. He saw himself slitting the leather of Steward's prized Eames chair and driving nails into his car's tires. Most gratifying of all was the idea of telling him what an A-one prick he was, how he couldn't analyze his way out of a paper bag. But he knew to keep his rage from boiling over into overt aggression. He managed to dial down his feelings to a manageable simmer.

Gold's approach did prove helpful in steadying him: he told him to focus on what this experience of a move to Germany meant to Susan, to help her express all her feelings about the anticipated move and how it affected her. Torman had been open with Gold about his feelings for Susan. He recalled in supervision his first encounter with her: he'd opened the door to the waiting room where four or five patients were seated. Calling Susan's name, he observed a young woman rise from her chair, and the association that entered his mind was of Botticelli's *Birth of Venus*, only the Venus approaching him had dark hair and eyes (and was fully clothed and not riding on a sea shell). Tall and elegant, she moved with an unassuming grace. Now, five years later and facing the end of her analysis, he found her just as lovely and knew he would miss her when her treatment ended. Perhaps most difficult for Torman was her repeatedly asking what he thought she should do about her husband's decision to move. So far, Torman emphasized the need to explore in as much detail as possible her fantasies about how he felt about her leaving treatment. He often thought how much easier his job would be if he weren't needing her "success" in treatment to graduate from the institute. Urging her to stand up to her husband and insist on staying in treatment might be in her best interest, but her continuing treatment clearly was in Torman's best interest as far as his graduation was concerned. He worried that his self-interest might bias his judgement. He felt paralyzed by his concerns, unable to step back and think how best to respond to Susan's dilemma of whether to stay or leave. As he often did when uncertain, he backed away into silence, leaving his patient in the dark.

Torman knew the tension with Claire added to his difficulty concentrating at work. He felt a sense of unease whenever his relationship with Claire seemed unsettled, disconnected. She blamed the stress at work for being preoccupied. It galled him that she believed her struggle to make partner far exceeded his struggle to become an analyst. Yet maybe she was right, maybe his whining was childish and he didn't fully appreciate how hard a time she was having. Nevertheless, her remoteness tried his patience.

Torman's relationship with Claire began a decade ago. In the summer months, he swam laps after work at a neighborhood swim club. Sometimes they shared the lap lane, but neither spoke to the other. She hadn't escaped his notice. Her one-piece Speedo bathing suit revealed the smooth, toned muscles of an athlete, a narrow waist, and small, shapely breasts. Her face, skin taut over its contours, was striking for its slender, prominent nose, with a slight sideways deviation at the tip. Out of the water and freed of her goggles, she revealed grayish blue eyes that in Torman's mind suggested a softness that counterbalanced an otherwise austere face, a face you would never mistake for anyone else's. One night, finishing laps at the same time, they found themselves standing hip deep in the shallow end, opposite each other as they removed their goggles. "You're always faster than me," Torman said. "How do you do that?"

Claire laughed. Her laughter, like her eyes, softened her features. "You have to learn how to relax in the pool. You look as though you're wrestling the water." They sat side-by-side on the edge of the pool, legs dangling in the water, talking comfortably about swimming, exercise, staying in shape. That summer they developed a routine of swimming laps together, then lying poolside on lounge chairs and sharing stories about their lives. Besides his attraction to her, Torman enjoyed her tales of outwitting opposing lawyers and conjuring up subtle legal arguments, told with a mixture of amusement and pride. They also shared a disdain for much of Cincinnati's backwardness, its intolerance of non-conformity, its hostility to liberal causes, its rah-rah sports fanaticism. They ridiculed hometown heroes like Pete Rose, baseball's "Hit King," who lied for years about gambling on the Cincinnati Reds, and longtime Sheriff Simon Leis, who unsuccessfully took legal action against Larry Flynt and supported the city's obscenity charges against a local museum for exhibiting Robert Mapplethorpe's photographs.

One night, leaving together, Torman asked if she'd like to go to the nearby Dairy Queen. Their relationship quickly and easily developed into a romance. Now, ten years later, Torman wondered what had changed, what had transformed the romance into a co-existence. How much of that was expectable and temporary and how much was a sign of something seriously wrong? It was as if, Torman thought, they were back in the pool, before their introduction, swimming in a shared lane, but at different speeds, unknown to each other.

Claire often thought back to that summer she'd met Torman. Before their introduction in the shallow end, she'd been aware of his presence, felt his eyes on her. Her affair with her former law school professor, Ezra Segal, consumed most of her attention at that time of her life. In addition to an appointment on the law school faculty, Ezra headed a non-profit organization whose mission was advocating for immigrants. As a third year student, Claire had signed up for an elective course with Ezra's non-profit. From the outset, she'd been enamored with Ezra, whose intelligence and idealism touched her and whose charm captivated her. On her last day of the elective, Ezra invited her to lunch. Fifteen years her senior, he nevertheless possessed a youthful energy, a flair for unconventional clothes, and a directness that surprised her. At lunch he told her how much he admired her. "You're one of the brightest students I've ever had. I'm very attracted to you. I need you to know that I'm married, and my wife has MS. I don't intend to leave her, but I want to keep seeing you. How do you feel about that?"

Stunned, Claire said, "I'd like to see you. This feels weird, but I think about you a lot and dreaded our contact coming to an end." They spent two hours over lunch, talking about themselves, about life and the law. Claire hardly noticed the surroundings, unaware of time and anyone else but Ezra. Before parting, they agreed to meet later in the week. Claire kept their affair secret, which lent it an excitement that she couldn't deny. Not seeking more of a commitment from Ezra than their planned trysts, she relished their time together, even when it felt rushed. During the two years their relationship lasted, they did manage to spend whole weekends together at out-of-town conferences, though such excursions were infrequent. Often he surprised her with small gifts, each one associated with a shared experience and accompanied by a tender note. She'd never been with a man so attentive and attuned to her. Over time, Claire allowed herself to imagine a life with Ezra, but these fantasies risked her asking more of him than she knew he was prepared to give. She forced herself to keep these daydreams contained, occasionally savoring them lying in bed at night or driving home after a long day at work. She avoided asking about his wife, not wanting to know anything more than he'd told her at their first lunch. Claire managed to wall off thoughts about being involved with a married man. It was a subject she chose to ignore, made easier by Ezra's own apparent lack of guilt or anguish. Claire could almost believe that Ezra's wife didn't exist, a belief reinforced by his rarely mentioning her.

During the summer when Torman's presence became known to her, she began to notice that Ezra found it more difficult to find time for the two of them. He seemed as attentive as always when they managed to be together, so she was perplexed yet not threatened by this change. One day, needing to do some research at the law school for her firm, she stopped by Ezra's office unannounced. Claire breezed into his workspace and encountered a strikingly beautiful woman sitting very close to Ezra as the two of them peered at documents. Ezra jumped up, looking alarmed. Recovering his composure, he introduced Claire to his student, who avoided eye contact with Claire and immediately excused herself, saying she was late for a lecture. Claire and Ezra remained standing, silent as each looked the other in the eye. Finally, Ezra shrugged his shoulders, looked down, and said, "Sorry." Turning on her heel, Claire fled his office, willing herself not to cry. They never spoke again.

Two weeks after their break-up, when Torman asked her to go to the Dairy Queen, she felt a kind of weakness, a desire to let this man, so different from Ezra, so earnest and predictable, give her comfort. A voice in her head said, "On the rebound, Claire," but she did not heed it.

❖ ❖ ❖

Claire called Torman's office, leaving a message saying she'd miss dinner, so he should go ahead and eat whatever. She'd try to be home around 8:30, but her new client was very needy and tended to prolong meetings. This sounded reasonable, yet he knew that early in her career she'd learned that if she insisted on meeting during regular business hours, her clients invariably found a way to accommodate her. The idea that Claire was having an affair entered Torman's awareness with such force that, instead of going straight home after work, he headed downtown and parked near her office building. Feeling like a jealous fool, he waited in his car. Around 6:30, Claire emerged from the office building's revolving doors in the company of another associate from the firm, an affable man Torman had met at one of the law firm's social gatherings. They were laughing, looking very happy in each other's company. They walked to a nearby restaurant and went inside. Torman sat in his car for 5 minutes, wondering if he should confront them in the restaurant. He felt sick to his stomach. While his gut told him that his worse fears were realized, his head came up with reasons he was overreacting, with plausible explanations for their possible dinner date. Maybe her client was late, or Claire and the lawyer were just grabbing a quick cup of coffee or take-out before heading back to work. Driving home, his worse-case fears overtook his efforts to remain rational. He felt like screaming.

By the time Claire got home, Torman had regained some measure of control. He decided to ask how her meeting with the client went.

"I don't want to talk about work. I'm tired and just want to wind down without being questioned. That's all I do, answer questions and listen to complaints all day long. I'm beat." Then, perhaps sensing his upset, she gave him a smile, adding, "C'mon, let's go upstairs and watch TV in bed." In spite of all his inner turmoil, Torman let her lead him upstairs while he tried denying what he feared.

The following day he called an old friend, Ed Thompson, whom he'd roomed with in college and kept up with over the years. A lawyer living in Portland, Oregon, Ed listened to Torman's fears and tried to settle him down. Basically, he advised Torman to work at re-establishing closeness with Claire by listening to her and encouraging her to open up, even if he'd heard everything about her work before. Torman wondered if he should simply ask if she was unhappy with their relationship, and if she was, he'd suggest they see a marital therapist. At the same time, he feared what he might hear if he confronted her, and that fear trumped any impulse to explore Claire's apparent unhappiness with him. He might be tormenting himself with a baseless dread of her infidelity, but that seemed preferable to the discovery that what he feared was grounded in reality.

Eric started his session wondering if a very attractive woman he'd just seen leaving the building was a patient of Torman's. Torman remained silent but figured it was likely Susan he'd seen. She was, Torman reflected, the kind of woman that men certainly noticed, though not the kind of woman who expected it. After a brief silence, Eric noted how Torman looked tired, maybe a little worried, when he greeted him in the waiting room. He asked Torman if he was all right. In response, he urged Eric to talk more about his observation. At the same time, Torman knew this would probably annoy Eric, but it effectively took the heat off him as he attempted to act as though everything was normal. With some irritation at Torman's deflection, Eric speculated that perhaps he'd gotten a late night phone call from a patient and lost sleep as a result. The speculation went nowhere, so eventually he brought up the date he'd had with a woman he'd met through JDate, an online dating service that Torman was pleased to learn Eric had signed up with.

"She didn't look even vaguely like the photos she'd posted. She spoke non-stop about her recent divorce and how furious she was that her former husband's 'slut of a girlfriend' ends up babysitting their young daughter during visitation with her 'shithead ex.' Some of her anger got directed at me, especially as she quizzed me about my past relationships and why they hadn't lasted. At some point I asked if she'd gotten any counseling while going through her divorce. That was a *big* mistake. I got an earful about shrinks, how worthless they are, how all they care about is getting paid. I used that opportunity to mention I was coming here four times a week, and that really put a dampener on the conversation. I dropped her off at her home as soon as I could after our dinner, wished her well, and sped away."

"Not exactly a dream date."

"Speaking of dreams…I had a weird one that night. I don't remember much of it, but I was in a car, driving somewhere I didn't recognize and feeling lost. A couple, a man and a woman I didn't recognize, were hitchhiking and I stopped to pick them up. I asked if they knew the way. They didn't say anything, just sat in the back. It was kind of creepy. That's all I remember. I suppose it's related to the date, which clearly went nowhere. And the couple sitting behind me…I figure that's a reference to you back there, saying very little, not helping me find my way. Plus she'd been so critical of shrinks on our date, maybe that influenced the dream."

"Sounds like you've been feeling angry with me, with my

not providing direction."

"Not anger...more just a sense lately of your being more distant, hard to read. Like today when I sensed your looking tired and a bit worried. Makes me feel worried."

"Why a couple?"

"I don't know...what comes to mind is my parents...I mean, they died in a car accident. I guess I see you as standing for both parents?"

"Well, your parents died before you found your way in life, and now perhaps you have the hope that I will help you as you look for a relationship and for a career that's fulfilling." Torman found himself fidgeting, feeling unnerved by Eric's dream. He wondered if Eric somehow intuited the difficulties between Claire and himself and experienced Torman's recent unease as interfering with his helping him find his own way in life. He knew most people would regard such speculation as nonsense, that a patient couldn't possibly be aware of his marital troubles, but he was convinced of the unconscious mind's uncanny way of knowing another, even if that knowing was beyond one's ability to put it into words. At the very least, there was frequently a kernel of truth to patients' fantasies about their therapists, though often distorted by their past experiences. He remembered a case conference in which a fellow candidate told how his control case reported she'd begun lactating. She was one of those incredibly attuned patients who seemed to survive emotionally through her connection to her analyst. The analyst's wife was in the early stage of pregnancy, and he insisted in their conference that there was no way his analysand could have learned his wife was pregnant. None of them in the class had known she was pregnant. They were about evenly divided between those who believed the patient had a premonition of his wife's pregnancy and those who thought her lactating was either a side effect of medication or simply chance. Torman was in the former camp.

Claire remained remote much of the time. Torman became solicitous, trying to suppress his fears and to bridge the gap between them. He wondered if he was trying to induce guilt in her or make her have second thoughts. He resisted the temptation to read her emails, thinking that was too risky and, if discovered, would really doom his chances of improving their marriage. He spoke regularly with his friend Ed about his fears, and that helped him manage his anxiety.

Claire was aware of Torman's efforts to probe her remoteness, yet his anxious watchfulness only drove her further into herself. At the same time, she looked forward to seeing Paul Anderson at work. An associate lawyer in her firm, Paul had arrived a year after Claire. Unlike the other associates, he appeared much more relaxed about becoming a partner in the firm, as if he could deal with whatever happened. He never seemed to compete with others yet made no effort to hide his confidence and self-assurance. The two of them flirted with each other, a seemingly innocent flirtation since Paul always seemed to have a girlfriend, though never the same one for very long. Claire teased him about his womanizing while Paul made light of her married life, referring to Claire and Steve by the names of TV couples ("So, how are things with the Simpsons?" "What's the latest with Alice and Ralph Kramden?" "What did Lucy and Desi do over the weekend?").

Claire welcomed Paul's ease and charm, much as she had Ezra's. Torman could be so serious, bordering on ponderous, as he struggled with his career. She missed being with a man who was impulsive, unpredictable, and fun. Sometimes she felt her marriage resembled her parents' life together, a life of routine and obligations and little else. If marriage was prison, then time spent with Paul was parole.

◆ ◆ ◆

Torman hoped Eric wouldn't give up on JDate, in spite of some admittedly disappointing experiences. Eric complained about divorced women with children and other "baggage." The ones who'd managed to avoid marriage and children seemed either odd or immature. However, his most recent date, a woman named Evie, had captured his interest, in large part due to her attractiveness and engaging personality. But as Torman listened to Eric's description of Evie, he worried he might have landed a woman with an unstable personality, one likely to create chaos in his life. It wasn't Torman's job to steer his patients away from troubled relationships, but a little education about another's behavior and its likely repercussions was hard for Torman to resist.

It was a good sign that Eric recognized, with no warnings from Torman, that Evie wasn't a good candidate for a longterm relationship. He told Torman that she'd been divorced twice, having a child by each husband. She'd railed against the legal system for granting custody of the children to the fathers. At least, Eric noted, she described those marital experiences with humor rather than rage. She spoke of traveling abroad by herself for a year after college and managing to get by in foreign countries with very little money. Eric had the impression she was skillful at engaging men's help. Between husbands she joined a traveling circus and lived for a year with the lion trainer who became, by her account, psychotic and abusive, so she escaped one night when he'd passed out after a bout of drinking.

In spite of his misgivings, Eric acknowledged that he planned to see her again. "For one thing, she's really pretty. And sexy."

"There's an expression in medicine that 'anatomy is destiny.' Being attractive definitely opens doors for women. And men. Did she mention if she's been in therapy?"

"No, she didn't. Your asking makes me think you feel she could use some."

"That thought never crossed your mind?"

"Well...it certainly does now. I think I was too bowled over by her to ask about that. I'm sure once I mention being in analysis she'll tell me about whatever experiences she's had in therapy. I'm getting the impression you want me to be careful about getting involved with Evie. That makes me feel you care about me, but, at the same time, reminds me of my mother who was always critical of the women in my life."

Torman knew he wanted to warn Eric about the possibility that Evie was someone he'd diagnose as "borderline." He felt tempted to describe how these individuals often make very good first impressions, are very idealizing of whomever they hook up with, and then, once entangled in a relationship, become very unstable, at times accusatory and hostile, at other times conciliatory and solicitous. Frequently, the person they attach to has no idea what's wrong and often feels to blame. In short, Torman wanted to tell Eric such people were a nightmare for all involved. Maybe he should just tell him to watch Glenn Close in "Fatal Attraction."

After hearing about their fourth date, Torman continued to struggle with his desire to give Eric a heads-up on Evie versus letting him come to the realization on his own that she was a walking land mine. So far, he reported the sex was great, though at times she apparently "zoned out" during these experiences and seemed to Eric as though she'd "left the planet." Torman suspected she was having dissociative reactions in which she was mentally cut off from what she was physically experiencing and needed to protect herself from painful memories.

Eric told her he was in analysis, and that led to his asking if she'd ever been in therapy. She said her parents sent her to a therapist while she was in high school because of some rebellious behaviors, but she didn't like the therapist and didn't stay in treatment very long. Her parents divorced while she was in high school, and she bounced back and forth between them. Torman decided to take a more passive stance with Eric, believing he was able to come to his own conclusion about Evie's stability. At least he hoped he would.

Torman felt some relief with Claire's being more like her usual self. They'd even had sex again, which reassured him. But he did notice that she'd been buying new clothes and spent more time in the morning with make-up and fixing her hair. Those observations kept him on high alert. Claire always maintained that men misunderstood women's attention to dress and appearance, claiming they were seeking other women's approval and notice more than men's. He wasn't so sure he bought that. However, the lessening of his anxiety allowed him to concentrate on his work, which, in turn, diminished his suspicions about Claire's infidelity.

Susan continued to struggle with their impending termination. She criticized her husband: "Dan has absolutely no idea how important this is to me. When I try to explain things to him, he gets this really annoying blank look on his face. Yesterday he said, 'I'd think five years in treatment would be more than enough. And, anyway, I'm sure they have therapists in Germany who speak English.' As if analysis is just like a box of Tide, the same around the world, just with different packaging!" Every session focused on her feelings about leaving, whether she'd gotten what she needed from the analysis, what she imagined Torman was feeling, how the anticipated loss of their relationship brought back the sadness of losing her grandparents, especially her grandmother who lived next door when Susan was growing up and with whom she'd spent so much time. She reported some return of the symptoms that brought her to treatment: fear of being in crowds, anxiety attacks that seemingly came out of the blue, a fear of gaining weight and needing to obsessively monitor calories. Torman found himself feeling better about the analysis, in spite of the termination being prompted by her husband's impending transfer. She'd made gains, had more insight, and even the re-emergence of some of her presenting symptoms was characteristic of patients in the termination phase.

However, Steward's assessment remained unclear. His resistance to giving any opinion about whether this phase of the analysis reflected genuine progress worried Torman. If anything, Steward seemed even more passive than ever. While Gold had been reassuring in their long distance phone supervision, he was so far removed from the struggles of lowly analytic candidates that Torman imagined his worries seemed infantile to him.

❖ ❖ ❖

Torman took note of Eric's anguished expression as he beelined to the couch. "Evie casually mentioned last night that she was late getting her period. I tried to hide my panic, but she quickly picked up on it, saying, 'If I'm pregnant, you won't have to worry, I'll disappear and you'll never hear from me.' Not exactly reassuring. Her reaction seemed crazy to me. I didn't know how to respond. Tell her that I want her to have a baby with me? Encourage her to vanish with my first born child? I've been careful, using condoms, but I know accidents happen."

"Having to wait to find out whether she's pregnant is understandably maddening."

"Waiting drives me crazy. I just want to end this relationship, but she's become clingy and tearful at times. Last night she said maybe everyone would be better off if she just weren't around anymore. That scared the shit out of me."

Torman wasn't surprised at the turn of events, at Evie's

reaction to Eric's anxiety. He wondered if she was really late with her period, if this was a test of Eric's commitment to her or a way to create conflict and distance between them. What he knew with certainty was how anxious her implied threat of suicide, on top of her possible pregnancy, made Eric feel.

"It's clear she's made you feel very anxious, not only with the possibility of an unplanned, unwanted pregnancy but also with her veiled threat of suicide."

"I couldn't sleep last night. My mind raced, full of thoughts of a baby I don't want, as well as fears of Evie killing herself or trying to. I know I want you to tell me how to handle this situation. But you never give advice, at least not so far."

"As you think about this now, what advice would you give to someone in your predicament?"

After a silence, Eric noted how he'd tell someone in his shoes to tell her that her comments were disturbing to him. If she's still feeling everyone would be better off if she weren't around anymore, then she should see a therapist. Just putting these thoughts into words allayed much of Eric's anxiety.

At the same time, Eric sensed that Torman still wasn't himself. He seemed remote and inscrutable, always insisting on exploring Eric's fantasies about what could be going on with Torman.

"They must train you guys to reveal nothing about yourselves. Sometimes it drives me nuts. If anything, it heightens my curiosity about you. I've told you about driving by your house and googling you. It's embarrassing, like I'm a kid with a bad case of hero worship."

Torman, sitting out of sight, smiled as he recalled experiencing the same frustrations with his own analyst. He wasn't sure that the analyst's insistence on remaining opaque, a blank slate onto which the patient could project all his unconscious fantasies, was always the best approach. Some balance between human responsiveness and mindful reticence was needed, but Torman was never sure how to provide that, usually opting for the blank screen approach, encouraging his patients to express their fantasies about him, at least as his initial response. But he had his doubts, suspecting he was hiding behind a wall which ultimately drove many of his patients away. He struggled to figure out if he was adhering to good analytic technique or using that technique to ward off deeper engagement with his patients. It disturbed him to think he was inflicting on his patients what he felt his analyst had inflicted on him.

❖ ❖ ❖

"I had a dream of going with Evie to a doctor to check on her health," Eric said at the beginning of his next session. "We were in an examination room, and a nurse came in and started asking Evie questions, all the while ignoring me. The doctor never appeared. That's all I remember." After a long discussion, Torman said he thought Eric's experience with Evie captured both his relationship with Torman and his relationship with his parents growing up.

"Your father never found a way to protect you from your mother's forcefulness and control, just as he'd never been able himself to deal with her effectively. Your father's escape was the family business, while you were left to deal with your mother on your own. Now, in your relationship with Evie, you feel the same kind of abandonment by me and are struggling to deal with another powerful woman all by yourself."

Torman silently congratulated himself for overcoming his own anxieties and offering what he believed was a comprehensive interpretation. Of course, he knew that Eric's response was the real test of whether he'd hit the mark. After a silence, Eric recalled a party he attended as a young teenager.

"Mom insisted I invite the daughter of one of her friends, a girl I barely knew and wasn't at all attracted to. I can't recall the threats she used but whatever they were, they got me to cave in. I'd gone to Dad to plead my case, but he refused to get involved, saying 'That's between you and your mother.'" Torman decided not to press the connection between his past experience and his present one. Instead, he simply noted how disappointed Eric was in his father for never standing up to his mother.

"I don't like the idea I was disappointed in Dad, a man I'd always loved, but you're right. I feel bad...like I'm being disloyal to him. He was well equipped to navigate in the world of men but could never stand up to Mom."

Later that week, as Eric entered Torman's office, he knew Eric had received good news. He practically danced his way across the room. Torman half expected him to do a swan dive onto the couch.

"Not pregnant! What a relief. I hardly missed a beat and told Evie I didn't want to continue seeing her. I thought she'd be crushed, but instead she turned things around and made me feel as though I was somehow unable to handle being intimate. She said how she understood that it was difficult for me to allow someone into my life and hoped I would eventually be able to tolerate closeness with a woman. Instead of becoming angry or hurt, as I'd anticipated, she seemed to take pity on me. Which was fine with me. I'm *so* relieved to be free of her." Torman said nothing but thought Eric might not have seen the last of Evie.

Susan often stopped at a nearby coffee shop after her appointment with Torman. She considered it a small luxury to while away an hour in such a cozy spot, sipping her coffee and watching the world go by outside the shop's window. She had a favorite seat in a corner that provided privacy and allowed her to think about her session and read whatever novel she'd most recently ordered from Amazon. Engrossed in her reading, she sensed someone looking at her and glanced up to see Eric hesitating by her table. He'd caught her eye in the past; there was something kind and gentle about him. Also a gracefulness in his gait.

Smiling, Susan said, "I know you...you're the 3:00 o'clock on Wednesday."

"Yes, and you're the 2:00 o'clock." Eric, spying the novel's title, said, "I liked 'State of Wonder' a lot. Actually, I like all of Patchett's books."

"Me, too. She's one of those writers you can't wait to get her next book. I'm Susan." She held out her hand, which Eric shook, all the while finding himself mesmerized by her large brown eyes and silken, wavy hair framing her face. After a silence, Susan, her laugh revealing perfect teeth, asked, "You have a name?"

"Yes, sorry...I'm a little slow on the uptake. Eric. I guess it's a little weird to meet someone who I've only encountered previously in a psychiatrist's waiting room."

"Well, let me assure you, I'm not crazy."

"I'm relieved to hear that. I'm not, either...just doing some, you know, fine tuning of my psyche. It's good to know we're both in relatively good shape." They were enjoying themselves. Eric wished he didn't have to go back to work.

An awkward moment followed, so Eric mumbled something about having to return to work. Driving off, he wished their encounter had lasted longer. He'd noticed her wedding ring, so he figured nothing other than a friendship could develop. He also wondered if she saw Torman or another psychiatrist in the practice. If she was one of Torman's patients, he'd have to talk all about her, why he was interested in her, and then he'd have to relate everything back to Torman, and how important he was in Eric's life and on and on. He wondered if there was a rule against having contact with one of your analyst's patients. Would Torman tell him he couldn't see her? That was hard to imagine. There really weren't any rules in analysis that Eric was aware of besides saying whatever comes to mind, to "speak as freely as possible," as Torman had instructed him prior to his lying on the couch.

And why shouldn't he show an interest in this woman? She's very attractive, likes Patchett's novels, has a sense of humor, and is in therapy. What more could you ask for? Even if she's a bit neurotic, at least she's taking care of her problems. Unlike Evie, who'd sent him a postcard from Costa Rica where she was spending a few months. Doing God knows what. She wrote that she hoped he'd be able to find the right woman some day. Too bad Susan's married, Eric thought, because she seemed much more appealing than the women he'd dated.

◆ ◆ ◆

The gods don't love me, Torman thought, when he learned that Susan and Eric had begun having coffee on Wednesdays after their back-to-back sessions. Eric was clear that he finds her very attractive, while Susan was more circumspect about her feelings for Eric. They quickly discovered they were both seeing Torman, but neither saw this as anything that threatened their treatments. If Susan wasn't a control case, Torman would simply have viewed her behavior as "acting out" unconscious impulses that Torman, in turn, needed to help her understand. But her contact with Eric further threatened his hope of neatly wrapping up Susan's analysis and earning the approval of the institute. He imagined Steward insisting Susan's behavior reflected her lack of progress in analysis and her being nowhere near ready for termination. From Steward's point of view, Susan's involvement with Eric would represent her reenacting a repressed childhood wish to have an incestuous relationship with her father (in this instance with Eric standing in for her father and Torman representing her mother). Steward would insist Torman work at helping Susan remember the past instead of simply repeating it without any awareness. As for Susan's being more circumspect about her feelings for Eric, Steward would see this as evidence of her defensive denial of the meaning of her behavior, as well as an effort to avoid direct competition with her rival (that is, her mother in the past, now Torman in the present). After all, this is what Freudian analysts expect to be the central drama of psychoanalysis: the re-living with the analyst of the Oedipus complex. Torman believed this expectation was too pat, leaving little, if any, room for novel discovery.

These thoughts brought back to Torman his previous experience with his analysand who refused to lie on the couch. Torman believed that young man not only needed to see Torman's face but also benefited from that visual connection in ways Torman could never fully explain. There were also moments in that experience during which his patient felt Torman really understood him, moments he greeted with a smile and an acknowledgement ("Yes, that's it exactly."). The accrual of these moments seemed pivotal in promoting his growth and in giving him the wherewithal to move out of his parents' basement and into the larger world. The visual and empathic connections seemed to Torman vastly more important than any interpretation of his Oedipus complex.

Aside from these theoretical reflections, Torman worried he was losing sight of what he was supposed to be doing and risked both analyses drifting out of control and blowing up in his face. Simultaneously treating in psychoanalysis members of the same family or intimate partners or even close friends was a recipe for disaster. Invariably issues came up with the analyst about trust, about who you love more, about whose version of reality you believe. And if he lost both cases, eight hours of his work week would go up in smoke. Torman didn't have a waiting list of patients eager to lie on his couch four days a week, or even to be seen in weekly therapy. He decided to call Gold to get some emergency supervision.

He doubted Claire wanted to hear the latest development in his analytic work, though he knew he'd tell her about it. He remained anxious about what was going on with her. She continued to work late and seemed disinclined to talk much. He made a point of asking about her work, her struggles in the firm, but she seemed reluctant to share much with him, often protesting she was tired of talking about work. He was tempted to ask about her colleagues, to see if she'd mention the lawyer he'd seen her with when he spied on her that one evening. Instead, he tortured himself with images of their having an affair. Sometimes Torman considered talking to Gold about Claire, but that felt wrong, as if it violated a tacit boundary in their supervision, a supervision he needed and valued.

"The usual?" asked the barista as Eric headed towards Susan's table. Eric nodded yes, then smiled at Susan, who'd put down her book and greeted him with a smile of her own. Their pattern of meeting weekly had evolved naturally. Eric typically consumed something sweet with his coffee, while Susan never indulged in anything other than coffee. He'd begun to tease her about resisting sweets, while she'd lament having longstanding "issues" with her weight.

"I'm not exactly anorexic, but I'm super careful about how much I eat. As a kid, I was overweight and my mother, who's rail thin and obsessed with her weight, made me feel guilty whenever I ate something she didn't approve of."

"Well, you look fine to me." Holding up his pecan roll, he added, "And your example keeps me from ordering another one of these."

Conversations invariably touched on their analyses and their experience of Torman, as well as on their relationships with others. On this day, Susan talked with Eric about her marriage, how she felt ambivalent about moving to Germany and leaving Torman. Plus she'd grown up in Cincinnati and was reluctant to move away from all that was familiar. Eric couldn't believe she'd been seeing Torman for five years. He hadn't counted on analysis taking that long. "I never run out of things to say," Susan said. "It sounds incredibly self-indulgent, but I don't care." Eric confirmed that he too felt as though inside his head there was a bottomless well of things to talk about.

Eric sensed Susan's ambivalence not only about moving to Germany but also about her relationship with her husband. He wondered to himself if she was thinking about ending her marriage and if that was a topic in her analysis. He was very careful about how he responded to her, mainly just listening. He felt tempted to see more of her but that didn't feel right. He felt that would be taking advantage of her when she was in a vulnerable state.

As Eric predicted, Torman showed a lot of interest in his relationship with Susan, encouraging him to explore what it meant to get to know someone he was treating. Eric reported a dream: "I was back in school, junior high is what it reminded me of, and all the students were in the auditorium for some meeting. A fire alarm went off. The principal was on the stage and directed everyone to walk, not run, in single file to the marked exits. I didn't want to panic...I felt scared and kept looking around to see if there was any fire or smoke.

"Last night I heard on the news about a local school having a lockdown as a result of some threat made to the principal's office. Turned out it was a prank, but you know how threats are taken very seriously nowadays. I guess that triggered my dream."

"What in your current life are you feeling scared about?" Torman asked.

"Well, I'm uneasy...I guess scared...about how you might be reacting to my seeing Susan for coffee. I worry you see me as misbehaving. In junior high, I started to get interested in girls, and my mother had a way of making me feel bad about this, as though it was somehow abnormal or excessive. If she even thought I found someone attractive, she'd make negative comments about the girl. I learned to keep my interests to myself."

Torman said, "In the dream, the principal urged everyone to walk, not run, to the exit. What do you make of that?"

"Well, he was trying to get us out of there without a stampede. I guess the principle's a stand-in for you. You never seem hasty, always taking time to explore everything rather than jumping to some conclusion or decision. I've sensed your uneasiness with my seeing Susan. It's not exactly disapproval but more a feeling you think it could interfere with things here."

"Like, in your dream, it'll interrupt school?"

"Yeah, that it's somehow a threat to my analysis, though you've never actually said that. *Is* it a threat to what's going on here?"

"It's not uncommon for someone in analysis to know another person in treatment with his analyst, but the more intimacy between those two people, the greater the potential for conflicts with the analyst over issues of trust. Do I sympathize with you or with Susan, do I like her more than I like you, who do I believe more, and so on. If you and Susan were partners, I wouldn't recommend that the two of you see the same therapist for individual treatment."

"But it's not against the rules to know someone who also sees your analyst?"

"The only rule, as you already know, is to speak as freely as possible about such a relationship so that we can understand the meaning that relationship has for you. So far, from what you've told me today, it sounds as though you anticipate that I'll disapprove of your interest in her, much like your mother disapproved of any interest you showed in girls when you were growing up. And the image of the principal directing you and the other students to the exits suggests you think I might eventually tell you to leave."

"Well, you did say that greater intimacy with her could cause problems here."

"I can't ignore something that could potentially get in the way of your analysis. I can see how calling attention to that danger feels like my disapproval."

◈ ◈ ◈

Torman's anxiety about Eric and Susan lessened after supervision with Gold. He didn't seem overly concerned and offered suggestions about how to discuss this involvement with each of them. Gold always emphasized the importance of understanding the meaning an experience had for the patient. Having a consultant outside of the institute allowed Torman to put aside his fears of jeopardizing his academic progress. He needed an ally, and Gold fit the bill.

Eric correctly surmised Susan's increasing uncertainty about her marriage. In Torman's sessions with Susan, he noted how her husband's decision to move them to Germany intensified her uncertainty. Predictably, Steward, in diehard Freudian tradition, insisted this was a classic example of her penis envy, that she was enraged at her husband's being the one in charge of their lives, calling the shots. Torman imagined Steward's delight in seeing an old New Yorker cartoon showing two women gazing at the Washington Monument while one of them comments that she could see why he was called the father of our country.

Torman did agree that Susan was enraged at her husband for interfering with her analysis, yet he also believed her focusing on her marriage shifted attention away from her feelings about their likely impending termination. Torman was tempted to link this experience to her childhood experiences in which similar dynamics operated, but Gold urged him to stay with her feelings about Torman, to tolerate the uncertainty and anxiety she was experiencing "in the here and now."

Not surprisingly, listening to Susan's experience with her husband stirred up Torman's fears about Claire's marital unhappiness and possible interest in another man. He thought of following Claire when she went to her Pilates class on Saturday.

He was ashamed to think he'd slink around trying to spy on her. His friend Ed suggested hiring a private investigator, but Torman preferred to do his own sleuthing. One night he looked through her purse. He even went through her laundry hamper, checking her underwear, looking for something suggestive of her having had sex. The whole time his heart pounded in his chest, afraid of getting caught and having no idea what to say if Claire did catch him. He'd never been a good liar. He'd never wanted to be.

Seeing patients helped. Their worries took his mind off his own, at least so long as they didn't remind him of his own worst fears. Even the hassles with the institute allowed Torman to forget how troubling things were with Claire. At various times, he felt on the verge of telling her that he sensed distance between them and, depending on how that went, suggesting they see a marital therapist to try to improve their relationship. Yet he repeatedly came back to the idea that not knowing what might really be going on kept open the possibility that he was simply making all this up. And so he remained stuck in a nightmare of his own making.

Lying on the couch, Eric held up the postcard from Evie so Torman could see it. "She sure doesn't give up easily. This card arrived from Columbia where she's traveling with a man she met in Costa Rica. The last line, 'Hope you find the woman of your dreams,' is a recurrent message from her. Feels like a dig at me."

"She has a way of not letting go, all the while trying to appear independent of you."

"I had no idea what I was getting into with her. Never a dull moment."

Eric went on to talk about missing his dad, how hard it

was to sustain his interest in work without his father's presence. "I never cleared out his office, just closed the door to it. Occasionally I look inside to make sure everything's still in place. His old business cronies have started telling me stories about him from the old days, stories I've heard before but still like hearing again. Sometimes the competition for clients wasn't altogether friendly, but fences always got mended. Dad was known for being a softie." Torman let his mind drift to thoughts of his own father, a man most at ease in the classroom, lecturing students, discussing ideas, grading papers. A tenured sociology professor at a liberal arts college, he'd written a few papers early in his academic career, enough to get tenure, but not enough to attract the attention of a top university. Like Eric's father, Torman's father had been overshadowed at home by Torman's mother. Unlike Eric's father, his dad never found much common ground on which to bond with his son. Torman's father lost his own father to leukemia at a very young age. He'd admitted on one occasion to having no memory of him. His mother, whom he revered, never remarried and devoted her life to raising her two children. Torman realized that his father had no idea how to be a father to him and understood through his own experience on the couch how he turned to his mother for approval and direction. Listening to Eric, Torman envied the closeness that Eric and his father forged at work.

"I've started reading novels at work when business is slow. Incoming calls seem intrusive and annoying. I try to hide my lack of interest in work. Most of the time I succeed, but Johnny wouldn't have missed what's going on with me. And he's someone else I miss. I enjoyed going out in the yard just to joke with him.

"Before the car crash, I always went to my parents' house for Sunday dinner. Usually just a spread of cold cuts, potato salad, and cheese cake or brownies. If Dad was attempting a project at home, I'd usually help. These projects often ended up a disaster, though an amusing one. Dad hated being defeated by a leaky toilet or by some DIY assembly. Half the time we lacked the requisite tool. We watched how-to videos on YouTube, but they rarely helped us much either. Mom never had any patience with our struggles, usually yelling at Dad to hire someone who knew what he was doing. If we succeeded, we'd insist she admire our handiwork." Again, Torman's thoughts wandered to his own father, a man who could fix anything. He had every tool imaginable in his basement workshop, all lined up in perfect order, like troops in formation, waiting for commands. But his father's pedantic approach to even the simplest home repair sent Torman off to find something more enjoyable to do. However, once he became a homeowner, he'd call his dad for advice on how to fix something, suppressing his annoyance at his long-winded explanations. The truth of the matter was that his dad always knew how to fix whatever mechanical problem Torman presented. For life's more pressing problems, Torman looked elsewhere.

Claire's mother called from the hospital to tell her that Claire's dad had died unexpectedly. He'd complained of a severe headache earlier in the day, went upstairs to take a nap, and never woke up. By the time her mom checked on him, he was cold and unresponsive. In a panic, she called 911. There was nothing the paramedics could do. He was pronounced dead at the hospital.

Claire felt the ground falling away under her. She'd always felt closest to her dad, a man of few words but strong loyalties. His death seemed unreal to her, yet inescapable. Telling her mother she'd join her right away, Claire, standing at the kitchen counter, put down her cell phone and called out to Torman, who'd gone upstairs to change clothes after work. Waiting for him, she held on to the counter to steady herself. At first, hearing the news, Torman thought she might be joking, but he quickly realized Claire was devastated beyond words or tears. He held her close to him, though she seemed miles away. "Mom's still at the hospital."

"We can be there in 10 minutes," Torman said, placing his hand behind her back as he gently steered her out to his car. They drove in near silence. "Jesus, what a shock. I can't ever remember him being sick. I'm so sorry, honey." With his right hand he held hers for a while, but when he needed both hands on the wheel, she folded her hands in her lap. At the hospital, Claire and her mother hugged and cried, while Torman stood off to the side feeling useless and at a loss for words. He knew there was nothing he could say but hoped he could find some way to be supportive. Fairly quickly, Claire seemed to pull herself together and began comforting her mother and talking with the hospital staff. The three of them discussed how to deal with Claire's brother Don, who'd been left behind at home, watching TV and oblivious to his father's medical crisis and death. The problem of how to handle him provided a less painful focus. They agreed that Torman should leave to pick him up and tell him the news about his father. Finally, Torman had found a way to be useful.

Before leaving, he accompanied Claire to the room where her father lay. He looked like a man asleep. Torman stood aside as she approached the gurney. She put her hand on his arm. Bending towards his face, she whispered in his ear, so quietly that Torman couldn't make out what she said. She kissed his forehead, stood back, and stared at his face, as if trying to etch the image of him into her memory. When she finally turned away, Torman reached out to put his arm around her, and she let him guide her back to her mother.

When Torman arrived at her parents' home, Don was still sitting in front of the TV. He was watching the cartoon channel and barely looked up when he entered the room. Torman sat down beside him, tapped him on the shoulder, and, using the remote, turned off the TV.

"Don, your dad was very sick today." He looked at Torman, nodding his head.

"The doctors tried to help. But Dad died. Do you understand?"

`   "Dad died."

"Yes. Dad died. He won't be coming home."

"Dad died."

"Yes." Don fell silent, looking at Torman briefly, then turning his gaze back toward the blank TV. "Come with me to the hospital. To say goodbye to Dad." Torman wasn't sure what to do if he didn't move, but Don got up, and they left the house. "Your mom and Claire are there. They want to see you."

"Dad died."

"Yes, Dad died."

While Eric was cleaning up the dinner dishes, the doorbell rang. Not expecting anyone, he figured it was a neighborhood kid selling scented candles or unhealthy snacks for a school fundraising. Instead, he found Susan in tears on his doorstep. Apologizing for coming by without forewarning, she told him she'd had a terrible fight with her husband and left their house in a rage. "I didn't want to talk to my family or friends about what's happening. You're the only one besides Torman who knows what I'm going through." Eric invited her in, guiding her to a small den off the living room.

Susan sat down, clutching the box of Kleenex that Eric found for her. For a few minutes she remained silent, eyes and nose wet and red. After a final forceful blowing of her nose, Susan regained her composure and described their fight: her husband Dan accused her of being selfish for wanting to continue her treatment with Torman and not caring about his career. At first, she tried reassuring him she was thinking of just delaying her departure for Germany. She noted how busy he'd be, how not having to worry about her adjustment to the change would allow him to focus on his new position. But Dan became increasingly furious, recounting all the ways in which he'd sacrificed for the two of them and how unappreciative she was.

"I don't know, maybe I *am* selfish. My analysis is so expensive and time consuming. But I feel it's the first time I've taken care of myself and not tried to please everyone else. I feel it's my one chance to discover who I am and what I want for myself." Eric noted how hard it is for people unfamiliar with analysis to understand its importance.

Gradually, Susan relaxed and began looking around the room, taking stock of all the books lining the walls of the den. Getting up to make some tea, Eric felt giddy, almost light-headed. At the same time, he knew he'd be reporting this visit in his next session with Torman.

Handing Susan her tea, he said, "Well, I guess we'll be talking about our meeting tonight in our appointments with you-know-who."

Susan laughed. "'Dad'll have a field day with this."

"So, if Torman's 'Dad,' then we're siblings."

"That's right, Bro."

After more bantering, Susan got up to leave, apologizing again for showing up unexpectedly and thanking him for listening. As he watched her walk to her car, Eric thought about her use of "Bro" and how he'd always wished for a sibling. There was even some comfort in the idea that their relationship, complicated by sharing an analyst and by Susan's marriage, might still allow for some intimacy through their "sibling" status. But the image of her sitting in his den, tea cupped in her hands, stayed with Eric into the night, spawning incestuous fantasies.

Patients always react to unexpected cancellations, sometimes wanting to know why, sometimes denying obvious reactions, sometimes reacting with anger, annoyance, hurt, all kinds of feelings. Torman wished he could just say he had to attend a funeral and leave it at that, but invariably more questions arose, more feelings needed exploration. Simply canceling without giving any reason allowed more freedom for patients to express their feelings and fantasies but seemed, in Torman's mind, unnecessarily mysterious and unnatural.

The funeral for Claire's dad was mid-week. Torman stayed home the rest of the week, then returned to work the following Monday at Claire's urging. He felt she didn't want him hanging around, plus she knew how he hated to miss work, hated messing up his routine. She handled most of the funeral arrangements, called family and friends of her dad to notify them of his death, and spent a lot of time with her mother and brother. Torman helped out with Don, who showed no emotion over the loss except for repeating "Dad died."

Torman was surprised that Claire was dry-eyed at the funeral, but on reflection he figured this conveyed just how necessary it was for her to contain her feelings of grief. He knew how close she and her father were and recalled her saying more than once that she could always count on him to be there for her. He assumed she immersed herself in taking charge of the funeral in order not to be overwhelmed with emotion. His efforts to help her talk about her dad were rebuffed, though not with hostility. "Steve," she'd say, "I just can't talk about this now." Torman sensed something was not right with this, that he should be the one she could open up to, that he should provide her with some measure of comfort.

Upon returning to work Torman learned of Susan and Eric's evening rendezvous. Eric seemed contrite while Susan was more defiant. Torman could feel himself tensing as he listened to Susan's marital woes. Identifying with Susan's husband interfered with his ability to empathize with her. The image of Claire and the lawyer he'd spied her with erupted into his awareness as Susan spoke of Eric's kindness. At the same time, he struggled to put that image out of his mind's eye and to focus on Susan's emotional state. He felt grateful for the couch: his face, contorted with anxiety, remained out of sight. Even so, Susan asked, "Are you angry with me, disappointed in me?"

"Is that how you're experiencing me now?" (a typical psychoanalytic dodge but the best he could manage under the circumstances).

"Well, you've been pretty quiet back there, and when you do speak, your voice sounds...strained. Maybe you think I should be confiding my feelings to you, instead of Eric."

"Well, I'd cancelled last week's sessions, then there was the usual weekend break in our contact. It's hard to contain such strong feelings...perhaps you missed our meetings, felt abandoned by my absence. Going over to Eric's house provided a substitute for me."

"You guys don't make house calls. Seriously, though, it's unusual for you to cancel sessions. I did wonder what made you do that. I've driven by your house a couple of times, not that I would ever stop and stare in your windows. When I was young, really just a little girl, I would sometimes listen outside my parents' bedroom door. Sometimes I'd hear noises and giggling though I didn't really understand what was going on. Now I know. We had this rule: always knock if the door's closed."

"I wonder if my absence last week felt a bit as though my door was closed and you were left wondering what I was doing behind it."

"It did cross my mind that you and your wife might need some extra time together. But I know that's silly. I don't think you'd cancel on short notice to have a roll in the hay with your wife." All Torman could think was how true that was, how he and Claire needed extra time together, yet how unlikely this would involve a roll in the hay.

◆ ◆ ◆

Eric and Susan continued meeting on Wednesdays, though their time together extended for longer periods. Conversation, as before, covered books, movies, childhood experiences, likes and dislikes, and, of course, Torman. But now Susan also spoke more openly of her unhappiness with Dan. Eric told himself these weren't "dates." A tacit agreement evolved that they would remain friends. Eric confessed his romantic, erotic fantasies to Torman, while Susan expressed her relief to Torman that she'd found a relationship with a man free of the usual heterosexual entanglements.

They talked about Eric's writing. Susan believed his condolence letters represented a creative streak that he should pursue. Eric, in turn, revealed his insecurity about his literary skills and his conviction he lacked the innate talent required for a writer. In response, Susan said what she regarded as obvious: "C'mon, Eric, writing's a skill. It's learned, not something we're born with." Obvious, perhaps, but coming from Susan this comment had an enormous impact on him.

In a session with Torman, Eric reported a dream about a dental appointment: "My dentist diagnosed significant decay of my upper right teeth. In the dream I could see the X-ray of my mouth with a noticeable area of decay extending along the back of the teeth." Eric speculated that he was anticipating Torman's discovering significant problems of which he was unaware. The area of decay was hidden from view, revealed only on close examination (that is, via analysis).

"So," Torman said, "what's the decay about?"

"What comes to mind...my mother had all kinds of dental problems. She had root canals, gum grafts, implants. I worry I've inherited her bad teeth. She was very self-conscious about her teeth, even keeping herself from smiling a lot. And she hated seeing a dentist, hated the pain and fear associated with seeing one. She never tried to change her life. She just complained. I felt her life was very narrow, and I see my own life in the same way. I've never stepped out of my comfort zone, never taken risks, always following the path expected of me: college, the family business. I guess I need major work on my psyche."

"Perhaps seeing Susan is an effort to step out of your comfort zone, as well as something you feel needs to be kept hidden."

"Well, I sure don't want her husband to know about this, even though we're just talking. I know I can't keep this hidden from you, though I'm uncomfortable revealing how I feel about Susan because she's one of your patients."

This was one of those times when Torman thought about Freud's emphasis on the oedipal conflict. Eric struggled with what any card-carrying analyst would call rivalrous, sexual impulses for a forbidden love object that belonged to his analyst. The question for Torman was how to respond to Eric, how to acknowledge his fears while at the same time encouraging his moving forward in his life, finding and developing his interests and ambitions. He realized that Susan might be the one to provide the push that Eric needed to overcome his inhibitions, so Torman was careful not to respond in a way that might squelch Eric's relationship with her. Rather than following the dictates of traditional analytic theory, Torman, following his gut, acknowledged how much Susan's encouragement of his writing meant to Eric.

❖ ❖ ❖

Since the funeral, Claire remained quiet and withdrawn. Torman continued to try to draw her out and talk about how she felt about her father's death. When that failed, he would sometimes talk about work, though he knew she only half-listened. He decided to tell her about Susan's relationship with

Eric, thinking she'd welcome some distraction from her own sadness. Sitting together at dinner, Torman said, "You won't believe this, but that analytic patient of mine...the one whose husband got the job transfer to Germany...she's having regular contact with one of my other analytic patients, a single guy who's very attracted to her."

Managing a wan smile, she said, "I bet you thought things couldn't get any worse with her. What're you going to do?"

"At this point I think prayer is my only hope. If they have an affair, Steward will get apoplectic, and my chances of graduating before I start collecting Social Security will approach zero."

The day after that conversation, as Torman returned home from work, he knew something was wrong when he walked in the door. There was an eerie absence. At first glance, everything looked the same. Then he spied the note propped up on the kitchen counter.

Steve,

I know this is a terrible thing to do, leaving without talking to you first. I just couldn't face the conversation, not now... maybe later. I don't want to hurt you, but I feel I need to separate from you in order to save myself from unhappiness and loneliness. I've tried to deny these feelings, burying myself in my work and, to a degree, that worked. But with Dad's death that all fell apart. I've felt so unconnected to you, and our life together seems so lifeless. You are not a bad person, just not the right person for me. I think I've known that for a long time but couldn't face the truth and couldn't face your anger and hurt. Every conversation with Dad ended with his telling me he loved me. I've lost his unconditional love, and I don't feel it with you. I've taken some personal things of mine and am staying with Mom and Don for now. Please don't call me. I'll contact you when I feel ready. I'm sorry for the way I've left and for the pain I know you feel.

Claire

All his suspicions and worries hadn't prepared Torman for this moment. He re-read her note, searching for some hope, some sense this wasn't permanent. He called his friend Ed, who tried reassuring Torman that she'd "come to her senses" and return soon. Torman believed otherwise. Ed invited him out to Oregon, saying he could come any time and stay as long as he liked. Torman thanked him, adding he'd stay in touch, and hung up. Exhausted yet unable to stop his mind from racing, he tried taking a walk, but that failed to settle his mind. He thought of writing Claire a letter, of calling his former analyst, only to reject both impulses. He didn't want to burden his parents with this news, though at some point he'd have to tell them. Having no appetite, he skipped dinner. Others, he thought, might drink alcohol, but he had no inclination to do that and, besides, there was none on hand. He wanted to go to bed, to let sleep take him away, but he knew sleep would likely elude him. Finally, around 11, he took 50mg of Benadryl and lay in bed for hours hoping for sleep, for some way out of the hole he'd fallen into.

Torman cancelled a week of appointments. He just couldn't face work. He barely ate. Sleep remained fitful. He made himself work out at the gym. He kept hoping he'd hear something from Claire, but she maintained her silence. He decided to accept Ed's offer and flew out to Oregon for four days. They talked at length about Torman's marriage, about what went awry for Claire. He hadn't been unhappy in their relationship, and only recently had he been aware of her drifting away from him. He felt like a fool being so clueless. After all, he was a psychiatrist, he was supposed to understand people. Ed became critical of Claire, describing her as arrogant and critical of others. "Honestly, Steve, I've only met her a few times, but I never cared much for her. She reminded me of many of my colleagues: aggressive, sharp-tongued, and self-important." Torman found himself defending her and focusing the blame on his self-centeredness and blindness to her emotions.

He checked his email throughout the day, hoping for something from Claire. He carried his phone everywhere, even into the bathroom when he showered, not wanting to miss her call or message. He agonized over what he would say if she called. Should he beg her to come back? Insist they see a marital therapist as soon as possible? Having to wait, he felt totally helpless. He feared their marriage was over before he could respond to what she needed and missed, before he could try to change. He kept his anger in check, fearing it would drive Claire further away and seal his fate. Yet how could she withdraw so completely without at least telling him what she was feeling, without giving him a chance? He felt as though she perceived him as some sort of monster, as someone too dangerous to confront. How could that be? Many questions, no answers. And he berated himself for not having confronted her with his suspicions, with his sense she'd withdrawn from him. He'd been a coward. Maybe he deserved this fate. His thoughts kept going over and over the same ground, re-playing their conversations, imagining her having an affair, wondering how to get her back, blaming himself for being such a failure as a husband.

The evening Susan and Eric slept together occurred during Torman's weeklong absence. This time she didn't arrive unannounced, having called him and asking if she could come by. Eric anticipated her being upset with Dan, but was unprepared for her falling into his arms. While he was a willing partner in their amorous act, he told himself—and later told Torman—that he hadn't actively pursued getting Susan in bed. Perhaps he was being disingenuous about his role in their taking this step, but it was Susan who steered him towards his living room couch and started kissing him. As Eric subsequently acknowledged to Torman, he could have stopped what was happening but he didn't, and for that reason he shared equal responsibility for their actions.

When Torman returned to work and heard the news, he wasn't surprised. Analyst disappears, patients act out (shorthand for patients expressing feelings in action rather than in words). What he did experience was concern over how this would affect their treatments, especially Susan's since he'd invested so much hope in her "successful" analysis being the key to his graduating from the institute. He hated being so concerned about his career, but he couldn't deny the feeling. Thinking about how he was focused on his own career made Torman beat himself up even more. No wonder, he thought, Claire left him; he could barely see past his own needs.

The other disturbing feeling he had involved their screwing behind her husband's back. He couldn't help identifying with her husband and worried he'd be unable to set aside his feelings in order to understand Susan's and Eric's. As it turned out, neither "lovebird" (as he'd dubbed them in his mind) came across as gloating or gleeful. Eric, in particular, seemed upset with Susan's marital status. He spoke to Torman of his distaste for sneaking around, keeping things secret. Torman didn't get the feeling that part of Susan's appeal to Eric was her being a married woman, though he did acknowledge to Torman how he wanted to save her from a marriage to a man who seemed unable to engage with Susan on an intimate level. Eric wondered if he needed to see her marriage in that way to justify adultery. As for Susan, she expressed surprise at the sudden, unexpected surge of sexual feelings for Eric. Torman believed that these sexual impulses resulted from his unforeseen cancelling of the week's sessions, which created painful feelings that she succeeded in obscuring from her awareness by acting out sexually. He tried explaining how this was an instance of sexualizing her feelings of abandonment, especially in the context of her marital unhappiness and the impending termination of analysis. Susan listened but seemed unconvinced, noting how the idea of sexualizing her feelings of abandonment sounded contrived and theoretical ("I don't know, that just sounds textbookish to me.") Listening to himself, Torman tended to agree with Susan's assessment, yet, at the same time, this is what many analysts would have offered, and it did explain why Susan acted on her impulse during Torman's absence. For Torman's part, he tried to listen and respond to both Susan and Eric with what he hoped conveyed concern and an effort to understand their experiences. He realized his efforts sounded forced but told himself to do his best and try not to be so hard on himself.

◆ ◆ ◆

Torman's home reminded him of a mausoleum, lifeless and dark. Being alone had never bothered him but now felt burdensome. Minutes dragged on. He looked forward to bedtime, yet sleep remained broken. He would lie in bed and ruminate about Claire, her probable affair, her unhappiness with him, his helplessness, his aloneness. Was this what old people who'd lost their partners endured? No wonder the mortality rate was so high in the year after losing a spouse.

And what did he miss? He'd been attracted to her from the beginning, an attraction that never waned. Their diminishing sex life only intensified his desire for her. Early on, her teasing him about his habits and routines conveyed her grasp of his personality and her acceptance, even love, of him. He felt known. Her intelligence never threatened Torman, who always found smart women appealing. After all, securing the love and attention from such a woman boosted his self-esteem, made him feel all the more worthy as a person. And there was her sense of humor, as well as the pleasure he felt with their shared laughter, their history of amusing experiences they sometimes recalled and enjoyed for another round. He had to admit, though, that over time her working at the law firm seemed to have hardened her, made her more cynical, even arrogant. These traits he'd tried not to notice, and when he did, he excused them as necessary defenses in a hostile work environment.

Nothing from Claire. He finally called his parents, who were shocked at first, then bombarded him with questions he couldn't answer. His mother couldn't restrain herself from expressing anger at Claire, whom she'd never liked. That didn't help: Torman ended up feeling it was his fault that he'd married the wrong person. After asking a few questions, his father said very little and let Torman's mother dominate the conversation. "Let us know if there's anything we can do," her parting comment, only reinforced his sense of isolation.

Meanwhile, the lovebirds' romance marched along. Eric floated into Torman's office, his gait livelier, his hair now fashionably cut, his wardrobe casually stylish. His rangy frame looked more defined and toned. Even his speech resonated with more confidence. Torman accepted feeling annoyed at Eric's good fortune, reminding himself that it was important to monitor his feelings, not suppress them. Gold was on vacation, so he was unable to consult with him over this latest development. As for Steward, he simply shook his head and seemed on the verge of telling him to abandon Susan altogether as "unanalyzable" because of her insistence on acting out her impulses rather than exploring them in treatment

Susan told Torman how talking with Eric had made her aware of what she missed in her relationship with Dan. Torman had heard how they'd met in college. She'd been impressed with his seriousness and ambition, qualities that were lacking in many of the other men she met in school. And he was good-looking in a wholesome, all-American way. Except for a short-lived break-up in their junior year, they dated throughout college and married shortly after graduation. She'd had reservations about marrying so young, yet he clearly had none. She now realized that he'd set goals for himself and taking care of finding a marriageable partner was one of them. The next step was his career, which he dived into with abundant energy. He had a number of offers upon graduating, ultimately accepting a position at P & G. He also enrolled in a MBA program. Dan often left for work before Susan got up and routinely arrived home around seven in the evening. He worked most weekends and always brought work home. Not surprisingly, his bosses regarded him as a rising star, and promotions came quickly. All this led to little time for much intimacy between them. Eric's attentiveness opened up all the disappointment she felt with Dan and their life together.

At one point Susan told Torman, "That night I showed up at Eric's after a fight with Dan, sitting in his book-lined den, drinking tea and pouring my heart out…I didn't want to leave. It felt so safe, and Eric was so kind and thoughtful. I realized then how deeply unhappy I was with Dan."

Susan balked at Eric's suggestion that she and Dan see a marital therapist. She feared confessing in counseling her affair and then having to deal with the repercussions. In three months, Dan was scheduled to leave for Germany. The pressure on Susan to make a decision about the move mounted as the departure date approached.

Neither Eric nor Susan wanted to stop seeing each other. Eric had begun to talk about how much better he was feeling. Torman finally spoke with Gold about their relationship, and he reassured Torman that the sky wasn't going to fall, though he predicted, correctly, that Eric was likely to feel much better and no longer in need of analysis. He suggested that Torman allow him to retreat from treatment and to focus on Susan's analysis which was further along and likely to reach a successful resolution. He thought Steward would be mollified if Eric managed a "flight into health" and either terminated treatment or cut back to weekly psychotherapy, and if Torman was able to keep Susan on the couch and talking about what this affair meant to her. Gold thought it was quite possible that her marriage would not survive which might indicate increased emotional strength on her part. His observation about Susan made Torman wonder about Claire and whether her leaving and possibly ending their marriage represented her moving forward. A very depressing thought.

He knew he had to confide in Gold about his marital situation because it was clearly affecting both his mood and his ability to listen with any equanimity to his patients. Gold's voice noticeably softened, asking if Torman was in treatment. He strongly urged him to see someone. Torman wanted him to offer his own services but realized that he needed Gold to continue their supervision. Gold couldn't be both supervisor and therapist. Still, he wished he'd offered.

❖ ❖ ❖

Claire called. It was hard for Torman to get a reading on her. She wasn't unfriendly or hostile but seemed guarded, choosing her words carefully. She made it clear she wasn't returning but didn't say outright that she wanted a divorce. "I'm seeing Dr. Shapiro, a psychologist. I need time to sort things out." The name wasn't familiar to Torman, but that wasn't surprising since psychiatrists and psychologists moved in different circles. Torman said, "I've been thinking it would help if we could meet with a marital counselor, someone who'd be able to help us talk things out."

After a pause, Claire said, "I'll think about that." Another pause, then, "I'd like to pick up my mail and a few things. I can come by the house when you're at work."

"I've put your mail in a pile on the kitchen counter. You can come by any time to pick it up and anything else you might want. I have plans to be away all Sunday morning, so you could come over then if that works best for you."

"Thanks."

Another silence, which Torman broke with, "I miss you."

"Steve, I know this is hard for you. Right now I need to take care of myself. I've got to go. Bye."

Torman played over in his mind their conversation, trying to find some consolation, some hope for their coming back together. He felt like he'd been talking to an acquaintance, not his wife, not someone he'd known for years. And yet, he wondered, had he known her? Certainly not as well as he'd once believed.

Claire's relief upon hanging up felt almost palpable. She'd feared Torman would try to analyze her motives and insist she re-consider her moving out. Paul's laid-back manner contrasted sharply with Torman's intense scrutiny and moment-by-moment monitoring of her mental state. She'd grown so weary of Torman's watchfulness and his own need to maintain a secure, predictable backdrop to his life. In his reaction to the news of her father's death, Claire had sensed in him a subtle worry that his life would somehow be thrown into upheaval, that his schedule and routines, so important to his sense of security, would be disrupted and that he needed to guard against this. That worry tinged his effort to comfort her and led her to withdraw from him. Now, their phone call ended, she recalled seeing Paul for the first time after he'd learned about her father's death. She'd made her way through the throng of sympathizers to her office on her first day back at work and discovered Paul standing a few feet within her office, arms outstretched, waiting for her. Dropping her briefcase, she let herself free fall into his embrace, caring not at all about how far a drop it would be or whether she was tethered to a safety rope. The landing was soft and soundless.

Susan called Eric late one night. She and Dan had a real blowout, and she asked if she could come over and stay until she figured out what to do. Knowing she was upset, Eric tried to contain his excitement at the prospect of her staying with him. He set about tidying up his home, though it needed very little tidying. He dashed upstairs, brushed his teeth, and scrutinized his looks in the mirror to make sure nothing was amiss. She arrived suitcase in hand, with a sheepish smile and a soft-spoken apology. "No apology needed," Eric said, taking her suitcase and guiding her by the elbow into his home. They slept very little, talking at length, finally collapsing into bed too tired for anything except sleep.

Before going to work the following morning, he made breakfast while she slept. Feeling domestic and wanting to make a good impression, Eric was preparing blueberry pancakes and bacon. Susan emerged from the bedroom wearing nothing but his flannel robe and, smiling broadly from the top of the landing, asked if he wanted to come upstairs. Barely managing to turn off the stove, Eric all but ran up the stairs.

By the time they did manage to eat breakfast, Eric settled for some burnt bacon that had remained on the stove and a couple of cold pancakes from the one batch he'd finished. He watched Susan measure a half cup of cereal, then a quarter cup of milk. "Whoa, you *measure* everything you eat?"

"Almost everything. I also keep a daily account of the calories I eat. Is this going to be a deal breaker?" They both laughed.

"Does Torman know about this?"

"Torman knows everything. Besides, I looked in your closet. You are one organized guy. The shirts are lined up according to color. So are your pants."

"Well, let's hope these are the most disturbing things we

discover about one another."

Arriving late to work, Eric couldn't have been in a better mood. Even the news that one of the trucks had broken down on the road failed to annoy him. The day flew by.

At some point Dan called Susan, demanding to know where she was and when she was coming home. She didn't cave in, informing him she was staying with a "friend" and would decide what she was going to do.

One of her problems was not having an income of her own. If she left Dan, she was in no position to support herself and certainly unable to pay for her analysis. Staying long-term at Eric's didn't feel right to her, in spite of Eric's assurances that he was delighted with the arrangement. They talked about her looking for work. It quickly became clear that she wasn't qualified to do much of anything: her college degree in fine arts and lack of any significant work history didn't bode well for finding meaningful work. At the same time, she couldn't envision returning to Dan and accompanying him on his move to Germany.

One of Eric's cousins had gotten divorced and praised his attorney, so Eric gave her name to Susan and suggested it would make sense to schedule an appointment with her to find out just what options she had if she decided she wanted a divorce. Susan thought that was a good idea.

Torman listened to each of their accounts of these events, being careful to remain neutral and non-judgmental. When Eric announced his feeling he'd like to cut back treatment to once a week, Torman didn't put up the usual roadblocks by insisting on careful scrutiny of his request or interpreting Eric's resistance to continued exploration of his inner world. With their romance heated up, he figured it was best that Eric back off the couch. Susan was in significant turmoil and required the intensity of analytic treatment, while Eric, feeling elated with his relationship with Susan, lacked motivation to pursue in-depth treatment. After all, psychoanalysis was ill-suited for someone in love. At least, that's what Torman told himself. It also helped that Gold had predicted this development and supported Eric's cutting back on his sessions.

Claire agreed to see a marital counselor. They met on a Saturday morning with Deborah Stein, a well-regarded social worker. Her office resembled a comfortable living room, with a spacious floral print couch and a glass coffee table separating the couch from two facing peach-colored accent chairs. Torman, too anxious to notice much else about his surroundings, hesitated taking a seat as he waited to see where Claire would sit. When she sat on the far end of the couch, he positioned himself in the middle, giving Claire the space he felt she wanted. "So," Deborah began, "How about if each of you tells me what expectations you have for counseling...let's start with you, Claire."

"I want to use our time together to help me decide whether to stay in our marriage. I've moved out, and I'm staying with my mother and brother." Claire became silent, sitting stiffly, her arms crossed in front of her.

"And you, Steve?"

"I'm hoping we can repair the rift between us. I want our marriage to survive. I know we've drifted apart, both of us very focused on our careers. And Claire's father recently died, something that came as a total shock since he'd been in seemingly excellent health. I believe that's had a tremendous impact on Claire. I've wanted to find a way to comfort her. I'm hoping our talking here will help with that."

"Well," Deborah said, "there's certainly a difference in your goals for counseling...I hear Claire saying she's uncertain whether she wants to commit to making the marriage work, while Steve, you want it to survive." Turning to face Claire, Deborah asked her to talk about what's gotten in the way of their communicating with each other and if the death of her father contributed in some way to these difficulties.

"I guess I've felt alone in our marriage for some time, long before my dad's death. Steve lives a very regimented life, one dominated by work, exercise, and routine. It's true the two of us have been very focused on our careers, but I miss spontaneity and romance in our lives. At times, I feel as though I'm living with a roommate, a considerate and thoughtful one, but a roommate more than a husband or lover. At night, Steve is usually buried in a book. He loves reading, but, let's face it, that's not an activity you can share with someone else."

Claire and Deborah turned towards Torman. "Claire, I know I can be self-absorbed. I know I'm a creature of habit. Keeping a routine, it's true, gives me a sense of security and order. But I don't want to keep you at a distance. I can work on being more available, more flexible. I don't want us to be apart." Torman felt as though he was practically pleading with Claire.

"I can't help it. I'd kept my frustration and sadness hidden from myself for a long time. But when Dad died, it was as if my denial broke down, and I became aware of all I'd been holding inside me, all the disappointments. I could always count on Dad to say he loved me. He used to tell me I was his little girl..." Claire's voice cracked. She looked down at her lap, holding back the tears.

Torman struggled to find a way to respond. Her rigid posture and her position at the far end of the couch inclined Torman not to try comforting her with a physical gesture. After a silence, he said, "Claire, I know how much your dad loved you and how much you loved him. I'm so sorry..." Claire's continued silence left Torman in the dark, unsure what else to say. He'd noticed how, throughout the session, Claire toyed with her wedding band, sliding it up and down on her finger. Torman watched this unconscious display of her marital dilemma, afraid to comment on it yet unable to ignore it.

Deborah noted how a lot of feelings had surfaced in the session and how she could appreciate how the two of them were struggling to find a way to deal with their feelings and to find some common ground to work on. At the session's end they agreed to meet again. Walking out together, he looked for some sign of softening on Claire's part. A touch from her, even just her hand momentarily on his sleeve, would have alleviated some of his despair. But her detachment remained in place. Nodding goodbye, she got in her car and was gone.

◆ ◆ ◆

Susan met with the lawyer Eric referred her to and felt an instant connection with her. Susan figured Claire Daniels was in her early 30's and admired how she appeared stylish without being too fastidious about her appearance. She greeted Susan with a smile, ushered her into a cozy office, sat down directly across from her, and said, "Over the phone, you mentioned being separated from your husband, considering a divorce, and wanting to know what your options are. Let's start with your telling me more about your situation." To Susan's surprise, as she began describing her experience in her marriage, tears welled up, causing her to pause and reach for the Kleenex box that Claire had edged towards her. "I know this is hard for you," Claire said. "Take your time."

"I'm sorry...I feel I've just begun to realize what a huge mistake my marriage has been. Getting involved with Eric and experiencing for the first time how good it feels to share my life and thoughts with a man..." She trailed off and looked down at her hands, which had begun to tremble. Susan looked up at Claire and was surprised at the expression on Claire's face, which seemed to mirror Susan's emotions. Pulling herself together, Susan continued to explain her situation. Her thumbnail description of her husband ("An ambitious P&G executive who's married to his job") elicited a snort from Claire and a remark that she knew exactly the type.

As Claire listened, the story she heard became oddly familiar. When Susan noted that she and Eric shared an analyst, Claire's heart skipped a beat. Shit, she thought, I bet this is Steve's patient. "What's your analyst's name?" Claire asked, trying to look and sound as neutral as possible.

"Dr. Steve Torman. Do you know him?"

Putting aside her notepad, Claire said, "He's my husband."

"No! I…I don't know what to say. I had no idea."

"I'm sure this is a shock. For both of us. I know enough about analysis to advise you to tell Dr. Torman about our contact. Your treatment is of the utmost importance, and you don't want to do anything that will compromise it. It's likely that the two of you will decide it's best for you to choose another lawyer."

"Is that what you think would be best?"

"Frankly, yes. If you decide to pursue a divorce, the experience is very draining and stressful, just as, I'm sure, your analysis is. All kinds of feelings will emerge with me, not all of them pleasant. You don't want that to complicate your treatment. And clients tell me all the time about things their therapists tell them to do or say while going through a divorce, and often I end up telling clients that I completely disagree with their therapists. I could go on and on, but I think you get how complicating things would be if you were to seek my counsel. I want to assure you that I will not discuss our meeting today with Dr. Torman, nor will he discuss your treatment with me. We both maintain confidentiality." The latter statement was not entirely true, though Claire didn't want to make matters any worse for Steve than they already were. She imagined how upset he'd be hearing the news that Susan had consulted with her. Claire felt bad enough that she'd left him. She would never have seen Susan if she'd known she was Steve's patient.

"Should we stop here?"

"Well, I'm comfortable answering your concerns about what you can expect if you follow through with getting a divorce. I think that will be very helpful to you."

"I'd really appreciate that."

Claire explained that whatever assets she and Dan had acquired in their marriage were generally regarded as "marital" and likely to be split in half. She might get some spousal support for a couple of years, but probably just enough to help her get some sort of education or training to equip her for a career. The cost of her analysis was a special issue and continued time-limited support for that might be possible to include in the settlement, but likely to involve some concessions elsewhere. Claire couldn't be more specific on that matter, adding her chances for the best possible settlement would improve if her husband was feeling guilty about the divorce because, say, he was having an affair or she was suffering from some serious health condition. She then asked Susan about her mental health, whether she'd ever been hospitalized for psychiatric illness, if she'd ever been suicidal, what medications, if any, were being prescribed for her. As Susan answered her questions, Claire hoped she gave the impression that she had no prior knowledge of Susan's analysis. Susan reassured her that she was more of the garden variety patient with chronic low self-esteem, some anxiety and panic attacks, especially in crowds, insecurities about her abilities and appearance, and indecision about her future in regard to work, her marriage, and having children. Near the end of the appointment, Claire advised her to get her own apartment or find a living arrangement with a family member or female friend, explaining, "You don't want to make Dan's anger any more intense than it already is by living with a boyfriend." At the end of the appointment, Claire said, "There's a lot to think about when contemplating a divorce. Take your time, talk with Dr. Torman, and, if you decide to go ahead with a divorce, I can help you find a lawyer who'll give you the best possible representation."

"So, you don't want to represent me?"

"I would very much want to, but not when it could interfere with your treatment with Dr. Torman." Seeing Susan's disappointment, she added, "In the meantime, if you have any questions, don't hesitate to call me." Claire walked with Susan to the elevators, shook her hand and lightly touched her shoulder. As Susan entered the elevator, Claire said, "Susan, you're in good hands with Dr. Torman."

Prior to her encounter with Claire, Susan had told Eric a lot about her childhood and what she'd learned in analysis with Torman. "Dad worked his way up the corporate ladder and always prided himself on his work ethic. When I was young, he rarely took vacations, though work often involved a lot of travel early in his career. I remember, as a little kid, I'd get real excited when he'd come home from a business trip. I'd follow him through the house, waiting to see if he'd brought me a gift. But he was pretty remote, almost never affectionate. Not mean or abusive, just not fully present, if you know what I mean. He left the child rearing up to Mom, who was the original helicopter mom, always hovering anxiously around me, overprotective and critical of my efforts to take risks or challenge myself. And Mom had, still has, a problem with the bottle, something she's tried, unsuccessfully, to hide from me and Dad. I'd find alcohol hidden in all kinds of places in the house, under the car seat, in the garage. Mom never worked, and I'm not aware of her ever having any ambition to be anything other than a housewife, totally dependent on dad, who made all the decisions affecting our home life. Analysis has helped me realize how I don't want to lead the kind of life and marriage my mother has." Eric took all this in, thinking of the ways in which his own mother and father were so different from Susan's, as well as the ways in which they were similar.

"You know," Susan said, "that first time we spoke, at the coffee shop, you commented on the book I was reading. It made me realize that Dan never asks me what I'm reading. That really struck me, as if I'd been hiding from myself any awareness of how uninterested he was in me and what I was thinking or feeling. And then you and I started to meet, and it felt so good to talk about all sorts of things with you. I decided I needed to do that with Dan and I tried, I really tried. He'd look at me while I told him about what I was interested in and thinking about, but I could tell he wasn't really listening, or listening just enough to know when to nod or give me an 'Umhmm.' I felt so alone. It got so that I couldn't tell if I felt more alone when he was at work or when he was home."

At some point, Eric wondered how she felt about his being Jewish and she laughed, saying, "Well, you guys are all really smart and rich, right?" She'd had limited exposure to Jews, though one of her college roommates was Jewish, and Susan occasionally visited her family and participated in a few of their Jewish holidays.

"Well, I'm not what you'd call very Jewish," Eric said, "at least from a religious point of view. We didn't belong to a temple, and my parents didn't care about any of the typical traditions. No seder dinners or lighting Hanukkah candles."

That led them to wondering about Torman, who Eric believed was Jewish. "What makes you think that?" Susan asked.

"Jews can usually tell when someone's Jewish. It's an intuitive thing."

"Oh, come on…you're joking, right?"

"Well, some people really look Jewish, others talk kind of Jewish…I just have this sense about him. Maybe you have to be Jewish to know what I mean."

They did agree that Torman was no doubt happily married to a beautiful, accomplished wife and had two perfect children and a dog.

In the second therapy session with Deborah, Torman

risked asking Claire if she was involved with someone else. After an awkward silence, Claire said, "Yes, a colleague at work, Paul." An even longer silence followed. Finally, Claire said, "I'm not going to stop seeing him."

Mostly to Deborah, Torman said, "I'm not sure what point there is in our continuing here." He stared at the floor, not wanting to look at either of them. More devastated than angered, he wanted to be with someone who would simply hold him. For the first time he knew what his patients felt when talking about their divorces or the divorces of their parents when they were children. His well-ordered life no longer held together. He'd entered an unfamiliar, shifting landscape.

Deborah tried to find some common ground, some way to approach talking about Claire's affair and her uncertainty about their marriage. Claire said, "Actually, I'm relieved Steve finally knows. I agreed to counseling because I needed to be in a safe place to tell him about Paul and to make it clear I wanted to end our marriage." Torman listened but didn't respond to Claire, leaving it up to Deborah to find some way to bring the session to an end.

Aware of Torman's despair, Deborah asked, "Steve, are you in therapy?" When he shook his head, she said, "I know how devastating this is for you. I think it would be helpful if you got some individual treatment for yourself. I know you're aware of many good therapists in town…Dr. Steward might be someone to consider…."

Not hesitating a moment, Torman said, "I wouldn't send a dog to him." Later, thinking back to this moment, he wondered if Deborah had been in treatment with Steward, though he didn't regret his comment. Steward felt like a safe target for his hurt and anger.

On their way out, Claire told Torman she'd consulted with a lawyer, adding if he wanted the names of some lawyers, to ask her. "This shouldn't be difficult to unwind. I don't want us to fight our way out of our marriage. I know you probably hate me right now. I'd feel that way if I were in your shoes. I'm sorry." Not waiting for a response, she hurried off, relieved she'd told the truth about Paul and wanting a divorce, but also feeling awful at inflicting so much pain on Torman.

Sitting in his car in the parking lot, Torman's thoughts drifted from replaying their session with Deborah to recalling the last time he and Claire had sex. She'd reached for him in bed, something that had heartened and instantly aroused him. Yet when they were finished, she quickly retrieved her underwear from the crumpled sheets and withdrew from him, as if she'd finished some unwholesome chore. Thinking back, he wondered what was going on in her mind. Had she felt some momentary yearning for him, only to experience its evanescence or illusoriness? Had she wanted to compare how sex felt with him to sex with Paul? Or had she wanted to see if she still felt any passion at all for him? Weighed down with hurt and an aching in his chest, he was relieved the session came at the end of the workday. There was no way he could return to work feeling so low.

Susan, while still at Eric's house, began looking for work so that she could afford her own place. A friend of hers owned an art gallery, and she hoped she could work there, even if part-time. She'd also looked into a masters degree in fine arts. She knew that careers with that degree were limited and often involved teaching. She'd started drawing, something she'd done in high school. She set up an easel in Eric's basement. He'd been posing for her, but she was reluctant to show him anything she'd drawn so far.

Torman listened to the ways his patients' lives intertwined, hoping he'd find a way to contain his own sadness so that he could help each of them find the means to overcome their inhibitions and move forward with their lives. Being at work was infinitely preferable to being at home, where the only sound was the sound he made.

◆ ◆ ◆

Torman didn't need to ask Claire for names of lawyers. Over the years she'd mentioned a number of her colleagues whom she respected, and he called one of them. Her office was downtown in a small brownstone. It was bright and airy, free of the usual dark mahogany furniture and paintings of American eagles that he associated with lawyers' offices. He picked a woman because he figured his chances for an empathic response were greater with a female lawyer, all the while realizing what he had to tell was pretty run-of-the-mill to any divorce attorney.

Andrea ("Everyone calls me Andie") Bayer met him in the waiting room and escorted him to her office where he sat in a red suede swivel chair across from her desk. Andie sat in her desk chair, took up a pen, and said, "So, Steve, tell me where things are with you and Claire." Torman launched into his tale, soon became tearful, finally stopping when he sensed he'd supplied her with enough of a background to his marital collapse. All this registered with her as she kept her eyes on Torman during most of his story.

"So a divorce is not what you want, but you have no choice in the matter."

"Yes. And I've learned enough from living with a divorce attorney to know that such feelings have no bearing on the divorce. So, what else do you need to know?"

"Well, I always ask, what's your worst fear?" That caught him off guard. Not anticipating such a question, he sat quietly for a while, thinking.

"Living alone for the rest of my life, unable to find someone I love and can trust to love me back. If I'd done something obviously awful, like having affairs or being sadistic and abusive, then I could change those behaviors. But I feel she's leaving me because of who I am, because I'm easily angered and self-absorbed and insecure. And that's my character, something not likely to change."

"Steve, I've been divorced, I've talked with many clients in your shoes, and I can assure you there's life after divorce. I found someone whom I love, and you will too. There are many people out there. I know...I'm divorcing them!" They both laughed at that.

Sensing he was ready to move on, Andie started with questions about assets, including bank accounts, retirement plans, home and mortgage, credit cards, and so on. At some point, she noted that the divorce should be uncomplicated and not drawn out if he and Claire were able to forgo fighting over every asset and if Claire's lawyer was reasonable and collaborative. The hard part for him, she explained, would be the emotional piece. She asked if he was in therapy.

"No, I'm not, though you're not the first person to ask me that. I'm not sure who I'd want to see. I used to see an analyst for many years but he's really old now, and I'm not sure how helpful he'd be. To be honest, I'm not sure he was ever very helpful."

"Well, I know some names of psychiatrists and psychologists, but I think you're in the best position to choose someone for yourself, if that's what you want to do."

At the end, Andie told him her hourly fee and indicated that if he wanted to hire her, he would need to sign a fee agreement. "I don't need to think about this. I'll sign the agreement."

As he stood up, she came around to his side of the desk and held out her hand. For the first time he noticed how small she was, just a little over five feet. In spite of her diminutive appearance, she possessed a forcefulness, an engaging presence. Large brown eyes looked directly into his as they shook hands. "I'll be in touch," she said. After a pause, while Torman stood silent, she added, "Steve, you'll get through this," then accompanied him to the outer door. With her help, he figured he would.

◆ ◆ ◆

As if Torman didn't have enough to deal with, Steward informed him in supervision that he was withdrawing as his supervisor because of his assessment that Torman's work no longer conformed to good psychoanalytic technique in spite of all his efforts to steer him in the right direction. For good measure, he recommended that Torman re-enter psychoanalytic treatment to deal with his "countertransference issues" that were affecting his work. He didn't specify what those issues might be. Torman understood this was Steward's way of saying that Torman's unresolved conflicts were interfering with his ability to work with his patient. Steward then added that the institute would decide if he should be assigned another supervisor or if Susan's treatment simply no longer qualified as a bona fide psychoanalysis. That last statement stunned Torman. It took all his strength not to tell Steward to go fuck himself. At least he was freed from having to endure more of his worthless supervision. Cold comfort, he thought, as he stomped out of Steward's office.

The last straw for Steward was Torman's informing him in their previous supervision that he'd learned the divorce attorney chosen by Susan was his wife (who'd kept her maiden name when they married). Shaking his head in disgust, Steward observed she was already having an affair with one of his patients and now was seeing his wife for legal assistance.

"That's just over-the-top acting out!" Steward practically yelled, face reddened. "You've completely lost control of this case." Torman tried explaining that Eric was phasing out of treatment with him and that both Eric and Susan had no way of knowing she'd been referred to his wife. Torman added that when he learned who Susan's attorney was, he advised her to seek another attorney for legal counsel. But Steward was clearly on the warpath, and it was in the following week's supervision that he informed Torman of his decision to resign as his supervisor.

Torman called Gold shortly after Steward's announcement. Gold managed to settle him down: "Steve, the institute knows Steward's unpopular as a supervisor and doesn't want to drive people away from considering a psychoanalytic career by making graduation a herculean effort. This will settle down, and you'll be assigned another supervisor."

Meanwhile, Susan was not happy with Torman's agreeing with Claire that she needed a different lawyer. Claire, whom Susan described as empathic and reassuring, had managed to make her feel secure. At the same time, she had mixed feelings encountering his wife. It was one thing to imagine he had an attractive, successful, compassionate wife, quite another to encounter her and have her fantasies validated. How could Torman possibly admire and love Susan when married to a woman like Claire? Susan complained she could never achieve what Claire had, could never impress him in that way. She also wondered if Claire and Torman had talked about her, even though Claire had assured her they hadn't. Torman also maintained they both respected their clients' right to confidentiality. What Susan didn't know was their living apart and impending divorce. Torman hoped that information would not get leaked to Susan and cause even more turbulence in her analysis. He also felt grateful for Claire's apparent sensitivity in managing the delicate matter of finding herself consulted by one of his patients.

❖ ❖ ❖

"Jeez," Eric said, "I had no idea my cousin's divorce attorney was your wife. I already feel I've kind of broken an unspoken ground rule by my involvement with Susan. I hope you're not pissed at me. You didn't look angry when I came in today, but I know how good you are at remaining inscrutable. I bet they have a course on that in analytic training. Something like, 'Inscrutability 101A.'" Torman smiled, enjoying a moment of levity. "Susan really got worked up over the experience. She thinks your wife's a combination of Louis Brandeis and Cate Blanchett."

"What impact did the news have on you?"

"Frankly, I'm impressed, though not really surprised. I figured you'd be with someone really smart and attractive. I have wondered who wins the arguments in your house. Lawyers have different training than shrinks. More likely to put on the gloves and come out swinging. I bet if you two got divorced, you'd be reeling on the ropes."

Wishing their conversation could take a different course, Torman allowed that comment to hang in the air while he thought how he and Claire might have had a chance to salvage their marriage if they'd gotten in the ring and gone a few rounds instead of each retreating to their corners, nursing their emotional hurts and trying to maintain the status quo. He forced himself to return to the moment with Eric, to distance himself from his own regret.

"We've often talked about how your mother ruled the roost, so it's not surprising you'd imagine that I, like your dad, might have difficulty standing up to my wife."

"It's certainly true that Dad was no match for Mom. I can still recall a few of their fights. Dad always backed down, usually leaving the room. Never anything physical, just Mom getting very stern and not letting Dad get a word in."

After their session, Torman wondered about Eric's comment about a divorce between him and Claire. Maybe on some level, Eric sensed what was going on, just as Torman had previously speculated in connection with Eric's dream about the silent couple in the back of his car.

When Torman called Dr. Gold for supervision, he was surprised to hear a recorded message indicating that Dr. Gold was out of the office due to an illness. Callers were advised to contact Dr. Richard Jamison for further information. That sounded worrisome to Torman, who immediately called the number for Dr. Jamison. He left a brief message indicating he was in supervision with Dr. Gold and asked Dr. Jamison to call him on his cell phone. That evening he learned from Dr. Jamison that Dr. Gold had suffered a serious heart attack while seeing a patient and was in intensive care. "To be honest, Dr. Torman, it's not clear when, or even if, Dr. Gold will be returning to work. His condition is listed as critical and he's not stable enough to undergo surgery, though that may change."

"I appreciate your calling me," Torman said. "How can I stay informed about Dr. Gold's condition?"

"I've got your number, and when I know something more, I'll give you a call."

"This is a real shock. He's been such a help in my work. I really admire him."

"It's been a shock for all of us here. He's been a mainstay in the institute. We're hoping he recovers fully. I'll be in touch when I have an update to report."

From the sound of Jamison's voice, Torman inferred that Gold's prognosis was poor. Doctors, Torman thought, aren't supposed to get sick. A ridiculous thought, but it was a common belief among physicians, who typically neglected their own health and resisted being patients, sometimes even treating themselves. He imagined Gold was in his late sixties, around the same age as his father. Torman found himself thinking about his father, who's health had always been good in spite of developing hypertension in his early sixties. His father rarely consulted Torman about physical issues, and Torman now realized that he'd never shown much interest in his father's health. He made a mental note to ask his father about his most recent physical exam in their next phone conversation.

With Gold unavailable, Torman was on his own, waiting to hear from the institute if he'd get another supervisor for Susan's treatment. Torman realized how he'd gotten dependent on Gold's supervision, how Gold had a way of steadying him. Beyond helping Torman treat his patient, their working together had a conspiratorial element: Gold was in his corner, like a boxer's cornerman, offering advice on how to defeat the institute and gain the upper hand in overcoming resistance to his graduation. He felt awful about Gold's medical crisis and, at the same time, felt abandoned, forced to fend for himself. Briefly, Torman felt sorry for himself, but then made himself put those feelings aside.

Susan described a dream in which she was walking in the woods near her house. The sun began setting, and it became darker and harder to find her way. Finally she reached a clearing and had to decide which way to go. She walked along the edge of the clearing, looking for a path or something familiar to guide her. She felt someone was watching her and became very anxious and started running. "That's when I woke up," Susan said, "and I was scared until I realized it was a dream." After a pause, she said, "I suppose it's pretty obvious...I'm not sure where my life is heading and feel alone trying to find my way. I wonder how involved you are with my life, how much you really care about me. You've got your own life, your wife, your other patients..."

"And that someone watching you...that's me behind you, out of sight as you lie on the couch?"

"Yeah, I can always sense you're back there. I can hear

your breathing sometimes. It's not scary though, not like I felt in the dream."

"Maybe you're scared of what you'll discover here?"

"Well, lately I've wondered if you feel I've made a terrible mistake leaving my husband and having an affair with Eric. And that makes me wonder if those feelings are really my own. What you guys call 'projection.' It's really hard right now knowing what I really think."

"I think one of the problems for you is the sense of urgency you have about how our time together might be very limited because of the uncertainty about how long you'll be able to continue here."

"You mean, I'm going to lose the financial means to continue in analysis."

"Yes, so in the dream you find yourself running, no longer able to take as long as you need to find your way."

That seemed to make sense to Susan. Torman's thoughts drifted to his looming divorce and how little control he felt over the course his own marriage was taking.

Andie emailed Torman that she'd been in touch with Claire's lawyer and believed the divorce was likely to proceed smoothly and quickly. Claire's lawyer sounded reasonable and planned to send a settlement proposal for Andie to review with Torman. He reacted to the news with a mixture of relief and disappointment: relief that there wouldn't be hostile negotiations, disappointment that the divorce was marching ahead despite his wish that his marriage could be salvaged.

When the proposal arrived, Andie emailed a copy of it for Torman to review and scheduled a time for them to discuss it. Torman dreaded the appointment but tried to hide the dark mood that had settled on him like a shroud. They went through the document line by line. At the end, looking intently at him, she said, "So, what do you think?"

"Sounds pretty fair. We'll have to sell the house. I don't really care about that, but I don't like having to give up so much of my retirement plan."

"Maybe you can give her a larger share of the equity in the house in order to keep more of your retirement. We can certainly try negotiating that." As she spoke, she continued staring at Torman. "Steve, I know this is hard. You don't want this to move forward."

"Do they teach you how to read minds in law school?" He managed to laugh.

"I've been doing this work for many years. You pick this stuff up. At least you do if you're not a complete moron."

Andie told him how difficult her own divorce was, how painful it was, how she swore she'd never marry again. "But I did, and I'm happy about that. I saw a shrink for a couple of years, and that helped." He told her he was still uncertain about who to see, how small a world the psychiatric community was, how he wasn't even sure he wanted to see anyone.

"Sometimes I think I should see the social worker in our building. He's very popular, works long hours, seems to like his work. I know too much about most of the psychiatrists in town."

They talked for over an hour. As he got up to leave, she asked if he felt better. He realized he did and told her.

"Good, you should feel better at the end of our meetings." As before, she walked him to the outer door. Walking to his car, Torman thought how Andie would be a good choice of a therapist and remembered reading one of Irv Yalom's novels in which a psychiatrist did end up seeking treatment from his attorney. That made him smile.

Eric told Torman how his cousins who manage the two other branches of the business are capable of stepping in at the office and running things.

"If I decide to get out of the scrap metal business, I'm confident they'll want to buy me out. So far, I don't have the confidence that I could be a writer, though lately I've begun keeping a journal. I share it with Susan, who encourages me to keep at it." Torman was relieved to hear that Eric had begun to imagine writing something other than condolence letters.

Eric and Susan had talked about how important it is for her to feel she wasn't just going from one man to another. She wanted to develop a life of her own that was independent of her relationship with a man. "At times," Eric said, "I worry Susan will find me inadequate and will want someone with more imagination and creativity."

Torman was careful to keep to himself what Susan revealed about her feelings for Eric. He pretended as though all he knew about Susan was what Eric told him about her. He focused on Eric's uncertainty in knowing what he wanted in a woman and on the impact of his mother's invariably disapproving of any potential girlfriend.

"You never learned how to trust your gut instinct about a woman. Instead, you became preoccupied with efforts to either please your mother or frustrate her with your choice." Eric agreed but also sensed that Torman was being careful not to say anything about what Susan might be feeling, in part because it could get back to her. When he admitted thinking this and recalled Torman's warning of the dangers of his patients' seeing each other, Torman noted how, perhaps unconsciously, Eric had created the very condition he dreaded repeating, namely, having Torman in a position where he'd disapprove of a woman Eric chose to see. Eric became quiet, mulling over this idea, while Torman felt relieved to no longer dance around this topic and to be able to offer an explanation of Eric's behavior. After all, Torman told himself, wasn't that what therapy was all about? And didn't Eric need to learn to rely on his own feelings and desires, rather than those of others?

The institute, to Torman's relief, assigned another supervisor, Dr. Paul Gosz, for Susan's treatment. Torman thought they must've dragged him out of mothballs, just like they did with that ancient Dr. Schmidt who gave the introductory lecture to each new class. He'd heard of Dr. Gosz but had never seen him and hadn't even known if he was still alive. Supervision was at Dr. Gosz's house, an old Queen Anne in Clifton, a section of town in close proximity to the University and home to students, professors, and Birkenstock shod liberals who felt out of place in Cincinnati's more conservative neighborhoods. Dr. Gosz had retained his Hungarian accent. They sat in a book-lined study in late afternoon, the sun's rays slanting through the westerly windows. His dog, a rust colored vizsla named Baba, accompanied them and, after sniffing Torman's crotch, lay down by Dr. Gosz's feet and promptly fell asleep. Dr. Gosz kept a bag of hard candies by his chair, occasionally sampling one and inviting Torman to join in. His large head seemed precariously supported by his small frame and nodded as Torman began describing Susan and her nearly 6 years of treatment. Baba's snoring provided a vibrant backdrop to Torman's voice.

Dr. Gosz spoke very little and, as their time drew to a close, finally suggested that Torman pay attention to Susan's yearning for affirmation. He then smiled and added that he looked forward to hearing more of her progress in analysis. Awakened, Baba followed Torman to the door. Letting himself out, he felt relief that this man was not likely to increase his professional woes. On the other hand, Torman wasn't sure how helpful he'd be. "Yearning for affirmation"? Is this analysis, he wondered, or Hallmark Cards?

Susan broached the subject of terminating her treatment in 6 months due to the likelihood of her husband's no longer paying for her analysis. Torman didn't feel he could wait to discuss with Dr. Gosz how best to respond, so he offered to cut her fee in half and suggested meeting three times a week instead of four. He wasn't sure how the institute would view such an arrangement, but it was acceptable to him and hopefully would allow their working together to continue beyond 6 months. They agreed that she would consider this option and discuss it at further length.

Torman realized he needed to find some other kind of work to supplement his private practice income. Regardless of Susan's decision, she would soon be ending treatment, and Eric had cut back to once a week. That meant a lot of open hours in his schedule, not readily filled. One possibility was working as a consultant in one of the community mental health centers. The patient population in those settings was very different from the one he saw in his private practice. It would involve seeing patients with serious disorders such as schizophrenia and bipolar disorder, as well as prescribing medications that he rarely used in his current practice. He felt ambivalent about doing this, in part because it made him feel like a failure. Consulting in a community mental health center was hardly the sign of a successful career in psychiatry. On the other hand, he wanted to work, to use his training and skills, even if that meant in a setting where much of his analytic training wasn't utilized. Clinics emphasized diagnosis and medication management, with limited time spent with patients. However, he'd done this kind of work in his residency and recalled feeling gratified by the progress many patients made in spite of the limited clinical contact and the seriousness of their illnesses. Plus, keeping busy would keep his mind occupied, would serve as a barricade to his melancholy.

❖ ❖ ❖

Eric reported that he'd cleaned out his father's office of all his personal effects, keeping some things while donating the remainder to Goodwill. "I'm keeping his Mr. Rogers cardigan sweater. I could never part with that."

He also noted starting a short story. His desk, covered with ideas written on yellow post-its, resembled a patchwork quilt in need of some design. He was working on organizing all of this into some coherent story. Hesitantly, he wondered if Torman would be interested in reading whatever he eventually came up with. Torman smiled, saying he most definitely would be.

❖ ❖ ❖

Andie emailed Torman, informing him they had an acceptable divorce agreement. They met briefly so he could sign some documents. She told him the final step involved attending a hearing to finalize the divorce. Looking Torman in the eyes, she asked how he was doing in a way that suggested a genuine interest, so he told her that he was finally accepting having no control over the loss of Claire and had even entertained thoughts of dating. That word, "dating," caused him to feel self-conscious and uncomfortable, but he couldn't think of an alternative. Andie reminded him the world was full of good women and reassured him he'd find one. "Frankly, Steve, you're a real catch." Torman beamed.

Leaving Andie's office, his mood crashed as he recalled how, a few weeks ago, Claire had arranged to come over with movers to take possession of the furnishings and other home contents they'd agreed would go to her. She didn't have to ask him not to be present. Torman had arranged to spend the Saturday afternoon with Lou Genova, a neighbor who'd gone through a divorce and who'd proved to be very consoling, even inviting Torman to join him and his current wife and children every Sunday evening for dinner. It was Torman's return home after the movers left that came back to him. He'd wandered from room to room, trying to rearrange what was left to make his home look half-full rather than half-empty. Eventually, he'd made his way upstairs. The marital bed dominated the master bedroom. Claire had made it clear in their brief negotiations that she had no desire for their bed. A small bedroom had been her study. Her diplomas were gone, leaving their ghostly vestiges on the wall. All the framed photographs of the two of them remained, as did their wedding album. He felt she'd excised his very existence from her life and was reminded of newspaper obituary photos in which the deceased faces the viewer but only a small part of his or her spouse is visible, just a shoulder or a fraction of a face left in the frame. Only in Torman's case, Claire's parting from him occurred not in death but in life.

Weary from moving furniture, Torman found himself sitting in the one remaining chair in Claire's study, staring at the walls and thinking about what those walls had absorbed over the last 90 years. Home to at least three other families, what sadness and loss had seeped into this house's frame? Had hurt outweighed the joy? Had Torman's failed marriage tipped the scales? He didn't believe in haunted houses, but he wondered about ghosts of emotions, of cursed relationships, somehow haunting, even influencing, the lives of those who dwelled inside these walls. A kind of magical thinking, he knew, yet who wants to sleep in a room where someone has died?

❖ ❖ ❖

Torman interviewed at a local mental health center for a 15 hour a week consultant position. The medical director, Dr. Jane Rabin, who greeted him in the waiting room, had been a resident in the psychiatric residency program when Torman, a recent graduate, was a young faculty member in the department. She expressed delight in his interest, though he suspected she was wondering why he'd be looking for work in that setting when he was in a private practice associated with the analytic institute. The logical assumption would be that he was lacking referrals and needed work. But she did not question his motivation. Instead, she emphasized how proud she was of the quality of work the clinic provided to a patient population that typically received substandard care. Jane had decided early in her career to devote herself to community psychiatry and prided herself on treating severely ill psychotic patients. Tall, stylishly dressed, with perfectly coiffed auburn hair, she resembled a queen visiting beleaguered troops on the front line. After ten minutes, she let Torman know he could start any time he wanted, the sooner the better. Although not anticipating such a quick offer, he agreed to start in a week.

Walking through the waiting room on his way out, Torman paid closer attention to the waiting room occupants. One young man, seated off to the side, was talking to himself. Two middle-aged women were shouting obscenities at each other. An old man with a walker and oxygen was slumped over in his chair, either asleep or unconscious. It looked as though he'd pissed his pants. Sitting at a small desk, an overweight security guard, dressed in a blue uniform and consuming a large bag of Cheetos, listened to someone on a walkie-talkie. A couple of young children were running around while their mother, distracted by a crying baby in a stroller, called out to them to behave and sit down if they knew what was good for them. Outside, by the main entrance, a disheveled man asked Torman for a cigarette, then for money.

Did he want to do this? Was he fucking nuts? Shaking his head, he got in his car and drove back to his office, where the only noise in the waiting room was the rustling of magazines.

The MFA in creative writing at Iowa University, known as the Iowa Writers' Workshop, required, among other things, a manuscript of one's best work. Torman listened as Eric discussed his tentative plan to apply. Eric sensed Torman's unstated endorsement of his applying. Every time he raised some reservation, Torman either countered with a solution or employed sarcasm to undermine his hesitancy.

"Really, Eric, what's holding you back?"

"I don't want a rejection. That would be humiliating. And I suppose I don't want to be apart from Susan…and from you."

"Have you thought of applying to more than one program? Iowa's not the only well-respected writing program. There's no need to put all your eggs in one basket. The University of Cincinnati has an MFA program if you want to stay in town."

"Well, I've gone online and looked up other schools. It's just that Iowa has such a great reputation. And being Iowa, there can't be many distractions, just hayfields or whatever it is that grows out there."

"Eric, nobody ever asks me where I went to medical school. I suppose it might matter if I wanted to do research at a prestigious academic center, but in practical terms, where I got my medical degree is pretty meaningless. I'm judged by my work, not my degrees."

"The other thing, as I said, is being separated from Susan and you."

"Do relationships have to end just because of physical distance?"

"No, but it can't help."

"I'm not so sure about that. Distance gives a person the

chance to really think about a relationship and what it really means to him."

"So, if I were 2000 miles away, I'd still be your favorite patient?"

"Right up there at the top."

The final hearing was in the courthouse, in a wood-paneled room off a long corridor. Seated on a hallway bench, Andie stood to greet Torman, then ushered him inside. Claire, already present, sat between her lawyer and a female friend he recognized. Andie had warned him this hearing would be a brief and coldly perfunctory ceremony.

The judge, a portly, thin-lipped man in his mid-fifties, peered at them over his half-lens reading glasses as he asked each party identical questions, the essence of which was to ascertain that they'd voluntarily agreed to the signed dissolution document. Then came the final pronouncement that their marriage was dissolved, followed by the instruction to exit by the door on the left. In spite of Andie's warning, Torman felt as though he was being thrust into a cold, dark night, coatless and alone.

Andie had suggested he bring someone there with him, but he'd had the fantasy that he and Claire would leave together, perhaps going somewhere for coffee to talk, to say goodbye. He hugged Andie outside the courtroom, telling her how much he valued her help and genuine concern. Looking up at him, she reminded him that there was life, and relationships, after divorce. Managing to hold back tears, Torman turned to leave and noticed Claire and her friend were nowhere in sight. Once outside, he spotted them a half block away, talking animatedly to one another. Embarrassment over his foolish expectations compounded the hurt that threatened to overwhelm him on the street. He plodded toward his car.

Torman was reminded of how he felt with the flu, how he'd swear he'd never forget how bad he felt and how he'd cherish feeling "normal" again. That's how he now thought of his emotional pain. He told himself he'd never forget this moment, the sight of Claire walking off with a friend as if on the way to a party or concert. He also reminded himself how transient the memory of acute illness was, how quickly the return to health was taken for granted. He supposed the same sequence would occur with his present state of mind. He bolstered himself with a perverse pride in knowing he wouldn't be destroyed by his feelings, that he'd keep going, that he'd eventually feel better. At the same time, he didn't want to let Claire off so easily. He understood how thoughts of suicide entered a rejected person's mind. His suicide would inflict lasting pain on Claire to a degree his words could never match. And it beat feeling helpless; it was a way to strike back. Self-pity and rage, in equal measure, threatened his effort to ward off despair.

In their next session, Eric acknowledged that Torman was right: he needed to consider additional MFA programs besides Iowa's. Mostly based on location, he picked five others. "Now I need to start writing in earnest in order to have work to submit. The condolence letters hardly qualify for submission, nor do my prior efforts at creative writing in college. I've mentioned working on a short story; it's almost complete. I make notes about ideas for stories, and I've started reading some books on writing fiction."

He noted that Susan was encouraging him to apply. What Eric and Susan didn't discuss was the separation that would occur. They still spent a lot of time together and had settled into a comfortable routine of daily phone calls and frequent evenings together.

Torman thought to himself how Eric and Susan were using therapy as launching pads for a new life, both seeking to shed their current identities for ones more in tune with newly re-discovered interests. In some ways, they were spurring each other on to explore alternate paths. What he couldn't foresee was whether their relationship would survive these changes. Eric worried that Susan would discover other romantic interests, while Susan seemed more concerned with handling her separation from Dan and losing the support of analysis. She never expressed fears that Eric would leave her.

Nothing like work, Torman thought, to make you forget your unhappiness. Healthpoint Behavioral Services (HBS), where Torman now plied his psychiatric skills 15 hours a week, was the perfect antidote for self absorption. The long train of human misery and poverty kept rolling in, leaving Torman barely time to pause between patients. Unlike his private practice, where he saw patients for 50 minute sessions at least weekly, his role in the clinic was limited to diagnosis and management of medications. While he got an hour for the initial visit, subsequent ones were 30 minutes and usually scheduled every 4 to 12 weeks depending on the patient's stability. In his private practice, he'd managed to avoid electronic medical records and electronic prescribing of medication, but at HBS both were mandatory and time-consuming. While staring at a computer screen and typing progress notes, he tried to get to know the patients, to learn their stories. Almost all of them were on multiple medications, often at dosages and in combinations that would make even a seasoned psychopharmacologist squirm. Not much time was left for any meaningful conversation about how they conducted or experienced their lives. Such work presented different challenges to a psychiatrist like

Torman who'd been focused so intently on understanding the inner life of patients.

Some patients were referred from hospitals, often with few or no records from their inpatient stays or emergency room visits. Others were transfers from psychiatrists who'd left HBS. The legal community referred another wave of patients, often with extensive criminal histories.

Torman worked in a windowless office equipped with a grey metal desk, its surface dominated by a large computer screen. A faux-wood bookshelf, minus books, listed sideways along one wall, collecting dust and colorful brochures from pharmaceutical salespersons (aka "drug reps") touting miracle cures. Three mis-matched chairs provided seating for patients, case managers (the ones responsible for ensuring that patients received benefits, housing, and medical care), and the occasional relative willing to be involved in the patient's care. Most often, it was just Torman and his patient. If he felt threatened, he'd been instructed to push a red button on his desk that alerted the support staff that he was about to be killed. Torman figured the Cheetos-consuming, weaponless security guard would come to his rescue.

His first patient started their session by exposing her forearms, which bore the unmistakeable crisscrossing of self-inflicted wounds. "I'm a cutter," she announced. Ever the professional, Torman asked, with what he hoped was a measured calmness, "Tell me when you began cutting on yourself." That led to an outpouring of all her years of abuse—physical, emotional, and sexual—at the hands of every caretaker in her life, right up to her boyfriend who was currently in jail for domestic violence. While Torman ended up denying her request for Xanax and other addictive medications for anxiety, he urged her to accept a referral for therapy.

"That won't help. I've tried that many times. Therapists always end up disappointing me, and at clinics like this they never stick around very long. Most of them are still in training and can't wait to get into private practice. And I can't afford to see someone privately."

The next patient was in his early twenties and nearly mute. He smelled so bad Torman had to breathe through his mouth. When asked why he was coming to the clinic, he stared at the floor, muttering, "The devil...you know...Judgment Day." What Torman did know was that he was schizophrenic and desperately needed medication. He spent much of the time trying to convince him to resume a once-a-month injection of anti-psychotic medication.

And so it went, one casualty after another. Torman felt he was back in his residency, deep in the trenches fighting a battle against overwhelming odds.

Eric announced to Torman, "It's time to sell the business. I'm looking for an appraiser to give me a sense of what it's worth. Dad always used the same lawyer for the business, and I've put in a call to him to get the name of a reputable appraiser. Once I have a sense of what it's worth, I'll approach my cousins and offer them a chance to buy me out."

"How're you feeling about this decision?"

"Like I'm being disloyal to Dad, like I'm somehow bad. I can't imagine he would've ever encouraged me to leave the business. I know he'd want me to be happy, but he'd never understand why I'd want to walk away from the family business. And it's not like I hate Silver Iron and Steel. I'm proud of it. It's not a Fortune 500 company, but it's a profitable business that's sustained three generations of Silvers. I've worked there almost half my life. I've never worked anywhere else. It's scary to let go of that."

"Striking out on your own *is* scary. Your father didn't do it, deciding instead to enter his father's business. From what you've told me, that worked for him, but not for you."

"If my father were still alive, I'm not sure I could do this. I rebelled against Mom but never against Dad. I don't feel I'm rebelling now...it feels more like I'm trying to find out who I am and what I want to do with my life. Susan talks about listening to her 'inner voice' to guide her and urges met to listen to mine. She and I have many of the same fears. Her leaving her marriage and my selling the business force us to find different directions, to challenge ourselves. She and I support each other as we face these changes. It helps having your support, too."

Torman trailed Dr. Gosz into his study. On the way, he warned Torman that Baba was "gaseous," apparently the result of getting into the kitchen trash. Figuring this would be nothing compared to some of his recent malodorous encounters at HBS, Torman simply shrugged his shoulders. Unfortunately, this time Baba settled down by Torman's feet, causing Dr. Gosz to smile apologetically. "Baba likes you."

Torman described his proposal to cut Susan's fee and to reduce the frequency of sessions in order for her to continue in treatment beyond 6 months. Dr. Gosz listened to the subsequent material and focused on a dream she reported in the session following the offer. In the dream Susan was entering an office filled with diplomas and awards. Seated behind a desk was a bearded man in an elegant dark suit. He was smiling and offering her candy from a bowl. She reached for the candy but it was sticky and stuck together. She left the office feeling uneasy and confused. Susan and Torman had talked about the dream in relation to his offer to allow her to continue longer in treatment. She admitted to mixed feelings about the changes he'd proposed. Torman had asked about the "sticky and stuck together" candy, and her thoughts predictably led to sexual associations, in particular to fantasies about his motives for helping her continue in treatment, especially her feeling he was being seductive.

Dr. Gosz noted that perhaps Torman had prematurely offered suggestions about how to prolong the analysis without first seeing how Susan would approach the change in her finances. It sounded to Dr. Gosz as though it was demeaning to her to be offered the candy, that it was not something she really wanted. She doesn't, he added, want to feel stuck to Torman and to be treated as though she's unfit to leave treatment at this time. "Perhaps you're wanting to keep her in treatment for your own reasons, and she senses this?"

Torman confessed fearing the institute would reject this case as a "successful" analysis if they terminated in 6 months under these conditions. It would be years before he'd have another analysis approach termination. Dr. Gosz remarked that the diplomas and awards in the dream reflected Susan's sense that external rewards were important to the doctor. He thought the two of them, by pursuing the sexual implications of the candy, missed the more disturbing fear that Torman, like her ambitious father and husband, cared only about his career.

Baba let out a real stinker at this point, just as Dr. Gosz, smiling as he enjoyed the irony of his action, reached for the candy.

◆ ◆ ◆

Torman listened as Eric described the negotiations with his cousins for the sale of his share of the business. "I don't like haggling over the price. I like my cousins and don't want the sale of my share of the business to poison our relationship. At the same time, I want to get what I feel is a fair price."

He went on to describe how hard it was telling his staff and the men in the yard about his decision to sell his interest in the company. "Word leaked out about my intention to sell, so

I met with my staff and yard men to discuss the likely changes. I stressed that I anticipated their jobs would be secure and that the business would likely remain in the family. Many of our workers have been with Silver Iron and Steel longer than I have, and there's a real sense of attachment to the company. Even during hard times, Dad always avoided lay-offs, and I've continued protecting their jobs. We've never had a strike. I'm proud of that. In spite of my efforts to allay their anxiety, the men in the yard remained mostly silent, shooting glances at each other as if they'd heard all this before. I slunk back to the office, found Dad's old, nearly full bottle of scotch, and poured myself two inches worth in the lone shot glass."

"Even though you don't have to face your father, you had to face your employees with the news you're moving on. Their apparent disappointment is hard to accept."

"Yeah…at least I didn't have to look Johnny in the eye."

After a pause, Eric mentioned he'd finished a short story. He got the idea for the story after reading an article in the local newspaper about shoplifters and how the court often refers them for counseling. His story focused on a young woman in psychiatric treatment for shoplifting. She'd recently divorced and was obviously depressed though unaware of how her emotional state contributed to her stealing. Her nine year old daughter observed her mother's shoplifting and that set the stage for a painful confrontation between mother and daughter.

Torman wanted to know why he chose that particular topic for a story. Eric remembered getting caught stealing a bag of chips in a convenience store when he was nine. "I was with a friend from school, and we used to go there after classes and try to steal stuff. It was a game of sorts, seeing who could get the coolest thing. The man in charge of the cash register caught me on the way out and confiscated the bag. Threatening to call the police if I didn't cooperate, he demanded my parents' phone number and left a message on the answering machine for them to call him. That night my parents told me how shocked and ashamed they felt. As punishment, I had to return to the store the next day and apologize to the man who'd caught me. My allowance was also suspended for a month. That was the last time I stole anything."

After listening to this tale, Torman said, "Didn't your father's dad die when you were nine?" Eric recalled he'd died early in his ninth year. He told Torman that he didn't think his death had deeply affected him. He was closer to his grandmother, who was the warmer of the two and often babysat Eric. But Torman wondered if he'd sensed a change in his father, who was extremely close with his father. Eric recalled seeing him cry for the first time at the funeral. "Dad wasn't his usual self for a long time after that. I remember sitting next to him watching TV at night. Dad wouldn't say much and often fell asleep on the couch. Mom even began complaining about how he needed to get a hobby or take more of an interest in fixing things around the house. Instead of rolling his eyes for my benefit, he'd just stare off into space."

"So," Torman said, "maybe the stealing was more than a game for you. Maybe it was your effort to make up for what you lost from your father, his companionship and camaraderie. You must've been very scared by the changes in your dad."

"I hadn't thought about my dad's reaction for years. Funny how that came back to me just now."

"Like the dreams you have at night, the fiction you write can shed light on your inner life."

Friday evening, as Torman settled down with a book, he received a call. Not recognizing the number, he let it ring and waited to see if the caller would leave a voicemail. It turned out to be from Susan, whose voice sounded strained as she asked him to call her. She answered after the first ring.

"Dr. Torman, I'm sorry to call you like this but I'm having

a panic attack and it won't stop. I've tried taking a shower and listening to music but nothing's worked. It's scaring me. I can't make it stop."

Speaking calmly, Torman asked when the panic started and then what she was thinking or doing before it came on.

"It started after reading an email from Dan. He accused me of being a selfish, childish bitch and said his lawyer would make sure I didn't get a dime from him. He said I'd never make it on my own, that I'd end up a whore on the street. It was so full of hate."

Torman could hear her crying and trying to catch her breath. "Susan, he knows your worst fears and he's playing on them. It's sadistic and awful. You should be madder than hell."

"I *am* mad. And that was only part of what he wrote. I can't believe I married him!"

Torman sensed that beneath her anxiety was a tremendous welling up of rage, so he encouraged her to talk about all the ways Dan infuriated her.

After a while, she said, "There's something else bothering me. Would you tell me if you thought I shouldn't end my analysis?"

"So you're wondering if I, like Dan, think you can't make it on your own."

"I guess so. But I think I need to hear you tell me whether you think I can manage without being in treatment."

"Susan, I intend to help you look at what it means to end your analysis, to examine all your fears and hopes. I believe it's important that your decision is based on your own assessment of how you'll do and what you need. However, after our careful analysis, if I believed you'd be making a terrible mistake to end treatment sooner rather than later, I would tell you." That seemed to allay her worries. He added that they should talk at greater length about all this at her appointment on Monday.

"Thanks for talking with me. I really appreciate it, and I can tell I've settled down. See you Monday."

Torman thought about the call, how Susan had never

called for help before and how, in a way, the rarity of reaching out in that way only magnified its potential impact. He knew he'd hear about its impact on Monday.

◆ ◆ ◆

Dr. Rabin, wearing a sapphire blue outfit and radiating Pilates vigor, knocked on Torman's office door, then glided into the chair nearest his desk to tell him how much his patients like him, how the psychiatrists and nurse practitioners praise his clinical skills, and how grateful she is that he'd joined HBS. Stunned, even blushing at this fulsome praise, Torman just sat there a moment before blurting out, "I'm really glad to hear that."

"You have so much to offer...we'd love to have more hours from you. I know how much time is taken up in your private practice, but just let me know if you're ever interested in adding more hours here." She went on about how interesting many of the patients are and how rewarding she finds helping these severely impaired people. Then, moving gracefully at her usual light speed, she vanished, while Torman geared up to meet his next challenge, James West, an Army vet who'd served tours in Iraq and Afghanistan and who wore sunglasses, camouflage trousers, and a T-shirt stretched tightly over muscles worthy of any film superhero. With not an ounce of fat, James barely squeezed into what must have seemed to him an office designed for midgets.

This was their second meeting. Torman had heard all about his psychiatric admissions, as well as his frequent run-ins with the police, who were constantly stopping him and subjecting him to lengthy interrogations. Torman could understand why he'd be approached warily by others. James' physical presence scared *him*. His flat affect—the lack of facial expression and James' deadpan delivery—alarmed Torman. The sunglasses certainly didn't help matters, either. He'd seen men his size bench press 450 pounds and toss 50 pound weights as easily as pitching horseshoes. Normally, veterans were served at the local VA Hospital, but James had worn out his welcome there and refused to return for services.

Today he sat down, looked straight ahead, and, in a soft voice Torman strained to hear, told him he'd killed a man on the way over to the clinic. All Torman managed to get out of his mouth was, "What?!" Quietly, James said it again. Torman sat there, unsure what to do. Then he saw a smile on James' face, and it hit him: he had a joker on his hands. Apparently Torman had passed the test and was okay in James' eyes. Their shared laughter felt good. Torman sat back in his chair, relaxed enough to ask, "So, aside from committing murder, what was the rest of your day like?" What emerged was a lengthy tale of how a former girlfriend, spurred on by jealous rage, kept telling anyone who'd listen that he'd been stalking her, stealing from her, and threatening her. This had been going on for years. No one believed his protestations of innocence. His only defense was to stay home all the time and work out in his garage.

Not having any easy solutions to offer, Torman simply accepted his story and acknowledged how restricted his life had become. Later, he imagined seeing James' former girlfriend as a patient and hearing an entirely different version of this tale, one that would also likely pull him in and have him empathizing with her pain and terror.

The orientation party for students entering the University of Cincinnati masters of fine arts program, which had accepted Susan's application, took place at the school's fine arts complex and capped a three-day series of meetings between the faculty and incoming students. Student and faculty artwork was on display in various galleries and studios in the fine arts complex. Eric told Torman how uncomfortable he felt in such situations. "Knowing only Susan," he said, "made matters worse. I'd tried to dress casually but still felt I stood out as a non-artist. No other man wore an oxford cloth button-down blue shirt, my khakis were too crisply pressed, and my hair looked too neatly combed. I imagined I looked like some kind of salesman or computer geek who'd shown up at the wrong party.

"Shortly after our arrival, one of the professors made his way over to Susan. Smiling broadly and calling her by name, he seemed totally unaware of me. He really looked the part of an artist with his faded, paint-stained Levi's, low-cut hiking shoes, and Hawaiian shirt. Susan made a point of introducing me to Max Samuels, but before I could say anything, Max, standing between Susan and me, turned his back to me and spoke softly and very close to Susan's face so that I could barely make out what he was saying. Taking Susan's elbow, Max said, 'Let me show you something.' Clearly I was not included in this invitation and was left standing there as they made their way toward one of the studios.

"I tried to look calm and circled the room with a glass of wine in my hand, feeling really out of place and pissed off that Susan had blithely gone off with this man who clearly was attracted to her while I was excluded and left alone. Making matters worse, Max looked like Robert Redford in the movie "Jeremiah Johnson," with long hair, full beard, and rugged handsomeness. I felt jealous and, at the same time, ridiculous for feeling that way. I felt like leaving without Susan but figured Max would welcome the opportunity to drive her home. When Susan finally did return, she looked flushed with excitement and gushed about how creative Max's installation piece was. I barely responded. She asked what was wrong. I said I'd felt ignored by Max and uncomfortable being left by myself. Susan said I was overreacting and blowing things way out of proportion. She said I could've joined them but held myself back. We left shortly, and the ride home was a quiet one. I dropped her off at her apartment." Torman acknowledged how upsetting this experience was for Eric and how hard it was to deal with Susan's apparent insensitivity to his feelings.

Shortly after hearing Eric's tale, Torman heard Susan's version. "I think Eric's shy and uncomfortable in social settings. He holds himself back. I'm not sure why...he's really capable of making conversation and has a good sense of humor. I think he feels out of his element in situations that are unfamiliar to him. But I'm so excited to start my classes, and I find most everyone in the fine arts program to be so stimulating and interesting...I just got really frustrated having to deal with Eric's withdrawal and hurt feelings. I wanted to share my excitement with him but couldn't because he felt so out of his element and ignored."

Torman acknowledged both her frustration that Eric held himself back and her disappointment Eric couldn't appreciate how excited and hopeful she felt starting the fine arts program. After she left the appointment, Torman found himself recalling Eric's experience of being ignored by Susan and Max. Where was the truth in all this? Torman figured it was somewhere in the middle, in the grey zone where everyone, himself included, grappled with conflicting narratives of events and experiences. Torman thought of this as the Rashomon effect, which regularly threatened to rupture the tenuous bonds holding relationships together.

Susan informed Torman that she didn't feel the need to put off terminating treatment. She thanked him for offering a lower fee but didn't feel comfortable accepting it. She said she'd learned a lot about herself and believed her life was moving in a new—and desirable—direction. She spoke enthusiastically about starting the masters program in fine arts, then described how strained her relationship with Eric had become. He was jealous of Max, the faculty member who, she admitted, was clearly interested in her. She found Max, a divorced man with two children, charming. Rumors about his exploits with female students were rampant. While wary of his attention, she couldn't deny how attractive she found him.

"I hate to say it, but being with Max is like driving at full speed in a sports car with the top down, while being with Eric is like going to the grocery store in a minivan. Eric's kind and considerate and thoughtful, but he's not romantic or spontaneous. Max is so full of energy and enthusiasm. I don't think he sleeps. He's in his studio all hours of the night, yet in the daytime he's eager to teach and talk. And he's unbelievably good-looking."

Her description of Max evoked Torman's jealousy. He could only imagine how jealous Eric felt. But he struggled to stay with Susan's experience, with her burgeoning excitement not only with school but also with Max. She'd really come alive and, he believed, needed that acknowledged, not questioned or dampened. Torman's awareness of that brought back Dr. Gosz's seemingly Hallmark card comment at the end of their first supervision, that Torman should pay attention to her yearning for affirmation. That memory made Torman smile, and he responded to Susan by acknowledging her feeling for the first time that she'd taken charge of her life and was following her dreams. In response, she recalled having a dream about flying. "It wasn't scary, at least not too scary. More stimulating. My arms were outstretched, the wind blowing my hair, the ground whizzing below me. I wasn't sure how to land…or where to land. I passed over the tops of trees and managed to come down in a field." She laughed, saying she'd read somewhere that analysts interpreted dreams of flying as representations of erections or having sex. "*I* think it has to do with my new sense of feeling free, of finally taking off on my own."

Torman agreed, adding, "I think there's also some concern about how and where to land. There's still uncertainty about where your life is going. Maybe also a sense that your leaving analysis makes you feel somewhat unfettered, flying free of any restraints."

"Well, everything does seem up in the air, so to speak. My marriage is ending, my relationship with Eric is shaky, and my analysis ends in a few months."

Torman found himself recalling going off to college for his freshman year. His parents drove him to college in Massachusetts, and, once settled in his dorm room and having met his roommate, he was eager to see his parents leave. His mother maintained her composure, while his father, much to Torman's surprise, couldn't hold back his tears. Torman hugged them both goodbye, turned away, and didn't look back. That memory made him think that he was responding to Susan's desire to emancipate herself and not look back. What Torman couldn't figure out was whether he identified with her or with those left behind. Or both.

Eric felt awkward talking about his relationship with Susan to Torman, who no doubt knew what Susan was really thinking yet couldn't tell him. Torman limited himself to underscoring the importance of Eric's relationship with Susan. Eric imagined that maybe even Torman didn't know what Susan felt, maybe she felt constrained telling him because she knows he sees Eric and cares about him. Eric knew Torman cared about him and sensed his appreciating how painful the fear of rejection was. He couldn't say how he knew that, he just knew it.

He told Torman that the only positive side to all this anguish was the material it gave him for writing. Unrequited love, jealousy, fears of losing Susan were all material for a writer's workshop. Soon he'd have to choose which story to send to the MFA programs. In the meantime, he'd started reading books on writing and was thinking of attending a writer's conference. He read differently now: he thought about how the writer constructed the story, how characters were introduced, how the plot moved along. There was so much to think about.

"Many writers advocate writing about what you know. I know the scrap metal business, but I doubt I could find a way to make *that* interesting. If I were writing a murder mystery, a character could get squashed to death in an auto crusher, but I don't think that's especially original. I suppose what I know is what I remember, what I've observed, what I've experienced in my life so far. Hopefully, that's good enough. Susan thinks I just need to let go more, not be so controlled in my efforts, allow my imagination to lead me somewhere, anywhere."

◆ ◆ ◆

Torman looked forward to supervision with Dr. Gosz. He'd even become attached to Baba and offered to take him for walks after their sessions. Oz (the name he used in his mind when thinking of Dr. Gosz, a name that conjured up "a very good man, just a very bad wizard") also seemed to look forward to their meetings. He'd talked some of his past, how he came to the United States at 18, managing to attend college while speaking rudimentary English and eventually getting his medical education and psychiatric training. He shared stories about psychoanalysts and psychiatrists, many famous and long-gone, who'd had an impact on his development.

They discussed the session with Susan that ended with Torman's memory of his parents' dropping him off at college. Oz stressed how important it was to appreciate both aspects of his experience of her: the side of him that shared her excitement at leaving the analysis (and Torman) and the side saddened by her departure. "Such feelings," Oz noted, "are reliable signs that the patient is ready. It doesn't mean she's 'cured' or will never need more help…it means she's ready at this time to terminate."

Oz talked about his first time on the couch, an analysis which lasted two years (ridiculously short by current standards but not uncommon back in the dark ages of psychoanalysis), and about his subsequent treatments over the years with different therapists. He acknowledged that much of this therapy wasn't that helpful and that most of what he learned came from his patients and supervision. That made an impression on Torman, since most analysts reported their own analyses were the most formative experience in their analytic training, while his own experience on the couch had been so disappointing.

Torman also described his work at HBS. Oz seemed to get a kick out of the really outlandish patients and reminisced about working with hospitalized patients before the days of effective psychiatric medications. He recalled how really depressed patients were sometimes made to clean floors with ridiculously ineffective instruments, such as toothbrushes, in the hope that this would mobilize their repressed anger, thereby improving their depressive symptoms.

"Of course," Oz said, "this never improved anything, though it did succeed in making them angry. So much for the oversimplified notion that repressed anger was the root cause of depression."

He'd worried Oz might denigrate his clinic work as unworthy of a psychoanalytic candidate, but to the contrary, he seemed encouraging. "It's gratifying to eliminate hallucinations in a psychotic person," Oz said, "and frustrating to feel you have so little impact on symptoms in a person you've been seeing for years on the couch."

He asked Oz if he missed seeing patients. "Not really. It weighs on you, all those intense feelings directed at you. It doesn't matter that you call them 'transferences.' It got to the point where I just felt I wasn't up to remaining so focused on what the patient was experiencing. But you're young and have lots of energy. Speaking of energy, Baba would love a walk around the block if you don't mind."

Hearing his name, Baba looked up and followed Torman out of the study. Leashed, Baba led him outside, and the pair made the rounds of the neighborhood, Baba sniffing and peeing, Torman relaxing and forgetting for the moment his worries and sadness.

◆ ◆ ◆

Eric's lawyer called to announce they had a deal with his cousins to sell his share of the business. Eric told Torman how he felt a mixture of relief and regret, about in equal measure. "But I'm determined to move ahead with the sale. At least the business will stay in the family. The buyout, along with my inheritance, will allow me to finance a return to school and, if I'm careful, anticipate a secure future regardless of whether I succeed as a writer."

Susan had suggested they celebrate the sale, but he didn't feel in a celebratory mood. He knew she was trying to find a way to cheer him up since she understood his attachment to the business and his father, the two being inextricably linked. He attempted to hide his depressive side from her, as well as his tendency to look to the past rather than the future. The evening before his session with Torman, he and Susan talked about her anticipating her immersion in art and learning to express her feelings through various mediums. Lately, she'd avoided talking about Max, knowing how jealous and threatened Eric felt, though last night was an exception. Early on, she'd told Eric about all the rumors of his affairs with students, but believed (or wanted Eric to believe) that his interest in her reflected his appreciation of her nascent skills and enthusiasm.

"At some point last night," Eric said to Torman, "Susan mentioned Max and how encouraging he's been, and I couldn't restrain myself and said, 'C'mon, Susan, you're a very attractive...no, you're a very *beautiful* woman, and he's hitting on you.' She said something like, 'So, he's just interested in getting me in bed?' I said that's what I'd bet on if I were a betting man, and she replied, 'But you're not a betting man because that would mean taking risks, something you don't do.' I used my usual self-deprecating humor to steer us away from a full-blown argument. Maybe she needs to discover for herself what kind of man Max is. I know you can't comment on this, but I'm pretty sure he's one of those predatory males who takes advantage of his position to seduce his students. I could be wrong. Or maybe I'm right, but no different. After all, I insinuated myself in her life at a vulnerable time in her marriage and could be accused of being just as predatory as Max."

He told Torman how Susan had brightened his life. Not just figuratively. She opened the shades, put cut flowers in vases, turned on lights, and hung some of her paintings on the walls. She insisted he buy clothes that weren't black, brown, or grey. She even got him to throw out his favorite pair of shoes, old cordovan wingtips that he'd had since high school and found unbelievably comfortable. (He confided to Torman that he only pretended to throw them out; he'd stuffed them in the back of his closet, hidden behind a suitcase.)

"I don't want to think about life without her shining presence."

Torman hadn't seen Claire since the final court appearance. Thoughts of her, though, recurred daily. What was she doing, did she think of him, did she have regrets, had the shine of her new relationship started to dull, did she miss him. And he kept alive the hope that she'd come back, in spite of the finality of the divorce. While grocery shopping on a Saturday morning, he was immersed in examining apples, unaware of the two women by the melons until he heard her unmistakeable voice and glanced their way. Laughing about something with another female shopper, Claire was hefting a cantaloupe and comparing it to the protrusion of her abdomen.

The pregnancy was fairly advanced and unmistakable to Torman's eye. Claire's face glowed. She was unaware of Torman's presence. He couldn't bear to go up to her, to fake some sort of normal response, whatever that would be. So he turned on his heels, abandoning his cart, and rushed to the exit. He didn't want her to see how pained he felt. He drove away, hating her and hating himself for being so weak that he couldn't face her. When had she become pregnant? Around the time she moved out? Had the pregnancy been what prompted her to leave him? Was her saying she never wanted a child the result of never wanting a child with him? Had she known all along that he wasn't the man she should have married?

Something shifted in his mind as he drove aimlessly from the grocery store. The hope that she'd come back vanished, leaving behind a black hole sucking all the light from his life. He realized the hope he'd clung to had allowed him to seemingly make peace with the loss of her. He hadn't accepted the divorce as something final. Now he knew better. Maybe, he thought, he could start to let her go. Really, he had no choice.

At least he was spared any future surprise. When he hears the news of her pregnancy—and surely will at some point—he won't be bowled over by the shock and possibly humiliated in front of others. Maybe he'll even be able to say he's happy for her, even though he's not.

Torman also had the nagging thought that maybe her not wanting a child was a reaction to some sense she had that he didn't want one. He'd told himself he wanted to be a father, but he'd picked Claire, who'd been clear about not wanting children. Perhaps she'd changed her mind over time, while he hadn't.

Maybe, he told himself, he was over-analyzing all this to block out how goddam awful he felt.

Eric spent the entire session with Torman talking about Susan. He was embarrassed by his jealousy, which seemed so adolescent. He recalled Susan's description of Torman's wife as an attractive, successful lawyer with poise and compassion, and he imagined they had this perfect union. Torman didn't say much, though near the end he commented, "I think it helps to picture me as above such emotions as jealousy, or at least as having a grip on such feelings. That way I'm capable of guiding you through this painful experience with Susan."

"I could certainly use some guidance. I know shrinks don't dispense advice, at least not very often. My dad was never very helpful. He'd stay in the background while mom would criticize my choice of women. As I've said before, he could never stand up to her, and I never learned how to assert myself in relationships either."

"What do you want from Susan?"

"I want to feel secure in my relationship with her, not worried she'll find me wanting and dump me for someone more romantic and spontaneous, someone like Max."

"Do you want to marry her?"

"Well, I think about marriage...but I tell myself that she's just getting out of a marriage and now's not the time to be pestering her about another one."

"You didn't say what *you* wanted."

He couldn't say he wanted to marry her, but he didn't know why. She was bright, beautiful, loving. Even with Max hovering around her, he felt she was trustworthy. Torman suggested Eric was wary of ending up like his father, dominated at home by a woman he could never fully satisfy and using work as a refuge from her control.

Eric wasn't sure he was right about that. But he left the

session feeling Torman was trying to understand his dilemma and wanted to help him find some way out of his misery. For his part, Torman wrestled with trying to separate his own pain from that of his patient and worried he lacked the ability to help Eric when he struggled so hard in his own life to handle Claire's rejection. He felt like the fictional Oz, hiding behind the curtain, fearing exposure.

◆ ◆ ◆

With a week left before Susan actually finished her analysis, Torman had begun writing his final 6 month summary of Susan's treatment. Writing helped take his mind off thoughts of Claire and the image of her holding the cantaloupe in front of her fertile abdomen. After reviewing the summary with Oz, he planned to submit it and then wait to hear whether the institute would accept it as a successful analysis. He wanted that diploma on his wall. He'd suffered through almost 11 years as a candidate. His time had come.

The only thing he'd miss about the institute was supervision with Oz. He sensed Oz also shared his desire to maintain their contact. Oz had outlived his wife and most of his friends. He'd mentioned a daughter, also a psychiatrist, who lived out of state and occasionally visited. Torman had studied her photograph in Oz's study: almost gypsy-like with dark hair and complexion, slender proportions, and a mischievous smile. Oz remarked that she'd worked for the Indian Health Service in Arizona for a few years after graduating from her residency, then opened a private practice in Tucson. At the end of their final supervision on Susan, Torman asked if Oz would consider supervising him on other cases. Delighted, Oz agreed.

His caseload at HBS had soared to 150 patients. And likely to climb higher. Once a patient had stabilized, there was pressure to space visits at 3 month intervals. That was adequate for many of them, especially those with schizophrenia who were compliant with, and responsive to, medication. But others, who appeared stable, could benefit from meeting at least monthly, if not more frequently. Some, like his bodybuilder, pseudo-murderer James, talked with no one on an intimate level other than Torman. Those who seemed most likely to benefit from more frequent contact he managed to see monthly or every 6 weeks.

Occasionally, patients scared him, usually in the initial appointment when he wasn't sure what to expect. Though assaults on out-patient staff were infrequent, some patients were poorly compliant with medication and abused drugs such as crack, a combination that could lead to unpredictable behavior and violence. The emergency button on his desk and the out of shape security guard in the waiting room failed to provide Torman with any sense of safety. Perhaps he should hire James to sit all day in his office, thus providing him with employment and Torman with security. James could keep his sunglasses on and bring a set of weights to work out with. Somebody gets out of line, he'd kill 'em.

The rejection letter from the Iowa Writers' Workshop arrived two days before an acceptance letter from the University of Arizona in Tucson. Dejection quickly gave way to elation as Eric realized somebody wanted him. As a child, he'd accompanied his parents to a dude ranch outside Tucson, a vacation that left him with a nostalgia for the mountains, desert and cactuses of the southwest. Eric went online to look up the courses offered, then began a search for apartments. Realizing he needn't wait for responses from other programs he'd applied to, he sent off his acceptance letter the following day.

Susan seemed genuinely excited for him, yet neither of

them wanted to face what his decision meant for the two of them. A part of Eric wanted her to come with him and transfer to a fine arts program in Arizona. Another part wanted to go by himself and see how each of them felt about their relationship when there was distance between them. However, he knew Max would eagerly seize an opportunity to start an affair with Susan, and Eric's absence would no doubt embolden him. And he wasn't sure it was fair to leave town and expect Susan to remain faithful.

He'd chosen not to apply to the University of Cincinnati's writing program. In part, Eric acknowledged being a snob and taking a dim view of the local university. But there was more to his decision. He wanted to make a break with his past, to see if he could create not only a new career but also a new life, one very different from his current existence. Plus he'd felt irked by Susan's comment about his avoiding risks and wanted to prove to her, as well as to himself, that he could take risks. There was the possibility that he was looking for a "geographic cure"—Torman's phrase for the belief that moving to another location will bring about personal happiness—but he wanted to do this. He didn't feel he was looking for a "cure," either. He was searching for a new direction in his life, and now was the time to make the move.

Eric discussed his decision in detail with Torman, and they settled on a termination date. He believed Torman supported his decision, though Eric couldn't help wondering if that support reflected, at least in part, Torman's relief in not having to deal with both Susan and Eric in treatment, each vying for his allegiance and understanding.

Torman's last note of a patient's final session was always very brief. He wasn't sure why; he'd done this from the beginning of his therapy career. Maybe a way of letting go of the person. Or laziness. He told himself that he was trying to be in the moment rather than making an effort to retain it in memory so he could record it.

Susan's final session left him sad. Not because she was sad. Quite the opposite: she appeared genuinely excited about the life before her. And her appreciation of Torman's help seemed genuine. As she got up from the couch for the last time, she turned towards him and, as he stood before her, hesitated to approach him. Sensing what she hoped for, Torman opened his arms, and she moved toward him for a brief hug. He felt as though he was saying goodbye to a daughter whom he loved and hoped would remember him as she left for parts unknown. On her way out, she opened her purse, placed a gift on his desk, and walked out his door for the last time.

He chose not to open it until reaching home and having time to reflect on it. Inside silver wrapping paper was a small painting depicting the analytic couch and his chair beside it. Light filtered from left to right, illuminating and linking the chair and couch, which seemed to float in space. On the wall behind the chair was a small painting, a miniature duplicate of her gift.

He realized she was telling him both where to place her painting and of her wish to leave a part of her with him. At least, that's what he imagined she was telling him since she'd chosen not to reveal her intention of giving him a gift. As an analyst, he was trained to analyze everything, including gifts that patients wanted to give him. He was glad she never mentioned it. Analyzing a gift took away all its impact and could feel needlessly cruel, especially at the end of a "successful" treatment. Sometimes Torman thought he just wasn't cut out to be an analyst, that it went against his desire to be seen as a decent, kind man wanting to help someone feel better. He resisted the psychoanalytic task of examining every wish, thought, and act. At times such as Susan's final session, he wanted to forgo the truth-seeking scrutiny of motives and just allow himself to feel appreciated.

Eric and Susan ended their relationship quietly, over dinner. Eric thought they'd both come to the same conclusion that their relationship wouldn't be sustainable over such a long distance. Each wanted to focus on new directions, Eric's as a writer, Susan's as a visual artist. Neither wanted to inflict pain on the other, so they avoided discussing the deeper issues that prevented them from remaining a couple.

Eric admitted to Torman being hesitant about opening himself fully to Susan. Though they'd explored his mother's influence on his interest in women and his father's failure to counter her negativity, Eric continued to feel he needed to hold himself back, to protect himself from something neither he nor Torman could identify. It wasn't as simple as fear of loss or abandonment, frequent themes in pop psychology accounts of failed relationships. Not that these weren't issues of his, just that he felt there was more to his holding himself back. He wasn't happiest when alone, and experienced loneliness when subjected to long stretches by himself. But the cocoon of his own world felt safe, comforting, known. Perhaps, Eric speculated, he was becoming an old maid, set in his ways and wary of change.

The move to Arizona seemed to belie this, yet it took him away from Susan and the possibility of intimacy with her. Eric thought about whether his risk taking was all that exceptional, whether he'd relocate without the financial security resulting from his inheritance and the sale of the business.

As the final session with Torman drew closer, Eric wondered about continuing sessions over the phone when in Arizona, but Torman, while he didn't outright veto this idea, suggested first seeing how things go out there. Torman made it clear that they could always resume therapy over the phone if Eric felt the need. Eric got the impression he wanted him to test his wings without Torman being his co-pilot. It also meant having to say goodbye.

❖ ❖ ❖

Torman rang Oz's doorbell and heard Baba's whine behind the door. After a long wait, the door opened, and Oz's daughter, whom he recognized from her photograph in Oz's study, greeted him. Missing was the hint of her mischievous smile; instead, she wore the look of someone tired from an ordeal.

"May I help you?" she asked.

"I'm Dr. Steve Torman. I have supervision with Dr. Gosz today."

"I'm sorry, I didn't know anyone was scheduled to see him. I'm afraid he's had a serious stroke. He's in University Hospital's ICU."

Stunned, uncertain what to say, Torman blurted out that he was sorry to bother her at such a time and asked if there was some way he could help. Baba was nudging his legs with his muzzle while Torman petted his head. Seeing Baba's obvious pleasure in his attention, Oz's daughter, who introduced herself as Anna, asked if he knew anyone who might provide Baba with a temporary home. She had to return to Arizona in a week and would likely be shuttling back and forth between her home and her father's for some time. "I'd be glad to take him. I've been giving him walks after supervision, and we've become good friends. Right, Baba?" By way of response, Baba expelled some gas which both Anna and Torman simultaneously registered. Anna spoke first, "He's got terrible gas."

"I'm relieved we can agree on the source of the gas. Your dad seemed to think it was the result of his getting into the trash."

"Dad loves Baba..." She began to tear up. They stood there in the doorway, neither knowing what to say. Anna finally asked Torman to come in so he could collect Baba's food, bowls, leash, and medications. Having a task allowed her to avoid becoming overwhelmed with her sadness. Torman used this opportunity to study her face, which was framed by soft, silky black curls and dominated by her piercing dark eyes. Her features were delicate, like that of a young child, though he estimated that Anna was somewhere in her thirties. Her movements likewise suggested a child's nimble agility as she gathered up Baba's belongings. When Torman asked about Oz's condition, Anna slipped into the medical jargon that doctors use to communicate with each other. She noted he hadn't regained consciousness, and the MRI revealed extensive damage as a result of an ischemic stroke in the left cerebral hemisphere. She believed if he survived he would be severely disabled and require intensive care. They shared the tacit understanding that it would be a blessing if he did not survive.

Torman wrote down his name and cell phone number and asked her to call any time she needed help. He emphasized how much he liked her dad and hoped she'd keep him informed about his condition. Anna thanked Torman and extended her thin hand, which he took and briefly held in his hands. "Dad spoke to me about you when we last talked on the phone. He was so happy to have someone to supervise and said you reminded him of his younger self, serious and struggling to find a way to become a good analyst. He looked forward to your visits."

"I valued our supervision. He was such a welcome, supportive influence, something I haven't experienced very often with other supervisors in the institute."

Juggling Baba's paraphernalia in her slender arms, she accompanied Torman and his new companion to his car. Without hesitation, Baba jumped into the front passenger seat, facing forward, as if to say, "Onward!"

Torman felt awful about Oz. What a horrible way to go,

stuck in ICU limbo between life and death. He didn't feel bur-
dened by Baba. Quite the opposite. Torman welcomed him, gas
and all.

❖ ❖ ❖

Eric wasn't sure what to expect in his final session with
Torman. It felt strange to say goodbye to someone he'd been
meeting with regularly for three years. He'd grown to like Torman, who'd seemed remote at first but gradually loosened up.
Yet Eric still knew so little about him. They talked about how
the deaths of his parents and his subsequent depression brought
him to therapy, how the sadness had gradually lifted, and how
the end of his romance with Susan and the end of therapy were
now affecting his mood.

Eric admitted feeling both scared and excited about the
prospect of leaving everything familiar and heading out West.
Yet he was extremely busy handing over the reins at work to his
cousins, figuring out what to take to Arizona, finding a place to
live there, and getting his house ready to put up for sale. Aside
from his appointments with Torman, Eric had little time for
reflection.

"I guess I'll wake up in Tucson, and the reality of it will hit
me."

"You're worried about how that will feel?"

"I guess...I don't think I'll panic. I think I'm more likely to
start wondering if I've made a huge mistake and worrying about
my future. Even now, I wonder about letting Susan go. I'd never
felt so close to a woman. I'm still not sure I did the right thing.
Maybe my insecurity led me to anticipate her becoming bored
with me and rejecting me for someone like Max. I really didn't
want to deal with that."

"I have the impression you managed to keep the door
somewhat open with her."

"We plan to remain in touch, probably by email. Maybe by phone as well."

"Have you thought about keeping in touch with me?"

"Yeah, I've thought about writing once I get settled out there."

"I hope you do. I'd like to hear from you."

The session was near the end. Silence filled the room. Finally, sensing their time was up, Eric told Torman he really appreciated his help, and then his voice cracked. They stood up and shook hands, Torman smiling, wishing Eric well. After he left, Torman moved to his desk where he sat down to write his final note: "Last session. Sad but hopeful for his future." Then, looking at his note, he wondered if he was commenting on Eric or himself.

Last sessions often ended this way: Torman having grown fond of his patient and wishing him or her well, feeling there was more work to be done, and wishing he'd hear some day from his departing patient yet knowing he probably wouldn't. It was a bit like finishing a novel and wanting to know how the lives of the characters played out in the future, how their choices influenced the rest of their lives.

The letter from the institute was brief and to the point. Susan's treatment was insufficient to qualify as a successful analysis. Evidence of a thorough working through of her transference neurosis was lacking, and her acting out in the latter phase of her analysis reflected a lingering tendency for impulsive behavior and limited insight. The letter ended with, "The progression committee believes the candidate will eventually succeed in completing a successful analysis."

Torman pounded his desktop hard enough to send papers flying. He wanted to scream at the committee members that they were total fucking assholes, ignorant, stupid, vengeful jerks who got their kicks fucking people over. They surely knew all about "acting out" because they were acting out with him. Taking out their frustrations on a candidate they didn't like and were going to torture. And that last line! Throwing him a bone. He'd have been less furious if they'd simply written, "We hate you, Torman, and we'll make sure you never graduate."

Who could he turn to? Oz, whom he'd visited in the hospital, couldn't speak and was barely alive. And what could Oz do anyway? He'd written a thoroughly supportive letter to the committee recommending acceptance of the case as a successful analysis. Torman supposed they'd simply note that Oz was ancient and no longer considered relevant (though, at the same time, perfectly adequate to supervise Torman). He pictured Steward smiling in his Eames chair, delighting in the knowledge that Torman's progression in the institute had been thwarted.

He decided to call Anna. She'd returned to Arizona but had given him her cell phone number. The last thing she needed was to deal with his anger and frustration, but he couldn't hold himself back. She seemed like the kind of person who'd be understanding and receptive. Not to mention grateful for his adopting Baba. And she knew his feelings for Oz were genuine. Torman rationalized that his concerns might take her mind off her father's dire medical situation.

Luckily, she seemed glad he called. Initially, he talked about his visit with her father. She shared what she'd gleaned from the neurologists. He eventually segued to the case Oz had helped him with and the institute's rejection.

"Dad had little respect for most of the analysts running the institute. I also think he had mixed feelings about psychoanalysis and its claims of superiority over every other form of treatment. He discouraged me from becoming an analyst, saying I should get good supervision on my own and listen to what my patients tell me."

"I wish I'd talked to him years ago...I'm going on 11 years as a candidate. It's hard to walk away from this now, though that's what I feel like doing. Actually, I feel like barging into one of those committee meetings and venting all my frustration and anger. But that would just confirm their impression that I'm not ready to enter their hallowed ranks."

"Have you thought of getting a lawyer?"

"You know, I was married to one...that's another story... but, yes, I have. I'm not sure what legal issue I could present."

"Lawyers are good at making those up."

Anna asked about Baba. He told her Baba had been sleeping in his bed, taking up most of the space, and not only continued to have gas problems but also snored.

"Maybe he needs a sleep evaluation to rule out sleep apnea."

"Great, a C-PAP device will force air down his airway and make his gas all the more explosive. Other ideas?"

"Perhaps separate bedrooms."

"I should consult with you more often."

"Glad to be helpful. Seriously though, thanks for looking in on Dad. I really appreciate that."

Claire had mentioned various lawyers and their reputations over the years. One of them, David Levine, a solo practitioner and civil litigator whom everyone feared, was known for his aggressiveness and brilliance. Having a photographic memory added to his reputation. Lawyers dreaded battling him in the courtroom.

Using Claire's name and law firm as references, Torman managed to get an appointment with Levine. His office, high up in a downtown skyscraper, looked out on the riverfront, with views up and down the Ohio River. A secretary ushered him into his office, and the panoramic view so captured his attention that he didn't see Levine until he swiveled his desk chair around to face him. He had the look of a Marine: short-cropped hair, jutting jaw, absolutely no extra flesh on his face, pursed lips, and not even the suggestion of warmth to his greeting. His eyes, dark and sunken, took Torman in, measured him, then seemed to shutter themselves from view. The image of a motionless reptile lying in wait for its hapless victim came to Torman's mind.

Torman introduced himself. "I know who you are," Levine said. "Tell me briefly what sort of problem you have." So much for pleasantries. He summarized his situation: he's 36, in his 11th year at the psychoanalytic institute, has one hurdle left to graduate, and he keeps getting rejected. He explained that having a "successful" case takes years and he's managed to complete two that his supervisors regarded as successful, only to have a committee turn both down. He had no idea why this was happening, other than a personal dislike of him. None of his evaluations had ever criticized him for lacking knowledge or having personal issues that interfered with his doing analytic work, except for one final evaluation from a supervisor who clearly disliked him.

Interrupting him, Levine asked for the names of the committee members. He rattled off four names.

"None are members of the tribe," said Levine.

Momentarily caught off guard, Torman said after a pause, "Right. As gentile as they come." What immediately came to Torman's mind was the portrait print of Freud the institute presented each graduating candidate: Freud's face revealing a nose slenderized and straightened by the plastic surgeon skills of the artist.

"This isn't going to be difficult. I'll write a letter on your behalf informing them of our impression that you're the victim of prejudice. I'll scare the shit out of them. They don't want bad publicity, and they certainly don't want to pay a lot in legal fees. What is it you want?"

"I want a letter stating I've met the requirements for graduation. And I want the diploma. Nothing else. I haven't discussed any of this with anyone in this community besides you and will maintain my silence if I'm allowed to graduate. I believe I've done more than enough to fulfill the requirements for becoming an analyst."

Levine nodded his head. "My fee is $450 an hour. My secretary will have you sign a contract." He reached for something on his desk and began reading.

"So, we're done?"

Not looking up, he said, "Yes, I've got bigger fish to fry."

Eric hired movers to take his furniture and other belongings to Tucson. He'd found an apartment near the campus and planned to drive out by himself. What he chose not to move, he gave to Goodwill. The house hadn't sold yet, but his real estate agent was optimistic that they'd soon land a buyer.

Susan and Eric decided to go out for a goodbye dinner. Eric wanted to see how he felt about her and to gauge how she felt about him. They'd agreed to meet at the restaurant. That eliminated the element of a "date." Eric arrived first and, hoping for a modicum of privacy and relative quiet, picked a table in a corner. As Susan entered, she hesitated a moment to search the room for Eric. He felt his heart racing and tried to calm himself. Seeing him as he stood up to greet her, she wore a smile and glided his way. A brief hug, then some nervous laughter.

"So…how are you?" he asked.

"Good, good. And you?"

"Well, honestly, a bit nervous. I'm pretty much packed and ready to go."

"Yeah, well, it's a big move for you. I think it's great you're doing this. It takes guts."

"Yeah, especially for a guy who doesn't take risks."

"I wish I'd never said that. I was angry." Eric regretted alluding to her past comment, but it was too late to take it back.

She asked some practical things, like where he'd be living and when classes started. They talked about school, how she was doing in her classes and studio work. Susan appeared animated discussing her painting and her total immersion in creative pursuits. Eric sensed that Susan wanted to steer clear of whether either of them was seeing someone. Neither wanted their parting marred by hostility. They talked about Torman and how they felt about their treatment and its ending.

"I think Torman helped me realize how unhappy I was in my marriage, as well as in my life generally. My life was on hold...I wasn't deeply connected to Dan. I had no plans. I was just drifting. But you know all that. You helped me too. I'm very grateful for all you did. I'm not sure I would've had the strength to leave Dan if you hadn't been there for me."

Over coffee and dessert, they grew quieter. Eric watched her eat half of her gelato, then stop. "How many calories in a scoop of gelato?" he asked.

"90. But who's counting?" Susan, smiling, pushed her bowl over to Eric, who happily polished it off.

Eric felt anxious, unsure what to talk about. He asked what she'd been reading lately, and they talked about books, how inspiring they were. At some point she said, "I hope you find what you're looking for." He wasn't sure if she meant this in a critical way, as if he were running away from something, or in an encouraging way, as if he were on an important quest.

"I'm not really sure what I'm looking for or expecting. There's not much here I'll miss other than you. And Dr. Torman." Part of him wanted to ask her to join him there, but he held back, knowing it was too late and not wanting to make her uncomfortable. At the very least, he wanted to part as friends, with the understanding they'd stay in touch.

Smiling sadly, she nodded. "I'll wait for you to email me. I want to know how things go for you. And this is for you. I didn't gift-wrap it, but I figured you wouldn't mind."

Eric hadn't noticed the canvas she'd brought with her in a

tote bag. It was a painting of the coffee shop where they'd first met. There were no people in the scene, just the shop in early morning light, with colorful blooms in the window box and the familiar ginkgo trees lining the sidewalk out front.

Eric wanted to embrace her and not let go. "It's beautiful. Thank you." He stood awkwardly holding the canvas in one hand. She gave him a quick hug and kiss on the cheek and made a brisk exit.

◆ ◆ ◆

Levine prevailed. Not long after their meeting, Torman received a letter from the president of the institute stating the progression committee had re-considered Susan's case and re-commended awarding him a diploma as a graduate of the institute. The diploma arrived two days later in a large manila envelope. He studied it to make sure it was properly dated and signed, with his name writ large on it. Torman noted the absence of the gentile-looking Freud portrait that graduating candidates receive (and often frame for their offices). His only regret was missing out on the opportunity to tear it up.

He didn't feel like celebrating, but he definitely felt satisfaction in taking action and getting the desired result. He felt no inclination to broadcast his long-awaited achievement, nor did he feel particularly proud of it. Not because he doubted deserving the diploma. Torman believed he deserved it. Rather, because it was all so anticlimactic and because he'd really stopped caring about holding himself out as an analyst. He put the diploma in his desk drawer.

Levine had sent him a brief note indicating that the matter had been settled, with the understanding that the settlement between Torman and the institute was to remain privileged and confidential. Levine asked to be notified when he received the institute's letter and diploma. Torman called his office, leaving a message acknowledging receipt of both and thanking him for his help.

Shortly after he received the diploma, Anna arrived in town to check on her father, who remained comatose and in serious but stable condition. Torman found it very disturbing to see him, his large head and frail body lying motionless at Drake Hospital, where patients go who required long-term medical care. He'd managed to breathe on his own after being weaned off a respirator. Anna talked with Torman about her hope he'd just die rather than linger on in a persistent vegetative state.

Torman recalled the last time he visited Oz at Drake. He spent some time talking to Oz at his bedside, where he lay motionless and unresponsive. There was always the remote chance Oz could hear what he was saying, so he spoke of the institute, his seeking the help of a lawyer to pressure the powers that be to award him his diploma, his meeting Anna and how much he liked her, and, of course, his wish Oz would recover. He added that he'd adopted Baba and pledged to take good care of him. Before leaving, an aide entered to re-position Oz and provide skin care. As she ministered to Oz, Torman introduced himself.

"Dr. Gosz was my supervisor prior to his stroke. He's a really good man."

"So, you're a shrink, too. I saw one years ago in my twenties. For just a few sessions, over at Central Clinic at University Hospital...a nice man, still in training, I think, but he wasn't much help. A couple of years later I divorced my husband. *That* was my cure," Bonnie, the aide, said.

"Did you ever remarry?"

"No, and I have no regrets about that. You married?"

"Recently divorced. I think my former wife found the same cure you did." They both laughed.

"I've met Dr. Gosz's daughter," Bonnie said. "Now there's a psychiatrist I'd see, if I had to see one. Something kind and caring about her, you see it in her eyes."

"I know what you mean. I feel the same way about her." Torman thought how there was something about those dark gypsy eyes which seemed to see right into his soul.

As Torman left Drake Hospital, his thoughts drifted back to a conversation with Anna about how she ended up in Arizona. Her description of life there sounded appealing. She spoke of the ease of leaving Tucson and exploring the vastness of the desert and mountains. "The sky at night teems with stars. And the sun always seems to shine, so unlike Cincinnati with its overcast sky and general gloominess. You should consider coming out to visit, to see for yourself."

A level of comfort had developed between them that wasn't complicated by physical contact. Given Oz's condition, it just didn't feel right to Torman to try to be more than a friend to Anna. And that was fine with him. It allowed them to get to know each other without that passionate, hormonal rush that can leave one blind.

PART TWO

Arizona 2015

T orman drove into Arizona on route 80, dipping into Douglas at the Mexican border, then heading northwest to Bisbee, a former copper mining town that managed to survive the mines' closings in the 1970's. He parked near the post office on Main Street and walked the short shopping district lined with galleries, restaurants, a honey store, some old hotels, and shops either going out of business or reinventing themselves. There wasn't much traffic, and the cars he saw often displayed Feel The Bern bumper stickers. Torman also noted that the Honda Element had replaced the VW Bus as the counterculture vehicle of choice. Shacks littered the town's mountainous sides, some given a second chance, others letting gravity, sun, and time whittle away at them. People meandered along, rarely in a hurry. The buildings dated back to the early 1900's. No chain stores or fast food restaurants greeted visitors. Anna had urged Torman to explore Bisbee when they discussed his intention to move to Arizona. She intuited that he'd feel comfortable in Bisbee's laid-back environment.

Bisbee's appeal to Torman crept up on him over the course of the week he spent walking the hills, talking to the locals, and imagining a life lived in this off-the-beaten-path town. He discovered the local mental health clinic and residential facility for substance abuse, both in need of a psychiatrist.

He understood why Anna had urged him to spend some time in Bisbee. There was a sense that the residents had decided to live their lives however they chose in this town where pretension seemed non-existent and the only conformity was non-conformity.

On one of his walks around town, Torman's attention was drawn to a "For Sale by Owner" sign posted on the front gate of a house. A number of homes, most all of which were former miners' shacks, sported colorful exteriors, but this particular house stood out with its carnival display of lime green wood siding, purple window trim, yellow and rose accents, and all variety of sculptural displays on its exterior and scattered about its tiny yard.

On impulse, Torman knocked on the door. That elicited dog barking and, eventually, the appearance of an old man, who looked Torman over, then asked what he could do for him.

"My name's Steve Torman. I see your house is for sale. I'd like to arrange for a chance to look at it."

"No need to arrange. Just come in and don't mind Junior. He's all bark, no bite. Call me Jimmy, everyone does." Junior, sniffing Torman's pant legs, no doubt picked up the scent of Baba, whom he'd left in the rental house where he was staying.

"My wife died last year. She's the one who collected all this stuff. Can't say I was enamored of it, but I'd gotten used to it after 55 years of marriage."

Torman couldn't believe his eyes as he entered the living room: purple walls, artwork everywhere, ornate crucifixes, hand painted furnishings, exotic birds hanging from the ceiling, a skeleton seated in a chair, numerous images of Frida Kahlo on ceramics, Mexican blankets on walls and couches, doors trimmed in reds, blues, and greens. He couldn't take it all in and fell silent as he stared at the profusion of color and imagery. Finally, Torman emitted an enthralled "Wow."

"Yeah, it's pretty wild. She had a gift for putting all this together. Honestly, it's hard for me to bear. I miss her every day, this home is so much of who she was." Torman noticed Jimmy was still wearing his wedding band and had a habit of fingering it as they made their way through the small house. Every room was unique, yet each displayed the same riotous combination of colors and art objects. Even the toilet was emblazoned with painted cockatoos and flowers.

"So, you'll be taking all the artwork and furnishings?" Torman asked.

"Hell, no. I'll be living in my daughter's home in Indiana. No room for this stuff. I'd have to rent an amphitheater to store all of it. Everything stays. I'm taking my pills, toothbrush, scrapbooks, and clothes. You can keep the rest or find a good home for what you don't want."

"I need to think about this...how much are you asking?"

"150 thousand. And that's my bottom line. You want the house, you pay the price." Jimmy smiled at this, but, to Torman's mind, looked sad at the same time.

Leaning down to pet Junior, Torman said, "Junior comes with the house?"

"Naw, he goes with me." Jimmy smoothed out his scruffy beard with one hand, then reached into his shirt pocket with his other to extract a ball point pen. With a shaky scrawl he wrote out his full name, Jimmy Stratman, along with his phone number. "Call anytime. I don't go out much any more. Don't have an answering machine, so you might have to try again. And be sure to speak up. I don't hear so well anymore. What did you say your name was?"

"Steve Torman. I'll be in touch." They shook hands, and Torman walked out the door onto the front patio paved with Mexican tile and paused to admire the hand-carved wooden posts supporting the patio's roof. Just then a golf cart ferrying tourists stopped in front of Jimmy's house. The guide waved at Torman and asked how Jimmy was. "Jimmy and Junior seem in good spirits," Torman said. He noticed the couple seated behind the driver. They had their cell phones aimed at Jimmy's house and were taking photos. The tour guide waved goodbye as he stepped on the gas.

This is ridiculous, Torman mused, opening the gate and stepping into the blinding midday sun. Yet he was smitten with the house and with quirky Bisbee. Standing in the street, he fished out his own cell phone and snapped a few shots, thinking how he'd send them to Anna.

◆ ◆ ◆

Imagining Anna's response to the photos, Torman recalled how Oz had died of pneumonia a few months into his stay at Drake Hospital. Torman helped Anna deal with the funeral, as well as the disposition of Oz's possessions and house.

The night before the funeral, Torman drove over to Oz's house, and, as he pulled into the driveway, he noticed a short, somewhat stout woman standing next to Anna on the porch. Anna greeted him at the porch door and turned to introduce him to Val, who stood off to the side. "Steve, this is my partner, Val Sanders. We share a home in Tucson." Completely caught off guard, Torman forced a smile and held out his hand, which Val squeezed hard, then quickly released.

"I thought you might need some help tonight...I didn't mean to intrude." Anna reassured him he was not intruding and invited him in.

Torman felt deflated and foolish. How could he not have known? What had he missed? It was true that she hadn't been seductive or flirtatious, yet she'd always seemed receptive to him. He'd apparently misinterpreted her friendliness as something more. The three of them talked about Oz and the funeral. After twenty minutes, Torman got up to leave.

Anna came over to him and looked him directly in the eyes. He had difficulty meeting her gaze. Softly, she murmured, "Sorry, Steve." It seemed in that moment that she understood both his pain and his humiliation.

Torman turned to Val and said he'd see her tomorrow. He

couldn't read her emotions. Her inscrutability unnerved him. He wanted to make as quick an exit as possible.

◆ ◆ ◆

The memory of discovering Anna's relationship with Val remained an embarrassing instance of his naivete. It had taken some time before the three of them could laugh about how completely flummoxed he'd felt that night before the funeral.

Torman's thoughts drifted back to Jimmy's house. He tried dismissing the idea of wanting it. Too much money for what was basically a shack dressed up like a cheap prostitute. Hadn't he always preferred minimalist design, subtle hues, classic furnishings? He was a Design Within Reach guy, not a wild Mexican manic-inspired guy. Jimmy's wife probably neglected to take her lithium and let her bipolar enthusiasm for color and excess run amok. And yet, the appeal of it was unmistakeable. There was a method to her madness, a coherence to all that color and artwork that bowled Torman over. To live in that home was to live in an artist's creation.

After two days of mulling over his feelings for the house and for Bisbee, Torman called Jimmy. "Jimmy, it's Steve Torman. I was wondering if I could come over and walk through your home again."

"I'm not going anywhere, just come on by."

"Can I bring something? How about lunch?"

"A cold beer would be nice."

Torman stopped by the Cafe Cornucopia on Main St., picked up a couple of sandwiches, and brought along a six-pack of beer. He'd asked Jimmy if he could bring Baba, got the OK, and the two of them arrived around noon at Jimmy's.

Junior was on high alert but quickly made up with Baba, who was intent on pissing on every cactus in the small, fenced-in yard. Jimmy, dressed in the same clothes he'd worn on Torman's first visit, greeted him with a handshake and a smile, eyeing with delight the six-pack.

"Good to see you again, young man. Did you bring your checkbook?" Laughing, Torman noted he'd begun looking for a bank to hold up.

They ate in the shaded side yard on a redwood table, while Junior and Baba positioned themselves under the table in the hope of a tasty reward. Jimmy made quick work of two beers and half his sandwich. Sitting back in his chair, he asked Torman what brought him to Bisbee.

"That's a long story. The short version is that I got fed up with the group of psychiatrists I worked with and decided to leave the practice. I'd gotten divorced, had no children, and realized I could make a big change in my life. Normally I'd tell my patients that moving somewhere was unlikely to bring them happiness, but I wasn't fooling myself. I knew happiness didn't come with a change of address and, if it did come, it wasn't likely to be long-lived anyway."

"So you're a head shrinker...no wonder you take such a dim view of happiness. Here, you need another." Jimmy nudged a beer in Torman's direction but he waved it off. "See, that's why you're not so happy. When I was your age, I'd have drunk all these beers by now. Two beers is my limit since reaching my golden years."

Torman added that he'd gotten to know a woman, also a psychiatrist, who lived in Tucson, and he'd grown very fond of her.

"Tucson's almost two hours away. Makes romance kind of a challenge."

"Well, it turns out she's a lesbian."

"Shit, Steve, you're driving me to drink another beer. You don't need a house, you need your own head examined."

"Well, it's been examined, though I guess not thoroughly enough. How about I take another tour of your home?"

Torman was amazed by what he'd missed the first time he'd inspected the house. A carved burro held magazines in its saddlebags; dioramas depicting Mexican life and religious events sat atop antique tables, dressers and shelves; ducks and chickens rendered lifelike by taxidermy nested above kitchen cabinets; original artwork hung everywhere. No room painted the same color.

While Torman drifted through the six rooms, Jimmy explained the origins of some of the artwork. Most of the antique furniture had belonged to his wife's parents, while most of the paintings were from local artists whom they knew. Jimmy also talked about his own life, how he'd been raised in Kentucky until age 6, when his family moved to Bisbee so his father could find work in the copper mines. He'd followed in his father's footsteps, but soon hated the mining work. "It's awful dirty and dangerous. Men died down there. Most of them drank when they weren't underground. I didn't want that kind of life." He became a car mechanic, eventually owning his own shop. "A good thing, too, 'cause when the mines closed in the '70's, I had a job and didn't have to leave to find work. Of course, business really dropped off, but I hung on and made a living. Over time, the town attracted a lot of hippies and artists who saw the beauty in Bisbee and discovered they could afford the shacks abandoned by the miners. My wife raised our kids, then worked part-time in the library, which, by the way, is the oldest library in the state of Arizona. Thought you might like to know that." Jimmy's face crinkled into a grin as he watched Torman absorb this information.

The two men sat down again in the side yard. Torman knew he wanted the house but was unsure whether to offer a lower amount. He liked Jimmy and didn't want to offend him. And haggling was not something Torman was ever comfortable with.

"Jimmy, I want your house and I'll pay your price, but I'll have to get an inspection."

"I understand. It's an old house...built in 1904...I'm sure there are some things an inspector will find, but I can tell you it's basically sound. I was hoping you'd want it. I like you, and it would give me pleasure to pass my home on to you."

They sat in the shade for a while, watching the dogs nap on the shaded gravel path and talking about whatever came to their minds. At one point Torman confessed he wasn't sure how to move forward with the purchase. Jimmy informed him that it was pretty simple. He just needed to contact the local title company, and they'd do the paper work.

Torman noticed Jimmy nodding off, so he said he'd be on his way. They stood and shook hands.

◆ ◆ ◆

On Saturday morning, Torman drove up to Tucson to visit Anna and Val. He'd spent time at their home over the past couple of years. It was an adobe structure with a pool in the back where he'd swim laps in the morning and drowsily float on a raft in the afternoon. The house's large terra cotta tiles cooled his bare feet. Val had opened up the interior so that no walls separated the kitchen, dining area, and living room. Thick, rough-hewn wood beams supported the ceiling.

Val bought and renovated older homes in the Tucson area. She served as general contractor for the renovations. When the real estate market collapsed in 2008, she'd taken advantage of the falling prices, buying homes that were in need of considerable work. By the time the market began improving, she had finished the renovations and placed them up for sale. She was always on the lookout for properties that had been neglected, and she'd earned a reputation for bringing them back to life without cutting corners. Having toured some of these homes with Val, Torman was struck by her imaginative remodeling and attention to detail. Her reputation for honesty and quality workmanship attracted investors and enabled her to develop a successful business.

For some time, Torman and Val had remained cautiously

polite with one another. Gradually, trust developed between them. Anna gave them space to work things out, all the while understanding that jealousy might complicate and ultimately interfere with Val and Torman becoming friends.

For his part, Torman realized that he had no chance of supplanting Val and, at the same time, wanted to continue to have a relationship with Anna. He figured his best chance was to develop a genuine friendship with Val. He believed the most sensible approach was to be open about his initial romantic interest in Anna and his shock upon discovering the existence of Val. Torman wondered if his positive feelings for Oz influenced how he felt about Anna. And, similarly, perhaps Anna's warm feelings for her father were projected onto Torman at a time when Oz was so close to dying. What Torman struggled to accept was the notion that he'd simply been blind to her sexual orientation.

Val tended to be more guarded around heterosexual men than Anna. She'd grown up in a small town in South Carolina, had not been cute as a girl or attractive as an adolescent, and feared the ridicule that the local culture expressed toward any signs of gay or lesbian people. Boys, and later, men, were especially cruel and vocal regarding their disgust with homosexuality.

Upon arriving at their house, Torman was eager to show them additional photos he'd taken of his soon-to-be new home. Anna laughed as she looked at the shots, especially the one of the toilet festooned with cockatoos and flowers. Val, typically the more low key of the two, asked about the history of the house and offered to do the inspection.

Later, lounging poolside with Anna, Torman asked about her work, leading to a discussion of some of her cases. She always appreciated his ideas, especially with patients who seemed stuck in treatment. She saw him as a gifted therapist and puzzled over his claims that his own work frequently resulted in minimal, if any, improvements.

At some point Val joined them and challenged Torman to

a race. "What does the winner get?" Torman asked.

"The loser takes us out to dinner."

"You're on. Four laps."

They started in the water, with Anna calling out, "Ready, set, go!" Torman took the lead, arms flailing and feet furiously churning the water. At the halfway point he ran out of steam and by the fourth lap was swallowing water in Val's wake.

"Another victory for women!" Val shouted, arm stretched skyward, as Torman gasped for breath at the pool's edge.

"I want you tested for steroids. I bet you've done more doping than Lance Armstrong."

Amused, Anna chided them for acting like children, then said she was going inside to make reservations at a very expensive restaurant.

◆ ◆ ◆

Val drove down to Bisbee the following Tuesday, meeting Torman and Jimmy at the house. Her inspection took over an hour. Jimmy took a nap outside in the shade, while Torman followed Val on her methodical examination of every inch of the house. Starting with the foundation, she worked her way up to the roof, keeping up a running account of her observations. Torman asked if he should be taking notes. "Don't bother. I'll write this up for you."

"How'd you learn all this stuff?"

"Mostly from my uncle, who was married to my mom's sister. Dad was a drunk, pretty useless around the house and enraged when something didn't work. He never fixed a thing, just kicked whatever failed him. When mom had her crazy episodes and got hospitalized, I'd stay at Aunt Jane's. Uncle Bert could—and did—fix anything. Like most everyone in the town where we lived, they had no money and did all the home repairs themselves. I'd follow Uncle Bert around, and he showed me how to fix the toilets, patch leaks in the roof, mend broken furniture, add electric lines, you name it. He called me his 'silent shadow.' I loved his patience with me. He was the only man I felt comfortable with growing up. And Aunt Jane fussed over me and let me do whatever I wanted. I think she felt sorry for me. I used to wish they'd adopt me."

Some of this story Torman knew about, but he gained insight into Val's character each time she shared more of her past. His own past seemed cushy by comparison. "Did you ever visit your mom in the hospital?"

"Just once. She'd stay at the state hospital for months at a time. She got shock treatments, which seemed to help but made her zombie-like for periods of time. Aunt Jane and Uncle Bert drove me to visit her when I was around 10 or 11. It was just before Christmas. They thought a visit would cheer Mom and me up. There was this visiting area, a large room with just some chairs and nothing else. The walls were painted a sickly green and peeling. A nurse escorted Mom out to us. A stained robe covered her hospital gown. Mom asked for a cigarette and tried to light it with Uncle Bert's lighter, but her hands shook so bad he had to do it for her. I sat next to Mom. I wanted to hug her, but she seemed to be hugging herself, and her eyes just stared straight ahead. At one point she said, 'How you doin', kid?' I don't remember what I said. Really, it was awful."

When Val finished her inspection, they said goodbye to Jimmy and stopped for coffee at the Bisbee Coffee Company.

"Seems like there's a lot to fix," Torman said.

"There is. It's not terrible, but it'll cost some money to make it safe and comfortable. The good news is that you've got a new metal roof and the electric's been brought up to code. My main concern is the wood pillars supporting the house. They go right into the dirt! I counted 24 of them, and they all need to be on concrete footers. I'd put central air and heat in, and that's going to be costly. Could use double-paned windows, too. The gas wall heater is new but the bedrooms will be cold without portable heaters. The window a/c works but, again, a new central unit would eliminate the various heaters and a/c window unit and would make you more comfortable. You can see right through some of the floor boards to the dirt below. I'd put carpet down, maybe some tile or wood but that will get expensive...You look shell-shocked. Are you all right?"

Torman laughed. "Shit, maybe I'm foolish to buy this place. How expensive will this be?"

"Off the top of my head, I'd say about 35 grand."

"I wish you could do the work."

"Me, too, but it's a really long drive. I'd need to hire help down here, and I don't know who to hire. But I can try finding out who does good work, and I'll oversee the work as it goes along. I won't let you get screwed."

Torman felt relieved thinking Val would watch over the work that needed to be done. "Val, I really appreciate you're helping me with this."

"You can give me some free therapy on the side, and we'll be even. By the way, you know Bisbee has a large LGBT community."

"Yeah, I've figured that out. Jimmy introduced me to his next door neighbors, June and Marge, who've offered to show me around to some of the nearby sights."

"I hope you don't have your eye on one of them 'cause that will only bring you unhappiness." Val laughed as Torman tried to think of a clever comeback.

Torman drove up to Tucson, left his car and Baba at Anna and Val's, and flew back to Cincinnati. He needed to clear out the condo he'd been renting for the last three years and decide which possessions to keep and ship out to Bisbee.

He'd already closed down his practice, including his consultant position at HBS. He'd dreaded telling his long-term private practice patients that he was leaving town. Even though his caseload had been shrinking, a number of patients liked him and struggled to accept his departure. It was easier at HBS since he saw those patients less frequently and had been working there a little under three years. Dr. Rabin took it hard. Finding psychiatrists to work at the clinic was increasingly difficult, and the ones she found were either not very committed to the work or not very skilled as clinicians.

He recalled one of his final conversations with Dr. Rabin. "So, why Arizona?" she'd asked, sitting with perfect posture on her balance ball desk chair. Torman's gaze shifted to the awards on her walls, the uplifting sentiments engraved on cards atop her desk, the gifts from grateful patients scattered about the room.

"I've been visiting a good friend in Tucson over the last few years. There's something very appealing to me about the desert and mountains. And this gives me an opportunity to start over again, to put behind me some of the unhappiness I associate with Cincinnati...my divorce, my frustration with the psychoanalytic institute. I'm realistic, though. I know moving won't solve my problems."

"Well, I just want you to know there's always a spot here for you if you ever decide to return. The patients really like you. *I* like you. I'll miss you." Standing, she gave Torman a hug. Not the momentary kind with just minimal body contact and a hand lightly patting one's back, but a real hug, pulling Torman slightly off balance as he buried his face in her lightly perfumed neck. To his surprise, he felt like crying. Then, seeing the time on the wall clock, Jane said, "Oh, I'm really late for a meeting," and rushed out of her office.

Torman debated whether to contact Claire. He'd learned she'd had a healthy boy, married the boyfriend, and made partner at the firm. They had not crossed paths since his catching sight of her early in her pregnancy at the grocery store. (After that sighting, he'd made a point of avoiding places where he might run into her and was relieved to learn she and her future husband had moved to a neighborhood at some distance from the Belvedere condo he'd moved into.) What was the point in saying goodbye? To see if she felt anything for him? To see if he felt anything for her?

In the end he decided not to contact her. He dropped his rental car off at the airport and flew back to Tucson. The expression, "Go West, young man" entered Torman's awareness as he sat in the plane awaiting take-off. To his relief, sadness gave way to excitement. He didn't care that it might be fleeting, that he might land in Arizona only to discover that he'd packed all his unhappiness and self-doubt along with his few worldly possessions.

It was easy to find work as a consultant psychiatrist in various mental health clinics in and around Bisbee. In Sierra Vista, a half hour away and seven times the population of Bisbee, the local clinic offered Torman 20 hours a week of work. The pay wasn't much but neither were his needs. He filled out the rest of his week with work in Bisbee, Douglas, and Benson. Torman's responsibilities in those towns mostly involved supervising counselors and therapists, while patients needing more intensive psychiatric monitoring and medication were referred to the Sierra Vista clinic. For the time being, he decided not to open a private practice. He called upon the few psychiatrists in the surrounding areas and explored the nature of their practices, asking lots of questions. These psychiatrists were older, nearing retirement, and open about their likes and dislikes of their work life. They seemed to share a dislike of health insurance companies' intrusion in their practices, as well as frustration with government requirements for treating patients on Medicare and Medicaid. As a group, these psychiatrists were loners, preferring to practice by themselves and intent on treating patients as they saw fit. Torman was impressed by their focus on patient care and their disdain for status.

Having secured an Arizona medical license prior to moving, Torman quickly settled into practicing again. The patients resembled those at HBS, only with deep tans. On Torman's first day in Sierra Vista, the clinic scheduled just four patients for him, thus allowing time for Torman to settle in and get familiarized with the electronic medical records. Sam Gaston, a homeless man with a long history of psychosis and alcoholism, barely spoke, so Torman had to rely on information from Sam's case manager and the chart to fill in most of the blanks in his story. Sandy Myers, a strikingly beautiful young woman, spoke non-stop, eventually forcing Torman to interrupt her in an attempt to get a more coherent picture of her life. Similar difficulties arose with Jerry Hammer, who not only talked incessantly but kept returning to outlandish tales of government malfeasance. Court-ordered to treatment, Esther Martin, the last patient he saw on his first day, made Torman uneasy, and their encounter stayed with him long after he left the clinic that afternoon. A grey-haired woman in her 60's, Esther stared at Torman as if daring him to question her mental health. After introducing himself, he started the conversation by asking why she was coming to the clinic. Maintaining her stare, she said, "Cut the crap, Mr. Torman. You've got my records."

"Yes, I've got some records but it helps me to get to know you if you can tell me about yourself."

"I don't belong in this shithole clinic with a bunch of idiots asking me useless questions. There's nothing else to say."

"Your chart shows you've been prescribed Risperdal injections every two weeks, but so far you've not shown for any shots. Has medicine ever been helpful to you in any way?"

"I don't need any medication. So why should I take it?"

"I read in your records that you stabbed a fellow resident at a group home 6 months ago and were hospitalized as a result. That's when the Risperdal was started. Can you tell me why you stabbed her?"

Esther just stared at Torman in silence for at least a minute, then said, "You know why I stabbed her, don't pretend you don't."

"No, I don't know. I'd like to understand why you did that. Were you feeling threatened by her?"

Esther stood up, announcing she'd had enough of this "bullshit" and headed towards the door. Torman said he'd like to see her in a month. "I don't care what you'd 'like,' Mr. Torman," Esther said as she marched out of his office. She couldn't have been taller than 5 feet and weighed less than 100 pounds, yet there was an unmistakable menace about her.

Turning to the case worker sitting in on the session, Torman, looking worried, said, "I didn't get very far, did I?"

Sharon, the twenty-something case worker, admitted, "You got as far as anyone gets with her."

"Do you think she's dangerous?"

"She's real careful to avoid saying the things that are likely to get her sent back to the hospital. The minute we see any signs of decompensating or threatening others verbally, we'll get her picked up. But she's crafty."

"Any family or friends she's in contact with?"

"Nope. Everyone gives her a wide berth."

"I can see why."

Val emailed Torman the name of a general contractor in Bisbee who could get all the work done on his home. The closing was a week away, but Jimmy was glad to make his house available for the contractor to inspect what needed to be done and to prepare a bid for Torman.

Torman arrived early at Jimmy's, and the two men sat outside with the beer Torman brought. Whether it was the beer, Torman's company, or something else, Jimmy seemed in a good mood. He'd never met the contractor but told Torman his reputation was solid, and his trucks could be seen all over Bisbee. Just then, at the designated time, Ed Ramone arrived in a white pick-up truck the size of a yacht. Ed, short, wiry, in perfectly pressed khakis and short sleeve shirt, jumped out of the truck and stood momentarily in front of the house. As he met Jimmy and Torman, he remarked this was the only house on the street he'd never painted. Jimmy laughed, saying he'd always done his own painting. Without any more small talk, Ed asked Torman to show him what he wanted done.

Making notes on a clipboard and taking some measurements, Ed listened as Torman read from the notes Val had sent him. After they'd gone through the entire house, Ed said he had a number of on-going projects but could get him a bid by the end of next week. Torman felt comfortable with Ed and sensed he knew what he was doing. Plus he felt secure in Val's recommending him and in knowing she'd be monitoring the work.

After Ed drove off, Torman asked Jimmy how he felt about moving to Indiana to live with his daughter. "Well, I'm a bit worried about it. Her kids are grown, and now I'm showing up, and she'll be watching over me. Of my children, she's been the caretaker. But her husband can't be delighted. He and I get along okay, but he's bound to feel I'm a burden. At least they have a large house, and I'll be staying above their garage, a carriage house with its own bathroom and kitchen."

"Living alone is hard for most of us. I sure had to adjust to it after my divorce."

"Yeah, this last year has been lonely as hell."

The two of them sat in silence while Junior gnawed on a Nylabone. Jimmy said, "You shrinks always talk this way?"

Torman laughed. "Yeah, sorry if I'm being too nosy."

"Is the meter running?"

"No, this is on the house."

❖ ❖ ❖

At the clinic Torman's initial patient of the day was Jerry, the frenzied paranoid man he'd met on his first workday in Sierra Vista. This time he showed up with his "spy pen," a video and recording device that he held up for Torman's inspection. He asked Torman to take it home and plug the pen's USB port into his computer so he could see the evidence of police corruption.

"Doc, you got to look at this! It's all there, plain as day. I get nowhere with the legal system. But you could help; they'd listen to you, I know they would. This has been going on since before I was born. It's run by a group..." At this point, Jerry looked around Torman's cramped office, up at the ceiling, behind the metal desk, each gesture of his head an exaggerated jerk. Whispering, he asked, "Is this office bugged?"

"Jerry, I don't think so."

"But you're not sure?"

"I really don't think it is."

"But you're not absolutely positive." Torman chose to respond with a shrug of his shoulders. "You got to be careful. The people I'm talking about kill anyone who talks about what's happened. I saw a policeman stab a guy when I was 5. I wasn't supposed to see it. I ran home. I hid in our basement. Someone rang the doorbell. My dad opened the door. I couldn't hear the conversation, but later my dad told me never to talk about what happened that day or everyone in our family would suffer terribly."

Torman learned long ago to believe there's always a kernel of truth to even the most outlandish delusion. He had no idea what part of Jerry's experience was based in reality. He figured his best bet was to acknowledge how frightened he must have felt back then and how frightened he feels now.

Jerry responded by telling more elaborate stories from his

past. The more he talked, the more pressured his speech and the harder it was to follow the endless details of his stories. Torman became restless, feeling captive to Jerry's ceaseless flow of recollections and emotions. Their half hour was up, with no end in sight to Jerry's tale. Finally, Torman stood up and repeated for the third time that their time was up. Jerry kept talking all the way into the hall, even as Torman waved goodbye.

The closing on the house took place in the local title company's office. Torman had arranged for a mortgage, signed numerous papers, shook hands with everyone present, and walked out with the keys to his new home. He had a list of places to go: the post office to get his PO Box and key (no mail delivery in Bisbee), the gas and electric company to get the utilities in his name, and the water company. He'd arranged to meet the following day with the local cable company guy at his new address.

He'd driven Jimmy to the closing and dropped him off before doing his errands. Torman noticed how pleased Jimmy was getting the check. He took it out on the ride home, examining it for the third or fourth time.

"I've never held a check this big. Kind of makes me nervous."

"Do you know what you're going to do with all that money?"

"My daughter's husband works at a bank. He's been managing what money I've saved so far. He's honest. I may need to dip into it if I end up in some kind of nursing home down the road."

Jimmy's daughter had arrived the day before to help Jimmy pack the few things he was taking to Indiana. She drove a van large enough to accommodate his belongings. They planned to leave the following morning. She greeted them as Torman pulled up in front of the house. Jimmy introduced his daughter Aileen to Torman and, after shaking hands, she thanked Torman for being so kind to her dad.

"He's an easy man to be kind to. I'm sorry he won't be around for me to visit with."

"I know it's hard for him to leave all this…all his memories of Mom…"

"I'm fine," Jimmy said. "I can handle this."

Seeing Jimmy's lips quiver, Torman said, "I know you can." They stood outside, an awkward threesome. Torman asked if he could help them tomorrow as they prepared to leave, but Aileen said they'd pretty much loaded up the van and would be off early.

"I'll take good care of your home, Jimmy." Torman held out his hand. He could see that Jimmy was choked up, holding back his tears. So they just shook hands.

Torman called Anna to discuss some of his cases, to catch up on her life, and to hear her voice, the sound of which always had a soothing effect on him. She warned him to be careful with Esther, who sounded dangerous to her, and laughed as he described Jerry's spy pen and the chaotic video he watched at home of Jerry's encounter with the Bisbee police. Torman asked what was new with her and Val and was surprised by her response.

"I've never told you this, but I've been thinking about having a child. Val and I have discussed this, but I'm ambivalent about getting some stranger's sperm. A part of me would want to know the father and would want the child to know him. But that gets very complicated, not just legally but emotionally. And I'll be 35 next month, so the clock, as they say, is ticking."

"How does Val feel about this?"

"She says she'd welcome a child into our lives but is clear about not wanting to know the father. She doesn't want to be the one carrying the baby. She's clear about that, too."

Torman experienced an impulse to offer himself as the sperm donor. Immediately following that thought was the awareness of how crazy the idea was. While he wished some day to be a father, he didn't want it to be under these conditions. He could just imagine how confusing this would be for a child, not to mention the kinds of parenting conflicts this would present to the three of them. Yet he wondered if Anna had thought of asking him, and, with an effort to mask the uneasiness in his voice, he asked, "You said a part of you would want to know the father and would want your child to know him…had you considered any candidates?"

Even without seeing his face, Anna guessed the real question in Torman's mind. "You're wondering if I'd thought about you?"

"It crossed my mind just now." He knew it was pointless trying to hide anything from Anna.

"Steve, you're certainly a man whom I like and admire, but I don't want to ever mislead you about the nature of our friendship. Val and I both care about you and hope our relationship with you endures. I'd like to see you find a woman with whom you could start a family."

Embarrassed he'd considered the possibility of her asking him to be the father, Torman said, "Yeah, me too."

That night Torman dreamed he was in a house that reminded him of the one he grew up in. He was going from room to room, looking for someone but not sure who that someone was. He felt excited and scared. He ended up in a barely lit bedroom. A pale figure, a woman, lay on the bed. He wanted to get closer to her but a hand on his shoulder pulled him back and the room faded to black. Torman woke from the dream with an uneasy sense. A part of him wanted to brush the dream aside, but he knew it was important to look at it in the light of day. He realized the dream was triggered by his conversation with Anna. The idea of fathering a child with Anna had excited him and, at the same time, scared him. What wasn't clear was why he was scared. He rejected the idea that it was the mere prospect of having a child, of taking on such a responsibility. Then he recalled a childhood memory tucked away in his head. When he was four or five, his mother had a tubal pregnancy and needed emergency surgery. His grandparents picked him up, and he spent two days at their house. He remembered his father arriving to take him back home. His dad told him his mother was fine but needed to rest in bed. Torman was excited to see her, but the actual sight of her scared him. Awake but immobile, she stared at the ceiling and responded hardly at all to his presence.

During his treatment on the couch, Torman had realized that his mother was suffering from depression and that it was months before she regained her normal mental state. His analyst, a strict Freudian, had believed this incident lay at the root of Torman's neurotic conflicts and had reinforced his anxiety over his oedipal strivings to supplant his father. Such a formulation was to be expected from a classically trained psychoanalyst, but it never really grabbed Torman in a convincing way. What did make sense was his feeling somehow responsible for his mother's suffering and his feeling the need to find some way to make her feel better, to make her happy. He spent a lot of effort trying to bring a smile to her face, yet for what seemed like eternity, he could not. In his analysis, he'd speculated that his eventual decision to enter psychiatry originated in his early efforts to make his mother feel better.

He imagined this is what lay beneath the impulse to father a child with Anna: the desire to make her happy. And what scared him was the possibility that he could never make her—or any woman—happy and would instead lead to her sadness and withdrawal from him.

Torman reassured himself that he was no longer that little boy and that Anna was not his mother. (At the same time, he tried to dismiss the voice in his head—his analyst's voice—that asked him, so why the interest in a woman whom you can't have? And why did you marry a woman who refused to have a child with you?)

◆ ◆ ◆

At work the following day, Torman ushered Sandy into his office. Her blond hair, formerly streaked green, now sprouted red cornrows with small sea shells attached at the ends. Slender and athletic, she was wearing a very short skirt and a tie-dyed t-shirt. She accepted getting an injection of Abilify every month but refused to add any other medication.

"Dr. Torman, I feel great. I really do. I'm seeing a guy, well, actually, I'm seeing a couple of guys, the one I talked about last time that I live with and a new guy. He's very sexy, very cool. An artist. I model nude for him, then we have sex. Sometimes we have sex first, then I model, and then we have sex. He's really unbelievable. Wants to take me to New York next month. He's hoping to have a show of his work. His work is great. I'm thinking of starting my own business. I'm not sure what kind of business. I just know I can't stand to work for someone else. Are you married? I don't see a ring on your finger. Do you ever consider seeing a patient? We could go out for coffee, nothing serious. Just for fun."

"Whoa, slow down, Sandy. No, I don't socialize with patients, but I'm interested in hearing about your relationships. Does the guy you're living with know about the new guy?"

"Yeah, he doesn't mind. He knows he can't keep me on a short leash. Why don't you socialize with patients?"

"It's unethical and harmful to patients. You need to be able to trust me and not feel I'm using my position to take advantage of you."

"You wouldn't be taking advantage of me. I'd do all the advantage taking." Torman laughed, Sandy's humor and liveliness impossible to resist. In an effort to regain some control over the direction of their conversation, he said he was changing the subject and asked about her sleep, her mood, her energy level, and side effects of her medication. She answered his questions, then noted he was no fun, just like all the shrinks she's seen, though better looking. "You should think about my offer, Dr. Torman. I could bring a smile to your face." And with that she gave him a mile-wide grin.

Torman knew he'd think about her at night when he was in bed. She would no doubt bring a smile to any man's face. And then unimaginable regret.

Ed's bid for the work on Torman's house seemed reasonable, so Torman gave him the go-ahead and wrote a check for partial payment. The following week a mostly Mexican crew arrived and tore away the exterior baseboard hiding the foundation and started digging holes for the concrete footers. When Torman stopped by around lunchtime, the sound of Mariachi music blasted from a boombox under his house. Torman felt like an uninvited guest to someone's party. He ventured out and introduced himself to the crew sitting outside enjoying their lunch. Back inside his home, he noticed how the light from below shone through some of the floorboards. He was living in a SHACK!

The men returned to work while Torman was eating his lunch. The floor trembled as the high-spirited men dug and pounded away below him, all the while bantering back and forth in Spanish. Not knowing their language, Torman couldn't follow what seemed to be an amusing tale being shared below him.

On his way back to the clinic, Torman wished his patients

could find the sense of purpose and camaraderie that Ed's crew possessed. Sam, his alcoholic schizophrenic, spent most of his time wandering around town by himself or drinking cheap wine in the park where he often spent the night. Jerry, too paranoid to live with or near anyone, often slept in his old pick-up truck instead of his apartment and drank coffee all day long. No one seemed to know how Esther spent her days, but Torman imagined her holed up somewhere safe while she fantasized the destruction of those she hated. On the other hand, Sandy certainly had company and stayed busy, but her activity and so-cializing had a driven, frenetic quality about it. Nothing endur-ing or substantial resulted from her manic energy.

When he arrived at the clinic, a case worker informed Torman that Esther had threatened to stab another group home resident. A staff member at the home searched her room and discovered a kitchen knife under her mattress. Torman and the case worker agreed it was time to get her picked up and sent to the hospital. "She's really going to hate me now," Torman said.

"Yeah, this is likely to move you and the rest of us higher up on her shit list."

◆ ◆ ◆

During Torman's subsequent visit to Anna and Val's in Tucson, Anna announced, over dinner, that they'd decided to pursue her getting pregnant via artificial insemination using an anonymous sperm donor. Torman, raising his glass of wine, offered his congratulations. Both Anna and Val seemed excited by the prospect.

"I realized," Anna said, "that I want to know the basic details of the sperm donor, his race, height and weight, med-ical history, family medical history, and educational level. To-gether, Val and I will make the choice of the donor. It still seems strange not to know the actual person, but his being anonymous eliminates potential complications."

Torman listened as the two of them talked about how a child would change their lives. In spite of himself, he felt his mood slip, though he worked to keep this from becoming obvious.

Sensing Torman's becoming quiet, Anna asked if he could play some sort of male role in the child's life. "I could settle into an 'Uncle Steve' role. My mother had two brothers and one of them, Uncle Stan, I really liked. He'd been much more athletic than my father and encouraged me to pursue sports. Whenever he could, Uncle Stan attended my soccer and baseball games. He and his wife had no children. His involvement in my life meant a lot to me."

"Would I have to start letting you win our swim races?"

"Val, I've brought my suit and will see you in the pool tomorrow."

"Why wait, I'm ready now."

Anna's only response was a shake of her head.

Torman didn't recognize the number of the incoming call on his cell phone but decided to pick it up. "Dr. Torman?"

"Yes. Who am I speaking to?"

"This is Dr. Valquez from the Arizona State Hospital. I'm the treating psychiatrist for Esther Martin. She escaped last night from the hospital. The police have been notified, and we expect she'll be returned to us shortly. However, I need to warn you that she'd been making threats to kill you and other members of the staff at your clinic."

"Thanks for calling me. I'll alert my clinic staff and contact our local police, who know her well. She is one angry woman."

"Yes, she is. We had a court order to administer intramuscular medication if she refused oral meds. And she did refuse all pills. The injections we gave her were not longterm sustained-release antipsychotics, just immediate-release Haldol. The shots hadn't shown any signs of effectiveness prior to her escape. I'll let you know when she's picked up and returned to us. I have to say she's one of the scarier patients I've treated. We still don't know how she managed to escape."

Torman recalled a psychiatry resident he worked with who'd been stabbed in the neck with a sharp pencil by a patient and almost died due to a partial tear of his carotid artery. That got everyone's attention. But the only way to work with psychotic or severely agitated patients was to use some degree of denial in order to remain calm and helpful. At the same time, you learned to position yourself between the patient and the door, always kept the door open, as well as following other safety measures. But if fear took over, you were useless to your patients.

Torman called the clinic and spoke with Esther's case worker, who'd already been informed of Esther's escape and threats. The clinic was on high alert, as were the local police departments in Sierra Vista and Bisbee.

That evening, coming home, Torman was glad to see Baba at the front door waiting for him. The two of them checked the entire house, including the exposed crawl space beneath the living area. He placed a hunting knife next to his cell phone on the bedside table. As the sky darkened, his uneasiness mounted. Sleep would not be good, but that meant he was less likely to be caught completely helpless.

Val arranged to evaluate the work being done on Torman's house. Arriving after the workmen left for the day, she and Torman explored under the house. She approved the concrete footings, as well as the removal of the old galvanized water line and its replacement with pex piping.

"So far, so good. Where are you taking me for dinner?" Torman said he'd planned on cooking her favorite pasta dish. "Candlelight? Mood music? Trying to make Anna jealous?"

"I can't help it, you're just so hot." Val emitted an appreciative snort.

Over dinner, they talked further about how a child would affect Val and Anna's lives, how both of them planned to continue working, at least part-time, and how much they had to learn about raising a child. Torman brought up being warned about his patient's escape from the hospital and her threats towards him and others.

"Do you know how to protect yourself?"

"Well, not really. She's pretty old and small. I'm sure I could outrun her."

"I hope you run faster than you swim. If not, you're in deep shit."

"Hey, I'll have you know I ran cross-country in high school. Besides, I'm sleeping with a hunting knife by my bed, and I check the house from top to bottom whenever I've been out. Plus I've got Baba."

"I'm fond of Baba, but let's be honest: his only defense is his gas."

Hearing his name, Baba came over from the couch and nuzzled Torman's thigh.

Some days after work, Torman jogged around Bisbee. Often he'd stop to rest at a small park where the community swimming pool was located. Occasionally he'd see his patient Sam off by himself in a secluded area of the park, usually drinking alcohol. Today he was surprised to see Sandy doing yoga poses on the lawn. He waved from his spot on a bench. She soon bounded over, asking if he wanted to join her doing yoga and meditating.

"Thanks, Sandy, but I'm just resting from a run and will soon be off."

"You know, yoga is really healthy for you. Have you ever done it? I've been doing it for years. It helps center me. You should tell your patients about yoga. Maybe they wouldn't need so much medication. If I didn't do this, I'd probably need more meds. But this works really well for me. How far do you run? We could run together. How about it?"

"I think we already discussed this subject. You know, how it's not ethical to socialize with patients..."

"Oh, c'mon, it's not like a date. Well, not exactly. Anyway, I'm an adult, I can make my own decisions about what's good for me and what's not. You really need to lighten up, Steve." The last said with a winning smile as she stood before Torman in black tights and form-fitting top, shapely legs and ass on display, arms akimbo, staring down at her uncomfortable-looking shrink.

Torman, having dealt with seductive, attractive patients, always asked himself at such moments, do you want to throw away your career, do you want to get sued? That generally helped quell any impulses of his own. "Sandy, I have to disappoint you."

"What if I find another shrink? Then could we 'socialize'?"

"The rules are clear: never. Really, it's for the best."

"Such a stickler for the rules! You're really missing out on some fun." With that, Sandy turned and left, glancing back once to offer up one more smile. Torman followed her with his gaze, allowing himself to imagine how much he'd like to help her out of her yoga outfit.

◆ ◆ ◆

The administrative director of the Sierra Vista mental health clinic, Stuart Craven, a dapper man with a Yosemite Sam mustache and an eagerness to shake hands, entered Torman's office with outstretched hand, then gave Torman a letter from a journalist who wanted to write an article on the scarcity of psychiatric care in rural Arizona.

"I think we might get some good publicity out of this, Steve, and God knows, we could use all the help we can get. Would you be interested in letting a reporter interview you for this story?"

"Sure, just have the receptionist put whoever it is in my schedule. Maybe we could also have him join our staff lunch."

"Great idea, I'll do that." Out again with his hand, Stuart gave Torman a hard squeeze, then added, "I'll leave you to work your magic on our patients."

Later that day, Torman read the letter more carefully. The journalist's name at the letter's end grabbed Torman's attention: Eric Silver. He figured this was his former patient, who'd moved to Tucson to get a master's degree in creative writing. He hadn't heard anything from him after his leaving treatment except for a brief note thanking him for his help and telling him he was eager to start his classes. He was curious to know if Eric had remained in touch with Susan and if their relationship had managed to survive the break-up.

The letter was addressed to the clinic director. Torman figured Eric had no idea that he was the psychiatric consultant. Finding an email address on Eric's letterhead, Torman decided to send a brief note to Eric alerting him to his presence and saying how he looked forward to seeing him.

Upon entering Torman's office, Jerry checked around the room, looking for any "bugs" or other evidence they were being recorded or observed. Then he launched into a long tale about a recent encounter at a restaurant in which he'd seen a cook drop meat on the floor, pick it up, and flip it into a pot on the stove. No one was wearing hairnets or hats in the kitchen, either. Jerry confronted the owner/manager with his observations, only to be banned for one year for being too loud and interfering with business.

"Doc, they should be closed down! That's how food-borne illnesses get started. I didn't have my spy pen with me, or I'd show you what I saw."

"This is the third business you've been banned from."

"Yeah. I'm gonna miss that place. It's got great cheap food. Don't go there, though, or you'll get sick."

"You seem to have survived quite a few meals there, Jerry." Torman couldn't stop himself from trying to use some humor to soften Jerry's outrage.

"This is serious, really. All that owner cares about is money. Someone gets sick, someone maybe dies, that's just too bad. Money is what makes the world go round. Guys like that would steal from their grandmothers. My dad, when he was really drunk, would come into my room and start yelling at me because of something I'd done, like leaving a dirty dish in the sink or not making my bed properly. It was like living with some kind of drill sergeant. He'd hit me when he got really mad, and I was scared of him. I guess that's where I got my concern about cleanliness."

"Did your mom know he'd hit you?"

"Yeah, but she was scared of him, too. You didn't cross my dad, especially when he was drinking, which was pretty much all the time."

Torman absorbed this information, which helped him understand Jerry's difficulties with authority figures. In the future he hoped he'd be able to look more closely at Jerry's experience with his father, but it was extremely difficult to get a word in edgewise with him. Torman also wished he could find some way to help Jerry channel his energy and vigilante spirit into more acceptable and constructive uses. If only he could work for an outfit like Greenpeace or some other agency that investigates environmental disasters caused by greedy or thoughtless individuals, corporations, and governments. That would allow him to feel validated, part of a group dedicated to doing good, yet still working on the margins of society. What a perfect fit! But Jerry's world was too small, too centered on his immediate surroundings. Not to mention that Jerry's paranoia would likely spook even the most diehard Greenpeace idealist. Torman viewed Jerry as a would-be Dirty Harry intent on ridding the world of all the scumbags and evildoers, a character who could exist only in the world of make-believe.

As usual, unable to get a word in and running out of time, Torman stood up and moved toward the door. Reluctantly, Jerry got up to leave, all the while keeping up his running account of all the injustices perpetrated by various people in town and warning Torman to keep his eyes open.

"Doc, you gotta watch your back."

Eric sent an email to Torman expressing his surprise and pleasure in learning they'd be meeting shortly. He offered some dates for Torman to choose from and included his cell phone number in case Torman needed to reach him quickly. He explained that he was doing freelance writing as well as working on some short stories.

Torman looked forward to seeing Eric. Contact with patients usually ended with the termination of treatment. In some cases, people returned for more treatment. A few sent cards with updates on their lives around the Christmas holidays. However, most of them never resurfaced.

Aside from his relationships with Anna and Val, Torman hadn't made any close friends since settling in Bisbee. He did take up June and Marge's offer to tour the Kartchner Caverns and joined them and other neighbors for a holiday meal. He'd also begun to know some of his co-workers at the clinics, but being the only psychiatrist had set him apart from others. There was a certain deference shown to him which created distance. Perhaps that was a good thing: it gave him some authority and respect. He was listened to. But there was a loneliness that went with that.

He valued his contact with Anna and Val, though he worried that the arrival of a child in their lives would limit their availability to him. He'd observed how couples became totally preoccupied with raising a child and how their worlds tended to shrink with the focus on child rearing.

The work on Torman's house was moving along. Val met Ed, and they'd become friends, discussing their approaches to rehabbing. Ed took her along to see some of the other properties he was working on and appreciated Val's suggestions. Listening to the two of them talk shop, Torman interrupted with, "Hey, what about my place? How about coming up with some ideas about how to make it a dream home!?"

Val and Ed exchanged glances, then looked at Torman's house as if seriously considering Torman's request. "You know, Val," Ed began, "a house with this heritage belongs in the Smithsonian, or, at the very least, in the Bisbee Mining and Historical Museum."

"Right, Ed. It would be a terrible travesty to alter any of the primitive features of this shack."

"I totally agree. The slightest pressure, even leaning against a wall, could bring the entire house down. Which would be a shame, since they just don't make shacks like this anymore."

"Yeah, it's a lost art. Our job is to preserve the structural fragility and crude integrity of these places. Something I feel privileged to do."

"Amen." Val and Ed stood staring at Torman's home.

Going along with his role as the insulted homeowner, Torman said, "I'm paying for this abuse?"

Val noted she wasn't being paid a damn thing, and he'd better take her somewhere nice for dinner.

"The last time I came down here you cooked pasta, but tonight I want a steak dinner, and I want you to take me out. How about the haunted hotel's restaurant?"

"Next time you visit, I'll have you come over for a real Mexican meal that my wife'll make. Much better than what the restaurants offer. And certainly better than what the doctor serves you here."

"Hey, I may not be able to wield a hammer, but I know my way around a kitchen." Both Val and Ed stared at Torman, then simultaneously burst into laughter.

The night before Eric's visit, Torman decided he'd better do some house cleaning. He was scouring the bathtub when he heard Baba barking at the door. Thinking he had to go out, Torman got his leash, hooked him up, and opened the door.

Standing on the porch, Esther, whose recent escape and threats had receded in Torman's mind, had one hand in her pocket, the other in mid-air, poised to knock on the door. Torman froze, his eyes fixed on hers, which glowered at the sight of him.

"You fucking bastard...an eye for an eye..." She pulled out a small revolver, aimed at his face, and fired.

Baba lunged at Esther, pushing her backwards with such force that her head audibly cracked on a large rock in the garden.

Seeing the gun, Torman had managed to twist his head slightly so that the 22 bullet punctured his right eye, shattering and ricocheting off the outer bony structure of his eye socket. He collapsed and passed out.

❖ ❖ ❖

Torman hadn't noticed the man in the battered pick-up truck parked close by his house. Spy pen in hand, Jerry rushed out of the truck and jumped Torman's fence. He tried to stanch the bleeding as he cried for help over the frantic barking of Baba. Neighbors on both sides, already alerted by Baba's barking, rushed over and crowded around Torman. Within minutes, an ambulance arrived and paramedics assessed both Torman and Esther. Jerry ceded care of Torman to the paramedics and disappeared just prior to the arrival of the police.

Esther was dead, but Torman's injury didn't appear life-threatening. He was transported to Tucson for medical assessment and treatment. The police stayed at Torman's house collecting evidence, taking photographs of the scene, and interviewing neighbors. It was not immediately apparent to the officers what had led up to Torman's injury. Esther's gun was found next to her body but had fallen out of her hand upon her impact with the rock. No one interviewed had seen the events or heard anything other than Baba's barking and a man's voice calling for help. Nor did anyone know who that man was or where he'd gone. The police recognized Esther and recalled being on the look-out for her. They suspected the man who left the scene may have witnessed all or part of what happened. There was also the possibility that this man, who'd fled the scene, was involved in the shooting and/or the death of Esther.

The word spread around the small town as quickly as one of Bisbee's monsoon rains swept through on a summer day. The clinic notified Torman's parents, who were listed as his emergency contacts, and case workers contacted patients to answer questions and dispel any unfounded rumors.

Torman was awake and fairly alert in the emergency room. A young doctor explained to him that he'd lost his eye but was not in any serious danger. They needed to do a brain scan, then would likely do surgery to stabilize the bones in the orbit. He gave the doctors permission to proceed, then tried to absorb what he'd been told. He managed to get someone to call Anna, who arrived as he was being wheeled to radiology for the brain scan.

Trying to hide her reaction to the sight of Torman's face, Anna, walking beside the stretcher, asked as calmly as possible how he was feeling, if he was in pain.

"I've felt better. That patient I told you about, the crazy woman who'd threatened to kill me, who escaped a month ago from the hospital, she shot me in my face when I opened my door. I've lost my eye." He started to cry but all that came out were some sobs and choking sounds.

"Steve, I'm here, I'll stay here with you." She held his hand briefly, then watched as the orderly wheeled him in for the scan.

In the morning Torman awoke to a dull ache where his right eye used to be. His head was heavily bandaged. He knew last night's events were real, not something he'd dreamed, but wished he could go back in time and do things differently. Like not opening his door. Or grabbing Esther's arm the moment she removed it from her coat pocket.

He became aware of a man he'd never met before sitting by his bed. Seeing Torman rousing from sleep, the man stood and moved next to Torman's face. "I'm Jake Lawrence with the Bisbee police department." He flashed his badge and, without further ado, said he'd like to know what happened last night. Torman described the events up to the moment he saw Esther take out her gun and hearing it fire. Jake asked if anyone else was present. "No, I only recall seeing Esther on my porch. I was alone at my house and not expecting anyone that evening. Where's Esther?"

"No one told you?"

"Told me what?"

"She apparently fell or was pushed off the porch, hit her head on a rock, and died at the scene."

Torman felt relief, then wondered if there was some suspicion that he'd pushed her. He was quiet, except for saying "I had no idea. I have no memory of anything after she shot me."

"Well, if anything does come back, call me." With that, he gave Torman his card and left. Torman scanned the card, then put it on the tray by his bed.

A nurse came in with a note that Anna had left for him: "Steve, I left after you were wheeled into recovery. Surgery went well according to your surgeon. Val's coming by around 9 this morning and I'll see you at lunchtime. You're in good hands. Anna"

When Val arrived, Torman was feeling restless, wishing he could get out of there.

"You look like shit," Val announced.

"So do you. How about some sympathy?"

"After you ruined my night's sleep and managed to worry Anna to death?"

Torman tried not to laugh because it hurt his head. Before he could come up with a clever response, Val said she'd called Ed to check on Baba and learned that some young, very attractive woman was taking Baba for a walk when Ed got there. "So, who's the babe you've been hiding from us?"

"I've no idea who you're talking about."

"Ed said she's got some noticeable tatoos, blond hair with red streaks in it, and an ass that men would die for."

Torman felt panic in his chest but tried to dismiss her curiosity with "Oh, she's someone who lives nearby and must've heard what happened. A good Samaritan."

"Samaritan my ass. You're withholding something, Steve. I can't wait to tell Anna." Val pulled up a chair by Torman's bed and put her hand on his arm. "Seriously, how're you doing?"

"I'm trying to absorb all this. My head throbs, but I can deal with that. I'm glad I'm alive."

"So am I."

❖ ❖ ❖

When Val left, Torman's mood bottomed out. His right eye was gone. Eyes don't grow back. What if something happened to his left eye. He'd be blind. He felt panicky. And he kept re-playing in his mind Esther's face, contorted with hate, her arm rising and the gun firing. An image from the movie "Don't Look Now," seen years ago, flashed before him: an old, ugly female dwarf in a bright red coat slicing the throat of a character played by Donald Sutherland, who believes he was following a child in the deserted nighttime streets of Venice. As he's dying, he realizes that visions he'd been having were actually premonitions of his own murder and funeral. What stayed in the back of Torman's mind all these years was the image of the hideous dwarf's face, suddenly revealed as she turns around to face Sutherland, and his paralysis as she slices his neck with a meat cleaver. Now, in Torman's mind, the dwarf's image merged with the image of Esther, and the memory of this scene would repeat itself over the coming weeks and months.

A knock on the door caused Torman to recoil involuntarily. Seeing the look on his face as she entered his room, the nurse asked, "Are you all right?"

"I'm fine," Torman said. "You woke me up, that's all. I'm fine." He didn't tell her that he was probably experiencing some PTSD symptoms. He knew what he was dealing with. He should be able to get a grip on this. He'd talk with Anna. She'd understand. Thinking of her helped ease his anxiety.

After the nurse left, he gently probed his bandages to try to feel around his wound. Was it a bloody crater? Would he get a prosthetic eye? Wear an eye patch? Would he look like a freak? Part of him wanted to look in the mirror, but with all the bandages he wouldn't be able to see anything.

He thought about Esther. He was glad she was dead. He wondered if he'd somehow managed to push her before he fell. He hoped he had.

Maybe he should ask for some medication, something like Zoloft, to deal with some of the PTSD symptoms he was likely to experience. Nobody seemed to address how terrifying the shooting was for him. He reminded himself this was typical of the medical world where psychological reactions and symptoms were rarely considered, especially if the patient was quiet and cooperative.

When Anna arrived around noon, he felt grateful for her presence. She encouraged him to talk about the shooting, listened carefully to all his concerns, and acknowledged his fears.

"Steve, it's going to be rough going for a while. Let's see how you do when you get back home. I know a really good therapist who can help if you need to see someone. And you know you can talk to me. Anytime." She held his hand.

Torman cried. "I hate feeling weak. I hate feeling scared."

Later that afternoon, a soft knock on the door announced Eric's arrival.

"Dr. Torman, I hope I'm not bothering you, but the clinic director told me what happened."

Torman had completely forgotten about Eric's visit. "Eric! Good to see you." He was feeling no pain thanks to the narcotic he'd swallowed after lunch. "How do I look?"

"Like someone who did 12 rounds with Mike Tyson." They both laughed. "What happened?"

Torman recounted the story of his attack, as well as supplying some history of his now dead patient. He added that Eric might want to consider writing a piece on psychiatrists' risks of assaults by patients.

"I'd been swung at a couple of times...when I was a resident working in the emergency room. But this was the first time a patient ever tried to assault me with a weapon. It's a concern most, if not all, psychiatrists share." Torman was aware of trying to appear put-together to Eric, not wanting him to see how fragile he felt. So he turned the conversation back to him: "So, how are you doing?"

Eric talked about the masters program he'd completed, about his freelance writing and his short stories. Not wanting to burden Torman with too much conversation, Eric said he'd be staying at a rental home in Bisbee for a few days and would check in with him tomorrow.

After Eric left, Torman's surgeon, Dr. Reynolds, rounding on patients, marched in to update him on the surgery and plans for discharge and follow-up care. During the conversation, Dr. Reynolds removed some of the bandages, inspected his handiwork, and seemed pleased with the results. "A lot of swelling, but that's to be expected. We'll send you home tomorrow. Expect headaches for a week or so. Any discharge, bleeding, or sudden pain, call my office. I'll see you in a week. And we'll refer you to a plastic surgeon to make you a handsome man again." And with that, he was out the door. While Torman was not surprised the surgeon never asked how he was handling the loss of his eye and the experience of being shot in the face, he'd been tempted to remind him that these issues were as important to address as the physical damage. But Dr. Reynolds hardly left Torman the time to say goodbye as he sped on to his next patient.

As if someone had been reading his mind, Torman's next visitor was Janice Cook, a social worker, who introduced herself and explained that every victim of violence was seen within 48 hours of admission.

"I understand you're a psychiatrist, Dr. Torman, so you no doubt know the likely emotional consequences of such trauma." A plump woman in her late forties with a kind face and the husky voice of a smoker, she hesitated to see how Torman would respond.

"Yes, I do have a pretty good idea of what to expect. I just never thought I'd be on the receiving end of a bullet." Torman stifled the sudden urge to cry.

Moving closer to his bed, Janice spoke softly, "We have an excellent psychologist on staff who's available to talk with you if you feel the need. He can also make a referral to therapists in the community who have special training in PTSD." With that, she handed Torman her card. "Here's my phone number. Don't hesitate to call me if you feel the need, and I'll try to be of help."

Torman managed to maintain his composure, though he had a fantasy of burying his head between her breasts and having her cradle his head there with her hands. Not wanting to make a fool of himself, he thanked her for visiting and for her offer of help. After she left, he wondered if he'd have benefited from a female analyst, if there was something about a woman that would have opened him up emotionally in ways his former analyst was never able to do. He recalled the comfort he'd felt talking with Andie during his divorce and with Anna earlier that day.

That evening, listening to the evening news on TV to see if his shooting made the program, his parents entered his room. His mom burst into tears at the sight of him, while his father hung back a bit, looking uneasy and worried. Torman reassured both that he was fine, that he'd lost his eye but had sustained no other serious injury. Once again, he told the story of the shooting, but, sensing their anxiety, downplayed the dangers of working with psychotic patients. He didn't want to burden them with his anxieties.

"Why do you have to work in these clinics? Why not open a private practice and see more of the worried well? After all, you spent years learning how to do psychoanalysis," his mother said.

"Mom, really, this was a freak incident. You don't get struck by lightning twice."

"Actually," his dad said, "I read once that a U.S. Park Ranger was supposedly struck seven times by lightning over the course of some 30 years." Torman and his mom stared at him.

"I'm trying to have a serious conversation with our son and that's your contribution?"

"I was just trying to point out that Steve's reassurance that lightning doesn't strike twice is not altogether true." Steve's dad looked at his feet, adding, "I guess that was pretty stupid of me."

Before the conversation could take a turn toward the familiar bickering of a long-married couple, Torman asked where they were staying. They lingered for an hour, making small talk, bringing their son up-to-date with family news. As they got up to leave, Torman suggested they return tomorrow and, in their rental car, take him back to his home in Bisbee. They planned to spend one night with him in Bisbee, then return to Tucson to fly home.

Aside from a headache and drowsiness, Torman felt physically good as a nurse wheeled him to the hospital exit where his parents' car awaited him. He napped much of the way home, opening his eye long enough to provide directions for his father.

"Oh, my...what a...colorful house," his mom said as they entered his home. Before Torman could respond, Sandy, accompanied by Baba, emerged from the kitchen and greeted everyone with one of her outsized smiles.

"Hi, I'm Sandy. I've been caring for Baba. Steve, let me see your face...well, nothing a good surgeon can't improve on." Everyone, with the exception of Torman, laughed.

As Baba nuzzled his leg and outstretched hand, Torman introduced his parents, who clearly were uncertain about Sandy's status in their son's life.

Sandy didn't miss a beat: "It's about lunchtime. Mrs. Torman, would you like to keep me company in the kitchen while I put together some lunch for all of us?" Off they went, with Sandy keeping the conversation lively and Torman's mother tagging along, delighted to see such a warm, lovely woman being so helpful to her son.

"Sandy's a real knock-out," whispered his dad. "How'd you two meet?"

"That's a long story." It was rare for him to be at such a loss for words. He couldn't violate patient confidentiality, yet he didn't want to lie and go along with the pretense that she was his girlfriend. "She's a neighbor. Very friendly woman, a real caretaker."

"So how long have you been dating?"

"Well, I don't think we're actually dating, Dad. Hey, let me show you around." Father and son, accompanied by Baba, toured the small house. As Torman tried to keep his father off the subject of Sandy, he wondered how he was going to deal with her. In spite of his headache and anxiety, his spirits had picked up at the sight of her. She infused his home with her buoyancy, her fragrance, her laughter. He was also aware of the lively conversation going on in the kitchen. His mother would not be so easy to distract from wanting to know about his relationship with Sandy.

For lunch Sandy served a pasta salad with artichoke hearts, asparagus, watercress, and feta cheese, dressed with lemon juice and olive oil. She got his parents talking about Torman as a child.

"Oh, he was always such a good boy. Never got into trouble," his mom said.

"Why aren't I surprised to hear that?" Sandy said, giving Torman a look of mock surprise.

Torman could barely listen. He couldn't focus his thoughts. Unexpected noises startled him, he was self-conscious about his bandaged eye socket, and he felt an unfamiliar uneasiness that prevented him from relaxing. And then there was Sandy. How was he going to manage her?

After the meal, he pleaded exhaustion and retreated to his bedroom. Sandy took his parents on a tour of Bisbee after Torman assured everyone he was feeling all right being alone.

"I'm fine. I've got some medication to take, then I'm going to rest. Thanks for your help."

Shortly after his parents and Sandy returned, Torman got a call from Eric, who asked how he was feeling. Torman suggested he come by the following day and supplied directions to his house. He decided to take a short walk, thinking this might help clear his head. Before leaving, Sandy told his parents she'd be back to walk Baba in the early evening. If they needed help figuring out dinner, they should just call her.

Torman's mom was all smiles. "What an improvement over Claire. So much personality. Claire never gave me the time of day. Always in a hurry, always exercising or working or busy with something. And Sandy made such a good meal... something Claire never did. I think Claire's idea of cooking was microwaving a frozen dinner."

Finding himself in the odd position of defending his former wife, Torman said, "Claire had a very demanding profession, which didn't leave her much time to think about meal preparation."

"Or you, apparently. Too busy burnishing her all-important legal career. Well, enough of her." Looking at Torman, she added, "So, Steve, how come you never mentioned Sandy?"

"Mom, I really don't know her all that well. She's one of those people who's a natural helper. And full of energy." He hoped this would suffice.

"Well, I see she slept in the guest bedroom...seems like she's more than a neighbor."

"Hon, Steve's a grown man. He doesn't need to share his love life with his mother."

Torman was thankful for his dad's stepping in. Normally he'd have told his mother that he had no intention of discussing his private life, but persistent anxiety and the return of a headache interfered with thinking clearly. He said he'd be back in a half hour or so.

As he opened the front door, he felt a sudden panic. He looked right and left before actually stepping onto the porch. He reminded himself that Esther was dead. Looking around for any evidence of dried blood, he realized someone—Sandy?— had cleaned his porch.

He tried to think about how to handle Sandy. Her presence in his home, her involvement with his parents, her seeing him so vulnerable...so many boundaries crossed. He would have to transfer her care to another doctor, as well as talking to her about the impossibility of continued contact and, in so doing, restore appropriate limits to their relationship.

After ten minutes, he needed to sit down and rest. He sat on the bench by the Iron Man statue, a landmark in Bisbee. The sun felt good on his face, and he imagined the sun's rays speeding the healing of his wound. Anna had left a message on his cell phone telling him she planned to come down the following day and expected to spend the night. She definitely believed he should not be alone. In spite of his resistance to being cared for, he looked forward to her arriving.

Not wanting to worry his parents, he decided to head back home. While he appreciated their coming out to help him, he was eager to see them depart the following morning. Over the years, he'd managed to let go of his wish to please his mother and make her happy. He knew his mother blamed Claire for the change in their relationship and, to some degree, she was right. Claire had thought his closeness with his mother was excessive and encouraged Torman to rely less on her approval. And, to a lesser extent, his analysis brought about the awareness of how influenced he was by his mother and her needs. Reeling from Esther's assault and his injury, Torman didn't want to regress in his parents' presence and revert back to old patterns of behavior. Their leaving the next day freed him from that possibility.

Walking up the hill towards his home, he discovered how different the world looked through one eye, how much more vulnerable he felt.

❖ ❖ ❖

As promised, Sandy re-appeared in the early evening. Perhaps sensing Torman's unease with her unexpected intrusion into his life, she wasted no time gathering up Baba and heading out for a walk. It was apparent to Torman that she'd not only won over his parents but also Baba, who all but brought her his leash.

"Steve, if you want some time alone with Sandy, Dad and I can go out for a while."

"Thanks, but I don't get much time alone with you and Dad. I really appreciate your coming out here. I'm sure I'll be fine. Tomorrow a friend of mine is coming down from Tucson to spend some time, and she'll be able to help out with anything I need."

"Another woman in your life? How many are there?"

"She's a good friend and colleague who happens to be a lesbian. So you can forgo further questioning." He was pleased to see that this quelled her curiosity.

Torman noticed that, except for Anna, no one wanted to address the loss of his eye and the impact of being shot, at least not beyond hearing the description of what happened. He wondered if people were picking up on his reluctance to talk about this. Maybe they sensed his discomfort and anxiety. Anna, he knew, would remain concerned with the trauma's impact on him. She would gently probe how he was feeling, listening intently, empathic radar on maximum setting.

When Sandy returned with Baba, Torman thought about taking her outside and telling her she'd done enough and no longer was needed. He'd thank her and remind her that she was his patient. But he couldn't do it. In spite of himself, he was smiling as she told the three of them how Baba greets everyone they encounter on the street, how he always manages to defecate on the sidewalk in front of the busiest businesses on Main Street, and how she always shares part of her oatmeal cookie with him. He told himself he'd talk with her tomorrow. On her way out, she looked directly at him and asked how he was doing.

"I'm fine, Sandy."

"No, I mean, how're you *really* doing?"

"Well, I...I'm a bit anxious at times. I feel disfigured. I haven't absorbed what happened." He could feel himself wanting to talk with her at length but held back, simply adding how grateful he was for all she'd done.

"I know you feel I've overstepped what you guys call 'boundaries,' so I wanted you to know that I've transferred my care to a psychiatrist in Tucson. I'm meeting with her next week. I hope that allows you to relax a little in my presence, Steve. I've experienced a lot of trauma in my life, things I've not shared with you. And I know how long it takes to come to grips with that."

What surprised Torman the most was her seriousness and the absence of her flirtatiousness. Nor did she seem abnormally revved up. After a brief silence, she said how sweet Baba was. The dog, hearing his name, began wagging his tail as he stood by Torman's side.

◆ ◆ ◆

The next morning, a Saturday, Torman printed out directions to the Tucson airport, hugged his parents goodbye, and stood at the front gate as they drove off. Relieved, he sat in his yard waiting for Anna to arrive. He anticipated Sandy's appearing and figured Anna's presence would give her the impression that he had a girlfriend. He imagined this would dampen, if not dispel, any romantic notions she harbored for him. He would thank her again for her help and assure her that Anna would be providing all the care he (and Baba) needed.

Anna's car pulled up right on time. "So," she began, "how're you faring?"

"Well...I guess it could be worse. I've got one good eye. I hardly slept last night. I feel waves of anxiety, the free-floating kind that comes out of nowhere. I startle easily. And I keep replaying in my mind what happened. As a shrink, I'm not surprised by this, but at the same time I'm impatient with myself. I want to be rid of these 'symptoms' and get back to my life."

They'd gone inside, grabbed some coffee Torman had brewed, and returned to the shaded cedar bench where he'd been waiting for her. "Is this the first serious injury you've ever had?"

"Yeah. I broke my collar bone playing baseball as a kid, but that was nothing. And I injured my knee playing soccer in high school. I'd never given a thought to my eyes. Now I'm very aware of feeling unsure of myself, as if someone could easily come up on my blind side. I keep turning my head to the right to see if I'm missing something. And I'm aware I've got a crater in my face where my eye used to be. It's a weird feeling." Torman paused, sighed and waited for Anna to respond.

"What's your worst fear?"

"Losing my good eye. Being totally blind, feeling help-less, unable to defend myself." Said without hesitation or fore-thought, though her question echoed in his mind until he found its connection: exactly what Andie, his attorney, had asked him in the midst of his divorce.

"Defend yourself from…?"

"Another psychotic patient. Will I ever feel safe again doing my work? What happened that night with Esther, it hap-pened so fast, I couldn't react."

Anna didn't offer any reassurances or pat answers. She knew this was just the beginning for Torman, that he would need many conversations about the loss of his eye and the dan-ger he'd faced. He would need to rehash over and over the de-tails of the trauma in order to develop some sense of mastery, to prevent being overwhelmed emotionally from his memory of the experience.

Torman went back inside to get them more coffee. It was at that moment that Sandy arrived.

Anna looked up and knew this was the woman Val had mentioned.

"Hi, I'm Sandy. I'm here to walk Baba," she said while ex-tending her hand and smiling broadly.

"Anna. Now how is it that Steve has never spoken of you?"

"Likewise, how is it that Steve's never mentioned you?" Both women laughed.

"I got to know Steve a few years ago, when he was still in Cincinnati and being supervised by my father. Dad had a stroke and I traveled back and forth to Cincinnati to help oversee his care. I've lived with my partner Val in Tucson for a number of years. Steve's come out a few times and stayed with us."

When Torman returned, the women were in animated conversation. Baba's head was resting on Sandy's lap, eyes up-turned and centered on her face. "Steve, it looks like you've got competition," Anna said, gesturing in Baba's direction.

"No one can compete with Baba," Sandy said, kissing him on his forehead. "Steve, Anna agrees with me that yoga and meditation would be of help to you. Studies have shown they can decrease anxiety and promote a sense of well-being." Turning to Anna, Sandy added that she'd tried to encourage his doing this some time ago.

"Who said I was anxious?"

In unison, both women said, "You did." Once again, Torman could feel his resistance to Sandy's charm melt away. Having the attention of these two women lifted his spirits. He offered Sandy coffee, which she declined. Then he realized she'd most likely be a tea drinker, so he offered that. "Don't bother, Steve. I'll get it."

"I'm not an invalid. Stay put."

After Sandy left, Anna asked Torman why he'd been keeping Sandy a secret. "I can't discuss that." She looked at his face, then understood. Psychiatrists have a way of letting people close to them know when someone is a patient and can't be discussed. Since they can't come out and say so-and-so is my patient, it's this look they get.

"So...I can see there's a problem here with our going any further with this. Steve, I know you understand how such a relationship can lead to your undoing."

"I haven't *done* anything. I arrived home from the hospital and discovered Sandy had been caring for Baba. Perhaps you could tell her I'm being very mysterious about how I met her and then ask her how we met. You could even be very direct and tell her what you're suspecting. I'm in a real bind here."

"Why don't you simply tell her you can't see her?"

"I have! I'm not getting very far with her. I really can't discuss this, as I'm sure you understand."

"Well, I can certainly understand how appealing she is. Stevie, Stevie...what are we going to do with you?"

The remainder of the morning they talked at length about his being shot, the loss of his eye, his fears of returning to work and having to deal with angry, psychotic patients. At some point, Anna suggested that he go back to work as soon as possible and face his fear rather than avoiding it for a long period.

"I know you know this, but I'm going to say it anyway: you've got to get right back on the horse after you've been thrown. The longer you wait, the harder it will be to get back in the saddle." That led to talking about patients' inquiries about his eye, how he would deal with that, and how hard it will be to talk about.

"Hey, it's almost one o'clock, are you hungry yet?" Anna asked.

"Yeah, I am. There's a Vietnamese restaurant in town. Interested?"

"Get in my car and I'll drive us there."

On the way to lunch, Torman told Anna that a journalist was coming by that afternoon to interview him about the scarcity of psychiatrists in rural Arizona.

"I guess the reason for the scarcity is now obvious: we get shot. By chance, we knew each other in Cincinnati and will be catching up on old times."

"Not another patient, I hope." Torman looked at Anna, not bothering to answer.

"Jesus, Steve, I hope she's not another very attractive young woman who happens to love you."

"'She' is a 'he,' and love is not in the offing."

"Maybe we could fix him up with Sandy. That might solve your problem."

Eric had not changed much in the last three years. He remained an affable young man with an earnest air. His hair was longer, his attire more casual. Torman took notice of his cowboy boots, as well as his vehicle, a weathered Toyota pick-up truck. Like all visitors to Torman's home, Eric registered surprise at the sight of the harlequin shack. Seeing Eric's taking in his house, Torman warned, "Don't laugh, or I'll comment on those cowboy boots."

"Clearly, both of us have moved up in the world."

Torman took him on a quick tour inside, then they settled outdoors in the shade. "I'm really sorry about what happened to you, Dr. Torman."

"'Steve,' please call me 'Steve.' And thanks. I'm trying to get used to being one-eyed and gun-shy." As usual, Torman employed humor as a first line of defense. He didn't want to expose how disturbed he felt to Eric, though he talked some about the shooting before changing the subject.

"Eric, I have to ask: any contact between you and Susan?"

"We've kept in touch, mostly by email. She's been involved with a couple of men since our breaking up. A brief relationship with that art professor Max, who ended up screwing half the women in Susan's class. You may remember him, a guy I was really jealous of. And another with a fellow student. She's currently in-between relationships. I'm not sure where I stand with her. Friend, confidant, ex-boyfriend, confessor...maybe all the above."

"Not to get shrinky here, but how do you feel about her?" Torman felt much more comfortable shifting the focus onto Eric than staying with his own recent trauma. And there was an inevitable barrier of sorts that resulted from their former doctor/patient roles, a barrier that Torman knew to respect and not attempt to dispel, though of less concern between members of the same sex. This was especially important if there was the possibility of treating a former patient in the future. However, with Eric, Torman sensed that the issue of being available to

Eric in the future for therapy was not a likely occurrence.

"I miss her. I still love her. I look forward to her emails. At the same time, I try to keep my feelings in check. I guess I don't want to get rejected and lose her all over again."

"Better safe than sorry?"

"Something like that, yeah." Baba had sidled up to Eric, hoping for some petting, which he soon received. "I wish we were like dogs. They give and take affection so readily."

Torman nodded, but added, "On the other hand, they aren't always faithful. Sometimes I think Baba would go off with anyone who shows him some kindness. Come to think of it, that's how I got him. He'd belonged to a supervisor of mine who had a stroke and eventually died and whose daughter asked me to take care of him. Baba's been with me since. And the supervisor's daughter, who lives in Tucson, is visiting me. You'll meet her shortly."

In time, conversation focused on Torman's view of psychiatric care in rural Arizona. Eric took notes, asked questions, and finally got around to wondering why Torman would leave his private practice in Cincinnati for work in the "boondocks." Torman decided not to reveal too much about his private life, though it was pretty clear that he was no longer married. He mentioned getting divorced but focused on his feeling much like Eric had felt, wanting to make a real change in his life while he still had the freedom and opportunity to do that. He noted taking trips to Arizona and discovering Bisbee.

"That's the hardest part to describe. The appeal of this place. Some people visit, look around for an afternoon, then leave. Others visit and never leave. I never left. I feel comfortable here. At least I did until I got shot. Although even now, my discomfort isn't with Bisbee. What happened could've happened wherever I practiced."

Anna returned from exploring the shops on Main Street and, after introductions, joined the men in conversation. Eric and Anna began talking about their favorite hang-outs in Tucson, as well as the neighborhoods where they lived. When he expressed an interest in buying a house in Tucson, Anna suggested he check out some of the homes Val had rehabbed. They went inside Torman's house and got on his computer to view Val's website. Eric made a note of the website, thanking Anna and telling Torman he planned to visit the Sierra Vista community mental health center on Monday to interview the director and check out the clinic. Torman and Eric agreed to have lunch before he departed for Tucson.

After he left, Anna said, "Well, I must say, Eric and Sandy are engaging, likable people."

"Can't say the same for Esther. Though she's one patient of mine you'll never meet."

◆ ◆ ◆

Just as Anna and Torman headed out the door to go to dinner, Val called Anna from the emergency room. She'd been inspecting a dilapidated home for possible purchase and stepped on a rotten floor board, taking a bad fall. The doctor told her she'd broken her ankle in two places and required surgery. Anna said she would leave for Tucson in five minutes.

"Steve, I've got to go, but I don't feel good about leaving you alone. Can you find someone to stay with you tonight?"

"Really, I'll be fine. You worry too much. Tell Val I said she ruined our time together. And let me know how she's doing."

As Anna got in her car to leave, Torman spotted a battered pick-up truck parked a couple of houses down his street. He couldn't quite make out the man in the driver's seat but he thought it might be Jerry. As Anna's car pulled away, he ambled towards the truck. Sure enough, Jerry emerged from the cab and, glancing up and down the street, raced toward Torman.

"Doc, I've got to show you something. Is your place secure?"

"Secure? What do you mean, Jerry?"

"You know, not being monitored, no hidden bugs, that kind of thing."

"The FBI gave it a clean bill of health." Torman knew joking was a mistake but couldn't help himself.

"FBI?! You didn't let them in your house, did you?"

"Just joking. Sorry. Why're you here?"

"I've got to show you this tape, Doc." Jerry patted his shirt pocket where he kept his spy pen.

"Please, Jerry, not now...we can meet in the office when I'm back at work. I'm sure you know what happened to me." Torman gestured towards his bandaged eye.

"I taped your shooting." Torman was silent. "Don't you want to see it?"

"I'm not sure. The whole experience has been pretty disturbing." Jerry looked perplexed. "How did you happen to make this tape...were you spying on my house?"

"There'd been rumors about that woman, that she was out to get you. I was in my truck, parked a little closer to your house. I saw her and got out my spy pen. I should've gotten out of the truck and come over but it all happened so fast. I'd just started taping and then "POW," she fired that gun and you went down just as that dog of yours jumped up on her and sent her flying backwards. I got to you quick as I could. I left when the paramedics arrived."

"I'll tell you what, Jerry. Why don't you give me the pen, and I'll look at it when I feel ready."

"Okay. You know, you could use some security cameras for your house, plus an alarm system. I could get you one and install it. I know how to do all that stuff. I've got my apartment all rigged up. It's so sensitive, I can tell when the wind outside changes direction." That didn't surprise Torman, though he managed to keep himself from making another joke.

"I'll think about your offer." He took the spy pen and walked back to his house.

◆ ◆ ◆

Torman sat for a long time in front of his computer, trying to steel himself for what he was about to see. Finally, having decided that viewing the tape would help him come to grips with what happened that night, he connected the pen to his computer.

The images were clear, as was the sound. Once again, he heard her say, "You fucking bastard...an eye for an eye..." At the sound of the gun, Torman's head jerked sideways, just as it did on the tape. As he fell, Baba leapt at Esther, propelling her backwards. The tape stopped as both their bodies headed earthward.

Heart racing, muscles tensed, and breathing rapidly, Torman felt on the verge of a full-blown panic attack. Baba had started barking at the sound of Esther's voice. He quieted Baba, then re-played the tape. He hoped that repeating the tape over and over might help diminish his anxiety. On the fourth viewing, there was a knock on his door, causing Torman to launch out of his chair.

Cautiously, he approached the door, asking who was there. "It's Sandy." As the door swung open, he tried to appear normal. "What's the matter?" she asked.

He was so relieved to see her face, rather than the one etched in his mind, that he waved Sandy in, explaining what he'd been doing. "I think maybe I should give the tape a rest for a while." Sandy suggested they take a walk with Baba.

As they headed down the street, Torman explained how he'd gotten the tape, though he left out Jerry's identity. Sandy laughed at his efforts to protect his privacy. "That must've been Jerry, our local paranoid. He tapes everything with that spy pen of his. I'm sure the police would've confiscated it by now if they thought he wouldn't replace it." For a while they walked in silence, like a couple used to long walks together. By the time they returned to Torman's home, he was aware of feeling more like himself. At his door, he thanked her. Sandy asked about Anna, and he explained her having to leave prematurely.

"You shouldn't be alone tonight," Sandy said.

"Really, I'm fine now. The walk did me good." But he didn't turn to enter his house. Sandy reached for the doorknob, saying, "I'm staying tonight. I'll be in the guest room." Torman didn't protest any further. He realized he didn't want to be alone in his home. He needed someone there, and Sandy's calm assertiveness soothed him.

Once inside, she asked if he'd like some tea. She brewed the tea, then sat with Torman on his couch. "I know something about trauma," she said. "It stays with you a long time, sometimes forever. I was abused sexually by my father when I was thirteen. My parents were divorced, and I was staying at his home over my summer break. I think he couldn't handle my reaching puberty. He came into my room one night, clearly drunk, and got into my bed. I was terrified. He was much bigger than me and very strong. Afterwards, he just got up and left my room. I was awake the rest of the night and called my mother the next morning. I told her I couldn't stay any longer at Dad's. She picked me up that day but never asked why I'd called her. I was afraid to tell her. I'm pretty sure she knew what happened. I refused to stay at my dad's from that time on. Years later I confronted Mom in one of our family therapy sessions. She insisted she'd had no idea what happened. My dad died when I was sixteen. Some kind of boating accident where he drowned. For years I dreamed about the night he raped me. Sometimes I still do."

They sat in silence for a while, with Baba stretched out on the couch between them. Sandy scratched behind Baba's ears, inducing a kind of closed-eyes trance.

With Sandy's revelation, Torman felt even more guilty about their closeness. An affair with her would be a re-enactment of the damaging experience she had at age 13. At the same time, he tried to reassure himself that he was just allowing her to spend the night, that nothing would happen, that they would manage to remain friends.

"How'd you deal with your father's death?"

"I didn't. I refused to go to his funeral. I tried to keep him out of my thoughts. One of my many therapists urged me to talk with her about the rape, but I would just shut down, get very anxious, sometimes even go into one of those states where you detach from yourself and sort of drift off. What my therapist called a 'dissociative' state. That really freaked me out, so I avoided the subject."

"You feel okay talking to me about it?"

"Yes. I trust you. You're the first man who's been attracted to me who hasn't tried to fuck me."

"It would be wrong for me to ever violate that trust."

Around 2 a.m. that night, Torman woke Sandy and himself with shouts of "No!" Within moments, she entered his room where she found him propped up on his elbows with his one eye frantically looking about the room. She sat on his bed and lightly touched his arm. "Bad dream, Steve?"

"Yeah…I was going down these dark hallways. Opening doors, which led to other hallways. Then at the end of one, I opened the door and I saw a hideous old face and a gun explodes in my face as I'm shouting." Sweat soaked his t-shirt. "Geez, I hope this doesn't become a nightly occurrence."

Torman's attention shifted to Sandy's presence. He tried not to look in her direction, but the smell of her, something she used in her hair or on her skin, made him want to rest his head in her lap. "I'm all right now. Thanks, Sandy."

As she got up to go, she glanced back at him. "Call if you need me."

Adjusted to the darkness, his eye followed her as she glided out of his room, Baba in tow. He got up, tugged off his wet t-shirt, and found a dry one in a drawer. Lying back in bed and trying not to think about Sandy, he re-played the dream in his mind. He understood how such dreams are efforts to master the traumatic event. He'd learned that in psych 101A. But how long will that take? How many nights will he need to repeat this dream?

Torman spent the rest of the night trying to get back to sleep, succeeding fitfully.

❖ ❖ ❖

"Were you able to sleep after your nightmare?" Sandy asked over tea and oatmeal the following morning.

"I'm sure I slept some, but it didn't feel like it. I really didn't want to repeat my 'Don't Look Now' dream." Seeing her puzzled expression, Torman gave a brief synopsis of the movie.

"That sounds worse than Jerry's tape."

"Both of them, the movie and the tape, scare the shit out of me in my present state." He stared at his oatmeal and mushed it around with his spoon.

"No appetite?"

"Not much. Very kind of you, though, to make breakfast. It seems like I keep thanking you."

"You can thank me all you like. For that matter, you can give me your oatmeal." She proceeded to polish off his bowl in seconds.

"You always eat with such...gusto?"

"My grandmother always said that leaving food on a plate was an affront to God." Wiping her mouth, she added, "She also just happened to be morbidly obese." She flashed her wide smile in response to Torman's laughter. "So, Steve, what's on your agenda today?"

"I feel like taking a really long walk."

"I know a great hike not far from here. You end up at this mind-blowing view of mountains. We could take Baba the patient-killer."

"I don't know...I feel very uncomfortable being so comfortable with you. It doesn't feel right. I'm really torn about all this. Everything I've been taught warns against having any kind of relationship with you other than a therapeutic one."

"Steve, I'm here for you. Just let me be part of your life. You're not going to hurt me or damage me. I'm an adult. I understand why doctors, therapists, priests, etc. shouldn't screw the ones who trust them. But I believe I'm good for you. And that you're good for me. You're so kind, so principled, yet I feel you hold something back, some part of yourself. And not just with me. Don't shut me out. Don't use your medical ethics to keep me at a distance, to push me away."

"I've always believed...or at least told myself...that it's never right to get romantically involved with a patient, even a former patient. Ever. It's so easy to convince oneself of being in love and of not causing harm to another, but I've been taught how destructive and hurtful this is for the patient."

"I don't believe in absolutes, in rules that can never be broken. Like Baba, I'd have pushed Esther to her death to protect you. So much for 'Though shall not commit murder.'"

"I guess I need time to think about this." After a silence, Torman, pointing to where his eye used to be, said, "I need to change these bandages before we go for a walk."

"You'll need some help with that."

Torman imagined that her seeing the gaping, swollen mess that once housed his eye would put a dampener on any romantic interest Sandy had in him. That thought overcame his uneasiness about her helping him.

Upending his expectation, Sandy inspected the empty eye socket with an air of curiosity, gently touching the edges of the wound. She talked the entire time while cleansing the area and replacing the bandages, as if sensing his disquiet at having someone see his disfigurement. Afterwards, he thanked her, referring to her as Ms. Nightingale. "'Flo,' to you," she said. To herself, Sandy thought how his physical wound was no different than the emotional traumas she'd experienced. She realized his injury made her feel they had more in common, eliciting a welling up of compassion for him.

Torman returned to work on a Monday. The crater where his eye used to reside was still bandaged, but, according to the plastic surgeon he consulted, healing on schedule. The staff at the clinic were solicitous, trying not to stare at his face. He felt better once he began seeing patients. Work helped take his mind off the awareness of his loss.

Half the patients said nothing about his face or the shooting. The other half were curious, asking what happened, how bad it hurt, would he get a glass eye, was he scared seeing patients. Depending on the patient, after first asking what they'd heard and how they were doing with all this, he answered their questions in varying detail. Working made him feel useful again. Nothing like work, Torman mused, to allay anxiety and restore self-esteem.

Midway through the morning, Stuart, hand extended for a handshake, entered Torman's office.

"So good to have you back, Steve! What an awful, terrifying experience for you. All of us were so worried. How're you doing?"

"I feel a lot better now that I'm back at work. And thanks for dropping by the hospital last week. I appreciated the flowers and kind messages the staff sent me."

"Great, great…One thing…a lawyer called here asking to speak with you. Apparently he's representing Esther's family. Funny, no one knew she had any family. Anyway, the lawyer said it was very important that he speak with you. Here's his phone number. I hope you're not considering suing us, Steve…"

Torman shot a that's-crazy-to-think look to Stuart, who visibly relaxed, shook Torman's hand, and vanished.

Thinking he'd better get this out of the way, Torman called the number and was surprised that the lawyer, James A.

Hittleman, Esq., answered. After identifying himself, Torman listened to Hittleman's concern for his well-being. Then the lawyer explained that Esther's family had retained him to bring suit against the hospital and attending doctors for negligence in failing to provide a secure environment from which Esther could not escape. "Had she remained confined in the hospital, you, Dr. Torman, would not have lost your eye, and Esther would still be alive."

Torman took an immediate dislike to Hittleman, who seemed too smooth a talker. He knew this conversation was leading up to something, but he wasn't sure what that was, so he merely responded with "Umhmm."

"Doctor Torman, I don't know if you've sought counsel for yourself, but I wanted to inform you that I believe you have what we lawyers call an 'actionable cause' regarding the tragic loss of your eye, not to mention the trauma you endured in its loss. Legal representation could ultimately result in your receiving much deserved compensation for your loss, as well as helping to insure that the hospital in question will institute changes that will prevent such tragedies in the future."

"Thank you. I'll consider that."

"I hope you do. I've represented many patients and their loved ones over the years. Not many involving psychiatrists, though. I've always admired the psychiatric profession. The few psychiatric suits I've been involved with were ones in which a psychiatrist slept with his patients. But by far the majority of psychiatrists are most upstanding."

"Anything else I can help you with?" Torman wanted a quick end to this conversation.

"No. You've got my phone number. You can look me up on the internet. And, Doctor, if I can be of any service to you, please call me."

He tried to suppress Hittleman's comment about suits involving psychiatrists who sleep with their patients. He knew he needed to talk with someone about his relationship with Sandy, but at the same time was aware that no one was likely to support his continuing to see her, especially if this involved sexual contact. Even Anna had looked alarmed at his continued contact with Sandy.

Thinking back on his past supervisors, Torman figured Gold, who'd been so helpful to him, would have been his first choice to consult with, but Gold never left the hospital after suffering a heart attack, dying two weeks after an emergency surgical repair failed. Dr. Gosz also came to mind. Torman realized that he'd have been the easiest one to confide in. There was a kindness to Oz that came through in ways that didn't with other analysts he'd known, including Gold. He recalled Oz's telling him to pay attention to Susan's "yearning for affirmation." Maybe Oz would have explored Torman's yearning for affirmation, if that's what his interest in Sandy was all about. At least Oz didn't seem either foolish or rigid. But he'll never know how Oz might have reacted or what he may have said about Torman's dilemma. What was clear to him was his resistance to hearing either "Go for it!" or "Don't even think about it!" He needed someone who could give him a balanced, thoughtful assessment.

Eric, who came by the clinic to meet over lunch with Torman, was in good spirits. The editor of the newspaper that planned on publishing his article liked the idea of a follow-up piece on psychiatrists' risk of assaults from patients.

In the course of their conversation, Eric said he'd written Susan and invited her to visit him in Tucson. She planned on coming in four weeks.

"Maybe we could all get together," Eric said, adding, "though if that's not comfortable for you..."

"I'm okay with that, though you should discuss this with Susan and make sure she feels alright with our meeting. I occasionally spend the weekend at Anna and Val's home. We could all meet in Tucson. Which reminds me: have you thought about looking at one of Val's houses?"

"I have. I looked up her website again and emailed her. She suggested we take a tour of some of the homes she's rehabbing."

Torman felt a stab of envy at the thought of Eric rekindling his relationship with Susan. Why couldn't he find someone who was neither his patient nor a lesbian? One thing he was sure of: Sandy wasn't a lesbian.

❖ ❖ ❖

Sandy continued to come by every evening, ostensibly to walk Baba. Torman looked forward to her visits, in spite of his anxiety about fostering a relationship that could never be consummated without great foreboding on his part. He told himself he needed time to decide what to do and, in the meantime, allowed himself the guilty pleasure of her companionship. He didn't want to admit to himself that he enjoyed being cared for and cared about. He imagined that, in spite of his injury and loss, he was perfectly capable of managing on his own, that he wasn't a needy, dependent type who liked others helping him.

In the hope of attenuating his anxiety about his attack, he made a point of watching Jerry's tape every evening. The nightmares persisted, always involving his opening a door, seeing that hideous face, and being shot. And yelling, though without a witness, he didn't know if he continued to shout out loud.

In addition, he made himself drive his car to get used to the alteration in his depth perception and limited peripheral vision. His surgeon warned him about difficulties with performing tasks normally requiring binocular vision. Fortunately, his athletic interests were limited to hiking, swimming, and jogging, none of which required fine eye-hand coordination. His balance was somewhat off, and he tended to bump into things because of his decreased peripheral vision. Although he felt self-conscious about his appearance, he resisted an inclination to avoid being out in public.

One evening, while Torman waited for Sandy to appear,

Jake Lawrence, the Bisbee policeman who'd questioned Torman in the hospital, showed up unexpectedly at his house.

"Dr. Torman, it's Jake Lawrence, from the Bisbee police department."

"Yes, I remember you, Jake."

"We've been getting a lot of pressure from a lawyer hired by the family of your deceased patient to investigate the cause of her death. I told him we hadn't found any witness yet who could explain how she happened to hit her head with such force. But we are aware of a man who was the first to reach you after you were shot. No one could identify him, and apparently he left when the paramedics arrived. Have you learned or recalled anything more about that night?"

Torman debated whether to offer the tape or wait until he spoke with Jerry. Given Jerry's intense paranoia, especially in regard to the police, he decided to offer no information until he could speak to Jerry.

"Sorry, Jake, nothing new I can recall. I've got your number, and I'll call if I learn something."

"Thanks. This lawyer is really breathing down our necks."

Sandy arrived shortly after Jake left. Torman told her how he'd withheld knowledge of Jerry's identity and the existence of the tape.

"Well," Sandy said, "we certainly don't want Baba to get indicted for murder." Baba pressed himself against Sandy's leg.

"Nor do we want Jerry to have a complete meltdown at the prospect of the police questioning him."

"I bet if we looked out your window, we'd see him crouching somewhere with binoculars focused on your house. I'm sure he misses that spy pen of his."

Anna referred Torman to Dr. James Nelson for consultation regarding how to deal with Sandy and the aftermath of his attack. Dr. Nelson's office was in a low brick office building in Tucson. The waiting room was small, softly lit, with three molded plywood chairs and a couple of glass side tables with neatly stacked magazines. Out of curiosity, Torman examined the magazines and, not surprisingly, discovered a number of New Yorkers along with an Atlantic Review. As directed, Torman pressed a button next to Dr. Nelson's name by the door to his inner office. A light lit up inside the button. At exactly 5:00 p.m. the inner door opened, and Dr. Nelson, tall, thin, with thick grey hair cut short and laser-parted on the side, greeted Torman with, "Dr. Torman?...I'm Dr. Nelson...please come in." He stepped aside, an arm making a slight gesture towards the interior of his office.

Dr. Nelson sat in the leather chair beside the analytic couch while directing Torman to an identical chair across from him. Except for the oriental rug in the center of the room, there wasn't much color to the office, mainly hues of browns and grays. One wall was devoted to bookshelves lined with books, journals, and educational CD's. An iMac presided on his clutter-free desk, along with keyboard and mouse. What Torman imagined to be framed family photographs faced away from the patient's view. A clock, the remaining item on the dust-free shiny desktop, faced Dr. Nelson.

"You mentioned wanting a consultation regarding a patient of yours..." Dr. Nelson let this sentence hang in the air.

"Yes, her name is Sandy, and she's a former patient, someone I'd seen three times in my role as a psychiatric consultant in Sierra Vista's community mental health clinic." Torman went on to give some history of Sandy's condition, as well as the recent events that led to her becoming involved in his life and his struggling to deal with their relationship in a way that would not be exploitive of her.

"I know it's generally regarded as unethical to have a sexual relationship with a patient, even long after the treatment is terminated. Or, for that matter, to engage in any behavior that violates significant boundaries between patient and therapist. I've already allowed her to be of help to me and to spend time with me. I've discussed these issues with her, explaining why I feel so uncomfortable with our relationship. And I'm aware that I'm in a vulnerable spot in my life: I'm divorced, living alone, and dealing with the recent attack by a psychotic patient who shot me in the eye. All of which can impair my judgment and incline me to mistake Sandy's attention as justifiable and acceptable. Plus I know she's the victim of adolescent sexual abuse by her father. I understand how this trauma can get repeated in a sexual relationship with a psychiatrist. But I find myself feeling very attracted to her. She isn't seductive, at least not blatantly, or pressuring me for more intimacy. She also transferred her care to another psychiatrist. But I'm not fooling myself: I know what is likely to happen if we continue to spend time together."

"So what keeps you from re-establishing appropriate boundaries?"

"I have this sense that I'd be turning my back on an opportunity to experience genuine intimacy that would not turn out to be destructive to her or to me."

"There's no hope that such intimacy could be achieved with someone not your patient?"

"Well, it hasn't happened yet. I thought I had a close relationship with my former wife, but clearly I didn't. She left me for another man three years ago."

"I realize she's no longer your patient, but it seems clear that something's getting in the way of your doing what you believe your ethical requirements demand."

"It's the 'what's getting in the way' that I can't figure out. I want to do the right thing, but I'm not convinced that necessarily means I could never be in a committed relationship with her."

"I agree with you that we need to explore this further. In the meantime, it would be a good idea to do nothing until we can understand what this is all about."

The remainder of the session focused on Torman's past treatment, his family and medical history, and an account of his recent trauma and its associated symptoms. They agreed to meet the following week.

As Torman drove back to Bisbee from his appointment with Dr. Nelson, he struggled with his impressions of him. It seemed there was no room for the possibility that he could in good conscience continue to see Sandy. Dr. Nelson didn't come across as hostile but, at the same time, implied that a relationship with Sandy would likely be exploitive of her. On the other hand, he offered Torman the opportunity to explore the reasons for his vulnerability to the temptation of a relationship with Sandy. Perhaps if he could help Torman deal with his feelings about Esther's shooting him and his PTSD symptoms, as well as his subsequent feelings of dependence, then maybe Torman would be able to assess with a clearer mind what was going on between him and Sandy.

From all that he'd read about boundary violations with patients, he knew how essential it was to get consultation and/ or treatment. He told himself he was taking the appropriate steps and hoped it would lead him to a decision he could live with. He believed he cared too much for Sandy to hurt her by satisfying his needs at the expense of hers.

Yet there was something cold and clinical about Nelson that reminded Torman of Freud's comparing the analyst to a surgeon whose job it is to put aside all feelings, even human sympathy, and to concentrate his energies on performing the necessary operation (i.e., analysis) as skillfully as possible. Such a metaphor never sat easily with Torman. He believed that too much objectivity robbed therapy of its essential humanness, of its potential to promote genuine growth in patients.

Of course, it was possible that he was trying to undermine Dr. Nelson's efforts to prevent his taking advantage of Sandy, who, he had to admit, seemed quite vulnerable.

Torman arranged for a case worker to bring Jerry to the clinic. He ushered him into his office, explaining that he needed to discuss the tape with him.

"Jerry, the police are investigating the circumstances of Esther's death. Your tape would clear up any suspicions about its cause. I didn't want to turn over the tape without your permission."

Jerry began fidgeting, rubbing his hands on his jeans, unable to sit still, looking all around him. "I don't know, Doc... they'll want to know who made the tape, and then they'll try to pin this on me, claim I faked the tape after killing her, throw me in jail for the rest of my life..."

"Really, Jerry, the tape's very clear. If anyone's in hot water, it's my dog." Again, a mistake to make light of anything with Jerry.

"They could say I trained your dog to attack her. It'd still come back on me."

"Look, Jerry, I'll go with you and back you up one hundred percent. And this would allow the police to wrap up their investigation and stop coming around asking me and others questions about who the first responder was to my injury."

"They'll want to know why I was taping in the first place. I could get nailed for...something."

"I'll say I asked you to keep an eye on my place because of Esther's threats."

That seemed to satisfy Jerry, so they agreed to stop by the police station after Torman's last appointment.

Jerry rode with Torman to the station. He couldn't refrain from checking for surveillance devices, opening the glove compartment, peering under the seats, examining the window visors and various compartments. Finally, Torman suggested they could ride in silence if that would make him feel safer.

Torman had called Officer Lawrence that afternoon and arranged to meet with him. Standing near the entrance, Jake motioned for the two of them to follow him to his office. Torman started to introduce Jerry, but Jake interrupted him, noting no one in the station needed an introduction to Jerry. This set off Jerry, who began citing his rights as a citizen to freedom of speech and equal protection under the law.

"Jerry," Torman intervened, "we're here to clear up the matter of Esther's death." Jerry edged his body closer to Torman, as if using him as a human shield.

"Jake, Jerry happened to be watching over my place, at my request, and made this tape. He just brought it to me. I watched it on my computer today. I think it makes clear what happened to Esther on the night of the attack."

Jake held out his hand for the spy pen, attached it to his computer, and watched the tape. At the sound of the gun firing, Torman flinched but tried to look normal.

"I want to download this into my computer. There..." Jake removed the end of the spy pen and, with a dismissive look toward Jerry, handed it back to Torman.

Torman, unable to resist, asked, "Is my dog in trouble?" Both Jake and Jerry ignored the comment. "Well," Torman said, "I think this clears up any questions about what happened to my former patient."

"Yeah, I'd say so. This'll keep that prick of a lawyer off my tail." And with that, Jake informed them they could leave.

In the car, Torman said, "Jake wasn't very appreciative..."

"I'm telling you, the cops are assholes. Now you've seen it. They treat me like I'm some kind of vermin." Gesturing with his hand, Jerry added, "You can let me off down there by the Post Office."

Standing outside the car, Jerry poked his head through the open passenger window. "Doc, you really need to install a home security system. I could set it up for you. That way, with just your cell phone, you could check on your house any time of the day."

"Thanks, Jerry. I'll think about it." As he drove off, he looked for Jerry in his rearview mirror, but he'd already vanished. Much to his surprise, Torman was feeling inclined to have a security system installed. Since his attack, he found himself checking his house thoroughly whenever he returned from some errand or from work. Perhaps some security cameras would ease his anxiety, however irrational that anxiety was.

◆ ◆ ◆

Torman and Sandy, with Baba in the lead, walked up a winding road toward a water tower. Scattered about the mountainside and held in place by crumbling retaining walls and the grace of the gods, the former miners' shacks seemed to defy gravity's pull. With the sun's descent, the temperature dropped, prompting Sandy to say she wanted to stop at her house to get a jacket.

"I've never seen where you live."

"It's right over there." Sandy pointed to a small structure not far below the side of the road. They walked down steps which descended to her place and further down to other houses. A short gravel path led from the steps to the side door of her home. Torman noticed how her house was supported on thick wood beams mounted on cement footers, allowing it to float above the sloping mountainside. The back of her home merged with the mountain's rocks. Once inside, Torman admired a wall of windows overlooking the valley and Bisbee below. Pale yellow walls glowed in the remaining sunlight, as did the unadorned pine floor. Plants thrived everywhere. Low bookshelves along one side wall housed numerous books, mostly English and American literature with a smattering of Eastern philosophy. A simple galley kitchen lined the back wall. Open shelving revealed stacked dishes, bowls and platters, in the colors of a rainbow. A door on the other side led, Torman presumed, to a bedroom and bath.

"Your home is beautiful."

"It wasn't much when I bought it. It'd been gutted by the previous owner, who never got around to fixing it up. A guy I knew who could build anything installed the windows, floor, and kitchen shelves and put up drywall. I painted and sanded and sweated over all this. I feel a sense of peace here." She grabbed her coat hanging by the door. "Ready?"

Torman found himself thinking about some of the patients' homes he'd entered when, as a resident in psychiatry, he made home visits to check on reclusive patients who refused to come for appointments. Their apartments, filled with the castoff furnishings of others' homes, reflected the unruliness and disorganization of their minds. One person's home came to mind: open bags of garbage, seething with cockroaches, were strewn throughout the living room. When the patient lit a cigarette, Torman welcomed the stench-masking smell of tobacco. He felt relief seeing Sandy's home, with its simple beauty and thoughtful design.

"You're being quiet...penny for your thoughts," Sandy said.

"I was thinking how the interior of a home reveals a lot about one's inner world. Your home gives off a sense of calm. Makes me feel like taking a nap."

"Every morning I sit before the windows and meditate. New Agey, I know, but it feels so good. And this *is* a great place to nap."

"How'd you afford it?"

"Mom's family has money. When I showed signs of being unstable, her parents set up a trust fund for me. I get a certain amount each month. If I want more, I can try persuading the trustee, a guy I call Scrooge. He's what you shrinks call 'anal retentive,' but I prefer 'asshole.' His standard line is, 'Sandy, I'm just trying to protect your best interests.' And maybe he is, but he can be maddening."

As they set off again on their walk, Torman mentioned to

Sandy that he'd begun consulting with Dr. Nelson, a psychiatrist in Tucson. After a silence, she said, "Well, has your psychiatrist convinced you that you'll burn in hell for all eternity if you keep seeing me?"

"He's a Freudian, not a born-again Christian."

"There's a difference?" Sandy enjoyed making Torman laugh. "Seriously, though, I don't want to lose you because of some rigid fundamentalist. I worry you'll be blinded by your need to do what you think is right. You'd do better sometimes to follow your heart rather than your boy scout sense of duty."

Torman didn't know what to say. He knew what he felt for Sandy, but he couldn't let himself trust it. A line from high school French came back to him. "'Le coeur a ses raisons que la raison ne connait point,'" quoted Torman, pleased with himself for being able to recall the line so many years later. "The heart has reasons which reason cannot know. I think that's how it goes. I bet my recalling that would please Monsieur Pryce, my former French teacher, but not Le Docteur Nelson."

"Well, it pleases me."

Torman noticed that his nightmares were diminishing in both intensity and frequency. He wasn't sure whether this resulted from tincture of time or Dr. Nelson's encouraging him to talk about the trauma or Sandy's soothing presence in his life. Or perhaps from all three experiences.

"Where are things with Sandy?" Dr. Nelson asked.

Torman described their nightly walks, what they talked about, how he felt about her. "She's been open, talking about her life and family. I mostly listen. I've shared with her what happened in my marriage. She believes I hold back emotionally from others, but at the same time feels I'm basically a warm, if inhibited, man. She doesn't hide her wish to be closer to me, but she respects my reservations and doesn't press for more time with me. I've never had a relationship with an attractive woman go this slowly. We share an interest in books, we tease each other. I feel comfortable with her. She's easy to love."

"What does her psychiatrist say about her seeing you?"

"Sandy says she simply raised her eyebrows when she brought it up. I get the feeling her psychiatrist is pleased with her progress and is primarily focused on pharmacologic management of her difficulties."

"And those difficulties are…?"

"Well, she may be bipolar. That's certainly what her records indicate. My brief clinical contact with her suggested hypomania, but now I'm less certain what ails her. I wonder about the effects of growing up with an alcoholic father who abused her sexually, as well as her conflicted relationship with her mother, who she's estranged from. Some of the behaviors that have gotten her labeled bipolar may be better conceptualized as acting out her anger and rebelliousness."

"So, is it fair to say that what she's doing with you is a re-enactment of her incestuous relationship with her father and an expression of her spitefulness towards her mother?"

"It doesn't feel that way. It feels more like she's finally discovered a way to connect with a man, with me, where she doesn't feel either she's being exploited or exploitive."

"My concern is that she's extremely clever at manipulating you, that she's setting you up to believe she's suddenly cured and level-headed, when, from what you've told me, she's spent most of her life acting impulsively, without insight and in emotional turmoil."

"I don't think someone you've just described would have the capacity to deceive me so convincingly and for such a long period."

"Really, aren't you being somewhat naive? Isn't it quite likely that you're deceiving yourself in the hope you've found someone who really loves you? Someone who would never leave you? Or, looked at from a different vantage point, have you picked another relationship that has no future, that can only lead to disappointment and loss?"

"I can't deny that those are possibilities. That's why I'm here, to sort this out."

"There's another aspect of your relationship with Sandy that needs attention. You were traumatically injured by a patient and are in a period of recovery. That, as you yourself remarked, makes you vulnerable to feeling attached to Sandy by your desire to be cared for. She's functioned like a caretaker and could very well be using your dependence to manipulate your feelings for her."

Torman left Nelson's office in a daze, as if he'd been in a three hour exam for which he'd been ill-prepared. The sense of Nelson's disapproval weighed on him, as did Nelson's interpretations.

Torman arranged to meet Eric and Susan at Anna and Val's home for dinner on a Saturday night. He felt uncomfortable not asking Sandy to join him, but, at the same time, knew he'd feel uncomfortable bringing her. She didn't complain, saying she'd take Baba for his evening walk. In spite of his yearning for her, he'd managed to refrain from physical contact with her. No easy feat. He found himself envying Baba's closeness with her, his licking her face, her petting his stomach as he sprawled next to her on Torman's couch.

He was curious to see Susan, as well as seeing how she and Eric would interact with each other. He'd begun wearing an eye patch since the bandages were removed and felt self-conscious about it, especially around people who hadn't heard about his attack. He figured Eric had forewarned Susan.

Anna greeted him at her front door, giving him a hug and, arching back her head, examined his face. "How are you?"

"I'm trying to adjust to having one eye. Driving up here was challenging, but I'm making myself get used to navigating in the world with one eye. I'm still really self-conscious about wearing this eye patch. I worry I look ridiculous."

"If it helps, I think you look very handsome and distinguished. And I'm really glad you made the effort to drive up here. I have a surprise for you." Anna produced a slender plastic stick with a small window revealing two vertical lines. Seeing his puzzled expression, she said, "I'm pregnant!"

Torman congratulated her with another hug and stepped back to look at her midsection. "I can't say that I see any evidence, but you look great, and I can see how happy you are."

Following Anna to the backyard patio and pool, Torman caught sight of Eric and Susan. He shook their hands, then hugged Val, offering his congratulations. He became acutely aware of his eye patch, imagining they were all trying not to stare at it yet unable to think of anything else. Susan looked as lovely as ever. Her hair was cut short and spikey, her attire simple: tight black t-shirt with form-fitting jeans. Glancing at his eyepatch, she said how awful she felt hearing the news of his recent attack by a patient.

"I didn't know psychiatrists took such risks," Susan said, "but Eric's been doing research on patient assaults on psychiatrists and tells me this is not that rare. I hope you feel safe with us!"

"Not only safe, but grateful to see both of you again." Torman hoped he conveyed not even a trace of anxiety about the subject that still disrupted his sleep and made him jump at the sound of loud noise.

The evening proceeded smoothly. Eric talked at length about the house he was buying from Val and his research for the article on psychiatrists' exposure to patient violence, while Susan showed a slideshow of a recent exhibit of her artwork. Wine (except for Anna) and cheese gave way to grilled salmon, asparagus, and salad, followed by brownies that Torman had made.

In spite of his efforts to remain upbeat, Torman found himself feeling like the odd man out. Eric and Susan seemed to have re-kindled their affection for each other, sitting close together, sharing quiet asides, looking happy in each other's presence, while Val circled around Anna, keeping her plate full and wineglass filled with grape juice, not letting her carry anything heavy ("Val, I'm pregnant, not incapacitated!"). Torman was touched by the sweetness between them.

Shortly before Torman's leaving, Anna took him aside, asking, "Are you still seeing that patient of yours?"

"Still seeing Sandy, still seeing Dr. Nelson."

"I hope you'll do the right thing, Steve. I admit she's a very engaging, beautiful young woman, but it could cause so much heartache for you down the road."

"Trust me, I'm giving this all my attention. I haven't done anything that is potentially devastating to me, Sandy, or my career."

"The longer this goes on, the harder it will be to make a break. You know I care about you. I don't want anything bad to happen to you. Or, for that matter, to Sandy. I don't need to remind you that the APA's Principles of Medical Ethics is very clear that sexual activity with a current or former patient is unethical."

The drive home was long, filled with Torman's rumination about Sandy and what to do. He realized that many people outside the psychiatric profession would be puzzled by his struggling with the ethics of initiating a relationship with a former patient, especially one he'd seen for just a few sessions. The ethical issue is clearest when there's an ongoing treatment relationship. In that situation the doctor/therapist has so much power and authority in the patient's eyes that there is a profound imbalance in their relationship that makes the patient so vulnerable to exploitation. With a former patient this imbalance diminishes over time yet may never completely disappear. In Torman's mind, there was no absolute guideline, no defined timetable for engaging a former patient in an intimate relationship. Obviously, the safest path to take—the APA's formal guideline—is one of complete avoidance of an intimate relationship with a former patient. Yet Torman was uncomfortable rejecting out of hand any possibility that he and Sandy could form a lasting, healthy relationship. Torman struggled to find some clarity in all this uncertainty.

Traffic outside Tucson thinned, becoming practically non-existent once he exited the interstate highway and drove south on route 80 to Bisbee. An unidentifiable animal raced in front of his car, forcing Torman to slam on the brakes. Not wanting to run over anything live, he slowed down, keeping his one eye fixed on the road ahead.

"You haven't told me why you left Cincinnati," Sandy said to Torman on one of their walks.

"Partly because I could. Mostly, though, because my divorce devastated me and my career as a psychotherapist and psychoanalyst was such a disappointment. My wife left me for another man, and patients quit for various reasons, rarely because they got what they came for and felt better. I felt the psychoanalytic institute where I was in training for so many years had treated me unfairly. I finally got a lawyer to scare them into graduating me. All these experiences left me with a bitter taste. I'm not naive, though. I knew moving wouldn't change my life dramatically. But I felt like making a fresh start."

"Why Bisbee, of all places?"

"Why does anyone land here? It just seemed like a totally unpretentious, off-the-beaten-path place that felt right for misfits like me, for people who, for whatever reasons, stepped off the treadmill. Nobody cares where I went to school, what degrees I have, who I know. It's a place to be yourself or have a chance of finding yourself."

"Well, that part I get, but it's hard for me to believe you weren't successful in your practice. You come across as honest and sincere. And wanting to help. What more is needed in a psychiatrist? I knew I was making you uncomfortable, flirting with you and all, but I wanted to see if you were like every other professional I'd seen who either wanted to sleep with me or show me how smart he was. I was moved by your discomfort, your struggle to help me without overstepping your boundaries. You're still doing that. And that's okay, because this is such a hard choice to make, especially since I'm no longer your patient. You touch me deeply. I want you to know that. At the same time, though, I believe you've never felt comfortable following your heart and have missed opportunities for greater intimacy. And I want you to know that, too."

They walked for a while in silence. Deeply affected by Sandy's reaction to him but uneasy addressing it directly, Torman decided to talk about his career. "I don't fully understand why I wasn't more successful in my therapy practice. Sometimes I think I was just more inclined to focus on the failures than on the successes. I'm not sure how I stacked up compared to my peers. Therapists don't go around talking about their failures, their drop-outs. If they did, they would end up without any referrals. But I do believe something in me got in the way of allowing patients to open up, to feel safe with me. None of the supervision I had ever helped me understand what that was about. Nor did my analysis. No one suggested I wasn't cut out for that kind of work, but I felt something was wrong. At some point I might decide to try doing psychotherapy again and open up a private practice, but I'm not ready yet. Your experience with me, while it means a great deal to me to hear, wasn't typical of the feedback many patients gave me." Looking over at Sandy, Torman asked how she ended up in Bisbee.

"I'd hooked up with a guy, an artist, who had friends in Bisbee. We came to visit them. The boyfriend went back to California, while I decided to stay. My reasons were similar to yours. People were friendly and non-judgmental. I could live here cheaply, giving me a chance to think about what I wanted to do with my life. And it was far away from my family and their prying, disapproving eyes. My mother, especially, tried to squelch my enthusiasm, to undermine any accomplishment of mine. She'd say things like, 'Why do you always have to be the best at everything? Why are you so excitable?' She had a way of pouring cold water on everything I did."

"So, have you figured out what you want to do?"

"Don't laugh…I think I'd like to be a therapist. God knows, I've been exposed to a lot of bad or just plain mediocre therapy. I've thought of working with adolescents, even though I know they can drive you nuts. I remember how I felt as a teenager, confused and angry and vulnerable, and how I needed a lifeline, someone to hang on to, someone I could trust."

"Have you looked into getting a degree that would allow you to do counseling?"

"Yeah, but first I'd need to complete my undergraduate degree. Arizona State University offers online undergraduate and masters degrees. It's not expensive, and I wouldn't have to commute."

"I think you'd do well as a therapist. Your own painful experiences in life have made you sensitive to others' struggles. I find you easy to talk to and be with."

As they approached Torman's house, he noticed Jerry's truck out front. "Looks like I've got company."

"Lucky you. I'll be on my way so you and Jerry can discuss how satellites and drones are monitoring our most intimate moments." Handing Torman Baba's leash, Sandy turned around and walked away.

Torman approached Jerry's truck, unsure what prompted this visit.

"Doc, sorry to bother you, but I found this great deal on home security cameras. Just let me show you what it can do. I think you'll want to think about this." He opened a box and extracted a wireless camera, which Jerry praised for its discreet appearance, night vision, and high resolution. "I could install four of these and cover your entire perimeter. You could monitor your home from inside on your computer or from outside the house on your cell phone."

In spite of his reservations about yet another boundary violation with a patient, Torman couldn't help wanting to give Jerry something constructive to do. "You know how to install this?"

"No problem. I told you I installed my own surveillance equipment. Works like a charm. This is child's play by comparison."

"What do you charge an hour?"

"I don't know. I've never done any freelance work."

"I've noticed the local handyman wage here is $20.00 an hour. And I'll reimburse you for all expenses. Is that okay with you?"

Jerry lit up. "Yeah, I can get started right now."

"Whoa, it's getting late. How about waiting till tomorrow afternoon at 5 when I get home from work?"

"Great, Doc. I'll see you then."

Torman figured he'd either rue the day he agreed to this deal or it would be a turning point for Jerry, who would benefit from channeling his energies into something productive. Looking down at Baba, Torman said, "Don't worry, pal. You won't lose your job to modern technology."

"Don't you get cold at night, sleeping outside?" Torman asked Sam, who sat slumped in a chair across from him.

"Sometimes."

"What keeps you from staying in the group home?"

"Can't drink there."

"What if we found you a place where you could drink alcohol? Would you try staying there?"

"I could drink?"

"Yes. I think there's one place where they'd let you."

Torman knew that one of the group homes nearby turned a blind eye toward residents' drinking alcohol, at least as long as they were quiet and didn't get in fights.

"How's your sleep?"

"It's okay."

"If you need help with your sleep, let me know. I could prescribe something that would work better than alcohol. Alcohol helps people fall asleep but then they wake up in the middle of the night and can't sleep well the rest of the night." It wasn't clear how much of this conversation was meaningful to Sam, who stared at the floor most of the time and never spontaneously said anything. Just to keep things moving along, Torman had him step on the scale in his office and then took his blood pressure.

"Your pressure's a bit high. Are you taking anything for it?"

"I forget to take it."

"Well, walking a lot might help it. Not smoking could also help your pressure. When you come back, I'll check it again."

What Torman didn't do was harp on his taking medication. He knew Sam heard voices, but many patients preferred that to side effects of medication. The best chance he had with Sam was to gain his confidence and align himself with something Sam wanted help with, such as his sleep. A sedating antipsychotic could solve two problems with one pill. Torman was a patient man, he could wait. At least Sam didn't seem ready to bolt from his office. That was a good sign.

"Sam, do you have any family, any who live nearby?"

"I've got a brother."

"Where does he live?"

"Oregon."

"When did you last speak with him?"

"It's been a long time."

"If you want, we could track him down. Maybe you could speak with him on the phone, see how he's doing." Sam shrugged his shoulders. Torman made a mental note about his brother. Maybe in the future Sam would want to hear from him.

"It gets cold at night. We have some free gloves and hats. Let's get you some before you leave today."

Sam shuffled out of Torman's office, leaving an unpleasant odor behind. He called the front desk and asked the receptionist to help Sam pick out gloves and a hat. Torman opened his window for some fresh air, then finished his clinical note on the computer before moving on to the next battered soul in his schedule.

In the dream, Torman had returned to his parents' home, not their current one but the one he'd grown up in. He was in his bedroom, his throat very sore. His mother came into his room, had him open his mouth and looked down his throat, shaking her head and saying, "It looks really bad." He tried to reassure her that he was alright, but it was hard to speak because of the pain.

Dr. Nelson listened, tilting his head sideways and squinting his eyes to signify he was giving the dream his full attention. Torman added a memory of his tonsillectomy at age ten. He'd had recurrent strep throat infections, and the surgery was supposed to decrease their frequency. He recalled how sore his throat was and how he could barely eat or drink anything after the procedure. He'd spent three days at home recovering from surgery, missing school.

"Obviously," Torman said, "the surgery stands for this treatment. It's painful but it's supposed to prevent subsequent infections. It makes sense that my mother represents you, examining me and expressing concern about how 'bad' things look inside me. My mother always freaked out over any physical problem, always imagining the worst."

Dr. Nelson, unable to contain himself, jumped in at this point. "So, what we're doing here causes you pain, but it's for your own good. Letting go of Sandy is painful to contemplate but necessary for your ultimate well-being."

"When I was in medical school on my pediatric rotation, I learned that tonsillectomies were done far too often, that most children were better off not being subjected to the surgery and its possible side effects and complications. I'm more inclined to see the dream as reflecting my concern that the conventional wisdom in medicine is often not borne out over time, that patients are subjected to treatments and pain that are not warranted by research. So I can't agree with your interpretation that the dream reflects my belief I need to end my relationship with Sandy for my own good."

Barely able to let Torman finish the last sentence, Dr. Nelson said, "But what of your mother's reaction to what she sees inside you, something that looks 'really bad'? I think this suggests *you* feel that way, but you've projected this feeling onto your mother. It's been very difficult to own the feeling that you're doing something bad with Sandy."

Torman's face reddened, and his hands gripped the arms of his chair. He felt Nelson was trying to force him to see what Nelson had all along believed to be right: that the only ethical course of action was for Torman to end his relationship with Sandy. There was no gray area here as far as Nelson was concerned. He was just waiting to find the "evidence" he needed to prove his point. This is what many psychiatrists did, Torman thought, and it left little room for genuine discovery. Torman knew he'd done the same thing to some of his own patients and regretted it. "I think my mother's reaction reflects my experience of you and of Anna, who referred me to you. She recently reminded me of the American Psychiatric Association's Principles of Medical Ethics which states that sexual activity with a current or former patient is unethical. I came here knowing the position of the APA. I don't need it rammed down my throat. What I hoped for was to get a clearer picture of my unique relationship with Sandy, to explore what it meant to me and why I was in this experience, to weigh the pros and cons, so to speak, of pursuing such a relationship. I needed an unbiased therapist to help me achieve that goal, not one intent on getting me to see the light of 'reason.'"

Undaunted, Dr. Nelson, with the faintest of smiles, said, "There's a lot to be said for the 'light,' or voice, of reason."

As Torman left his office, he knew he would cancel the next appointment and not return.

Jerry worked with speed and efficiency on Torman's surveillance system. After two hours he was ready to test drive the equipment. With the installation of the security app on his computer and phone, Torman sat at his computer while Jerry dashed about his yard, hiding behind a tree, slithering along the ground, crouching by a window, and generally doing all the moves his vivid imagination could conjure up. Laughing uproariously made it difficult for Torman to notice if Jerry dropped out of sight.

Breathless, Jerry asked, "Any blind spots?"

"I kind of lost sight of you when you wriggled up the tree. You know, you moved like a quarterback evading tackles out there…"

Interrupting Torman's effort at humor, Jerry dashed outside and re-adjusted two of the cameras. He knocked on a window and gestured for Torman to look at the screen. Crouching, moving as if avoiding land mines, he reached the tree, scaling it with ease. When he returned inside, Torman gave him a thumbs up. For once, Jerry's face broke into a wide grin, like a kid at first base after hitting his first single.

Not wanting to blur boundaries any further, Torman paid Jerry, thanking him for doing such a good job. He figured it would be better to discuss in Jerry's next appointment their experience together and Jerry's obvious talents.

Torman believed work, of any kind, was good therapy. So many of his clinic patients settled for their disability payments, leaving them feeling worthless and disabled. Working, even part-time, risked losing that small but steady disability check, as well as their health insurance. Yet a few managed to find their way back into the workforce. He hoped Jerry would become one of those few. Someone like Sam, with a long history of schizophrenia, alcoholism, and treatment non-compliance, presented almost insurmountable challenges. For Sam, Torman's short-term goal was to get him off the streets and into some kind of stable housing. Just accomplishing that would be satisfying. Anything more—sobriety, medical care, employment—was unlikely. In his mind's eye, he found himself replaying Jerry's grin upon succeeding in his task. Torman felt good and tried to hold on to that feeling.

Spurred by the headway he'd made with Jerry, Torman decided to follow up with Abbey, Sam's case manager, and have her try to find his brother's whereabouts. She managed to find a phone number for Sam's brother, and Sam agreed to let her call him. She planned to sound out the brother's willingness to have phone contact with Sam, as well as providing his brother with an update on Sam's condition. It was always risky making contact with relatives who might very well have no interest in resuming contact with their very ill family member. Such news could cause more hurt to the patient. Torman was cautiously optimistic about the chance that Sam's brother would encourage some re-connection.

The following week, arriving at work, Torman was unprepared for the news that greeted him that morning. Abbey entered his office, closed the door, and said Sam was found dead in a park where he often spent the night. She sat down and cried.

"I feel I should have known something was wrong," she said. "He'd looked kind of pale lately and short of breath."

Torman had similar thoughts of responsibility and guilt. Sam's blood pressure had been high, and Torman knew that schizophrenics' life spans were significantly shorter than the average person's. "Was there any evidence of foul play? Or suicide?"

"Not that I heard. His body was taken to Tucson where they'll do an autopsy." Abbey, in Torman's mind so young and inexperienced, sat crumpled in her chair. Torman reassured her that, regardless of circumstance, it's very normal to feel guilty when a patient dies. He stressed that she had not been remiss and, in fact, had been very involved in Sam's care.

"This is the first client I've had who's died."

Torman nodded. "I remember the first patient I lost. It never gets easy. If it does, you're in the wrong field. You'll find you're not alone in having a patient die and feeling awful about it. My door's open to you. You can talk to me about this anytime. I mean that...anytime." They sat in silence for a while, then Abbey pulled herself together and thanked Torman. Torman hoped this experience, so early in Abbey's career, wouldn't drive her out of the mental health field.

Sandy invited Torman to The Bisbee Royale, the only theater in Bisbee, which was showing "Cinema Paradiso," a favorite movie of hers.

"I can't believe you've never seen it!"

"I missed a lot of things being so focused on school."

"Well, Dr. Torman, you need some educating to become a well-rounded member of society."

Torman felt uncomfortable with the idea of their having an actual date, but agreed to an evening of pizza (served at the Royale) and a movie. They decided to meet at the theater.

The movie captured Torman's attention. Near the end, Salvatore, the main character, has returned to the small Italian town for the funeral of the town's movie projectionist. As a child, he adored films and developed a close relationship with the projectionist to whom he became an apprentice. This is his first visit back since leaving the village as a very young man to make his way in the world. Over many years, to appease the village priest, the projectionist had to cut out all the kissing scenes in the films. He bequeathed to his former apprentice—now a successful film director—a gift consisting of all those kissing scenes spliced together. As Torman watched these passionate, romantic kisses through the director's eyes, tears welled up, not out of sadness but out of sheer joy. He felt too embarrassed to look over at Sandy, but he could hear her softly crying.

As they left the Royale, Torman thanked her for inviting him to see the movie. "It was very moving. Those kisses...a kind of triumph over the repressiveness of the church, as well as such a touching gesture by the projectionist." As he spoke, he saw the parallel with his own life and the disapproval of his profession for his wanting to act on his attraction to Sandy. He suspected she saw the connection too, though she remained silent. A part of him wanted to ask if she'd suggested the movie with the knowledge of how it might affect him in his struggle to come to terms with his feelings for her. Instead, Torman asked Sandy if she wanted to get some coffee and dessert. They walked down the street to the Bisbee Coffee Company. Finally seated and sensing Sandy was lost in her thoughts, Torman asked how she was feeling.

"You shrinks, always wanting to talk about feelings," she said with a laugh.

"I was never good talking about sports. Or the weather. Or politics."

"It saddens me that Salvatore can't commit to relationships. He's able to achieve success in his career but not in his personal life. The projectionist propels him out of the provincial town so he can pursue a career in film, yet at a great personal cost to Salvatore. Or so it seems to me. I like to think that what was spliced out of the films, the romance and passion, is what Salvatore finally appreciates as essential to life, as giving meaning to life."

"I guess that relates to our relationship and my hesitancy to act on my feelings for you."

"Yes. I understand your fears, but I don't want you to pull away. I feel you, like Salvatore, live at some distance from life, observing but not fully participating. Maybe that's what drew you to psychiatry. Or maybe psychiatry fostered that observant part of you. I don't know...I just wish you could move closer to life and to me."

Torman walked Sandy to her home, all the while thinking about her comments about him. What she said struck a chord. At her door, she turned to face him. He leaned forward, kissing her lightly on the cheek.

"Steve, you can do better than that. Give me a kiss worthy of the movies." And he did. "Going to have a heart attack, aren't you."

Torman laughed, waited for her to get inside her house, then headed home.

The letter from Dr. Nelson expressed his regret that Torman had decided not to continue their sessions. Nelson hoped Torman would re-consider this decision since the fallout from a relationship with a former patient could prove devastating to Torman and to his former patient. To Torman's surprise, he acknowledged how his concern for Torman had interfered with his ability to remain neutral in their discussions.

Torman had been on the other side of this experience a number of times. Often, he'd call a patient and urge him to return for one session so that they could talk about what happened between them or, if it seemed hopeless to repair the rift, he'd suggest one session to talk about the therapy coming to an end. Rarely did anyone accept his offer. Therapy dropouts were disheartening to Torman, who invariably took it as a professional failure. Other therapists seemed more inclined to blame the patient for quitting, claiming he or she was too defensive or too narcissistic or lacking the necessary insight and motivation.

He realized he felt satisfaction knowing Nelson was having to face a sense of failure or, at least, was having to defend himself from that feeling. Torman had never warmed up to him, felt he was being judged, and didn't like the feeling. He was puzzled that Anna referred him to Nelson. Maybe she thought he needed a psychiatrist who wouldn't beat around the bush, who'd set Torman on the right path. Clearly Anna disapproved of Torman's behavior, though he believed her disapproval derived, in part, from not wanting him to suffer any negative consequences. He ruled out jealousy on Anna's part. If anything, he suspected she'd be relieved if he found an appropriate woman to love so that he'd no longer be harboring romantic feelings for her.

He'd always wanted to "do the right thing," even if it meant denying himself some pleasure or personal satisfaction. But turning away from Sandy? Is that the right thing? How can he ever know, except by taking the risk?

◆ ◆ ◆

Jerry scurried into Torman's office. Satisfied their conversation was private, he asked how Torman's home security system was working.

"Jerry, it works great. You know, you did a very professional job. Made me think about the possibility of your doing this kind of work for others. You could set your own hours, work by yourself, have some extra income…"

Launching out of his chair and interrupting Torman, Jerry said, "Doc, no one would hire me. They've destroyed my reputation. I don't have a chance. I'm being followed everywhere. I'm a curse. It's dangerous for you to keep seeing me. Look what Esther did to you!" Spoken as he paced back and forth.

"What Esther did had nothing to do with my relationship with you." Torman knew how futile it was to argue with someone like Jerry but couldn't stop trying.

"How do you know that? How could she have escaped from the maximum security ward without some outside help? You think Oswald acted alone in killing Kennedy? Ruby was hired to silence him. And look what happened to Jason Bourne, continually hunted by government assassins. And…"

"Whoa, Jerry, Jason Bourne's a fictional movie character. C'mon now."

"Fictional, perhaps. But something so convincing must be based on real experiences. Doc, don't be naive."

"All I'm trying to say is that you've got some real skills, and you could put them to good use. You could help protect others, just like you've helped me."

Jerry sat back down, squirmed in his chair, glanced around the room, suddenly standing up to resume his pacing. "When I was a kid, I tried to help my dad do stuff around the house. I've told you how he could be really mean, especially when he was drinking. One day Dad was really drunk. I'd accidentally thrown a baseball through one of our second story windows, and he decided to replace the glass. He yelled at me to hold the ladder. I swear I was holding it, but he was really unsteady and fell. He broke his leg and arm. He never let me forget that. Used to call me 'shithead' and 'fuckup.' Never let me forget that I'd caused him to fall off the ladder."

"You know that it wasn't your fault. He was drunk and should never have gotten on that ladder."

"I'm not sure. Maybe I let my mind wander and didn't hold the ladder tight. Maybe I wanted him to fall."

"How old were you?"

"I'm not sure. 7 or 8."

"Jerry, a child that age can't be expected to steady a ladder. And even if the ladder was perfectly steady, your dad was drunk and should never have gotten on the ladder in the first place. It was not your fault."

Jerry sat down, fell silent.

"What did your mother say about the fall?"

"She said I should've been more careful. She never challenged anything Dad said. He was plenty mean to her, too."

"What you've told me helps me understand why you feel you're a curse to others, and how, for example, you could feel responsible for what Esther did to me. You were unfairly blamed for your father's accident, and no one, not even your mother, came to your defense and helped you see that your father brought this accident on himself. Now, when bad things happen, you're quick to blame yourself."

"I don't know, Doc. That seems far-fetched. All that happened a long time ago."

"Well, my guess is that similar things happened, all of which reinforced this conviction you have that you're to blame for bad things and that authority figures are hostile to you."

"Doc, I know you mean well, but you gotta believe me. You saw how that policeman treated me when we brought him the tape. Treated me like shit."

"That's true, he did. Policemen are human, flawed like the rest of us, but not all of them mean you harm."

"Well, I've never found one who didn't mean me harm."

There were limits to Torman's capacity for empathy which he struggled to overcome. At least Jerry believed that

Torman meant well. That was something. And learning more about his father and mother deepened his appreciation of what Jerry dealt with growing up.

"I'm thinking of wearing protective glasses to safeguard my good eye. Do you think that would look really bad?" Sandy looked at Torman as if she were imagining how he'd look.

"You're worried about your good eye?"

"Yeah, I mean, if something happened to it, I'd be blind. I don't think I could handle that."

"I think anything that makes you feel more secure about your vision is worth trying."

"I've noticed I'm anxious at work, especially around angry patients. It could happen so quickly. Getting jabbed in the eye with a pen or hit in the face by a thrown object. Esther caught me totally unprepared and unprotected. It could happen again with someone else."

"Let's see how sunglasses look on you." Torman got up and retrieved a pair he kept on the table by his front door. He put them on and faced Sandy. "You look just fine with them. You might want to get the kind that wrap around the sides of your face, you know, like bicyclists wear."

Torman found it easy to talk with Sandy about most everything, except for his internal struggles over their relationship. She listened intently, remembered what he'd told her, and offered advice only when he asked for it. Their evening walks with Baba had stretched to over an hour and often ended with their sitting outside his house watching the sun set behind the mountains. Physical contact remained minimal, usually consisting of Torman's accidentally bumping into her as they walked. His decreased peripheral vision on the right often led to his bumping into things, something he'd begun to accept and laugh about.

Sandy enrolled in Arizona State University's online undergraduate program. Sometimes she brought her laptop to Torman's house and completed work for a course or listened to a lecture.

Torman pictured their life going on like this indefinitely. That way he'd never be forced to make a decision. They'd just drift along. Maybe physical intimacy would develop so gradually that it would barely cause a ripple in either of their lives. Yet he knew this was a childish wish to avoid making a decision, like attending religious services but never making the leap of faith.

One night Sandy cancelled their walk. Torman and Baba headed off, eventually circling back via Main Street. As they approached a bar, a man exited and approached them.

"You're the guy I see with Sandy," he said to Torman, who hesitated, not sure he wanted to engage in conversation with him. The man was dressed in jeans and a plaid flannel shirt, his hair pulled back in a ponytail. His tone of voice bordered on hostile, and his weathered face suggested menace. Torman instinctively turned his good eye away from the man. "I hope you know what you're getting into. She begged for sex, then claimed I'd raped her. That's her MO. Fucking nut case."

Torman decided not to respond. He pulled on Baba's leash, moving past the man, who said to Torman's back, "You'll wish you'd listened to me when she calls the cops."

Torman did listen. It was his worst fear, that Sandy would suddenly react to sexual intimacy with feelings of rage and victimization. He thought again of her father, his molesting her as a teenager. This is what Anna and Nelson warned him about and what every psychiatrist learns early in his career, especially when treating manipulative, volatile patients. For that matter, Sandy might not even be aware that she'd react that way. And it wouldn't be her fault if she did. What more did he need to know? Anna was right. The longer this goes on, the harder for both of them to end the relationship. If he ended the relationship now, she might feel so hurt, so exploited, that she'd accuse him of having sex with her. It would be her word against his. Everyone sees them walking together. Neighbors see her at his house. Who'd believe him?

By the time he reached home, he was in a frantic state. He called Sandy and said he needed to talk with her. She was on her way back from Tucson. He said he'd meet her at her house. "Are you all right?" she asked. "You sound really upset."

"I'm okay. We need to talk. I'll see you shortly." He got off the phone, not wanting to explain what this was about, though he imagined she knew.

Torman got right to the point. He said he'd given a lot of thought to their relationship and had decided it would be best if they stopped seeing each other. Sandy asked him to tell her why, what he was worried about.

"I know you've reassured me that you believe I've been different from the other men in your life, but the minute I cross that line, I'm just like the others. Sure, I've shown more restraint, but in the end I'd be crossing a line I shouldn't cross. I could be wrong. Perhaps we would be able to be a couple without injury to you, but there's no guarantee of that. I'm afraid to take that risk."

"I'm not. And I'm not asking you to do anything other than allowing us to be close. I'm not pressuring you to take me to bed. What's made you decide this? It seems so sudden..." Her voice cracked slightly as she looked at him intently.

Torman felt his resolve sink. Sandy was close enough that he could smell her body wash, that same smell he'd noted the night she entered his bedroom after he'd shouted in his sleep. He'd wanted to hold her then, and he wanted to hold her now.

He reared up from the couch. "Sandy, I can't. I'm sorry. I care for you, I do. This is the hardest thing I've ever done. I've got to leave."

He all but ran out of her house. He didn't look back. If she was standing at the window, watching him flee, he didn't want to glimpse that. He didn't want to think. The night sky was cloudy, so he walked home in darkness. He recalled how he felt reading Claire's farewell note. Now he was the one doing the leaving. He hated himself for hurting her, for prolonging their relationship. He'd been weak. He blamed that on his injury, his needing her comfort. She took his mind off his eye, off his attacker. She loved him just as he was. But...that man said she'd accused him of raping her right after having sex with him. He couldn't ignore that. It wouldn't just damage Torman. It would damage her, her trust. He did the right thing. He did the right thing. He kept repeating that forlorn mantra all the way home.

Work and exercise took Torman's mind off Sandy. He began each day with a run up and down Bisbee's winding streets. He added hours at Sierra Vista's clinic and swam laps during lunch time at the Aquatic Center. In the evenings he took Baba on an hour long walk.

Seeing patients helped him focus on their difficulties instead of his own. His loss made him more responsive to the suffering of his patients. So many of them were lonely, cut off from family, lacking friends, drifting through their lives. Sam came to mind, a man so withdrawn, so alone in the world. The last time he saw Sam he was huddled in a corner of the Bisbee park where Torman often rested when he was jogging. Torman made a point of checking in with Abbey, Sam's case worker, to see how she was dealing with Sam's death. And he made himself more available to other case workers, many of whom struggled with worries about their patients.

He reached out to Anna and Val, visiting them on weekends. Anna approved of his decision to break up with Sandy, though he didn't tell her about his encounter with the man who claimed Sandy had accused him of rape. Anna asked if he wanted her to fix him up with someone, but he declined. "I'm really not ready to get involved with anyone. I'll let you know when I feel the time is right."

The idea of dating never appealed to Torman. Now that he sported an eye patch, he was even more reluctant. He certainly didn't want someone to see the crater under the patch. Sandy had seen it when she helped change the bandage early in his recovery, but her not being repulsed seemed an anomaly to Torman.

"By the way," Torman told Anna, "I stopped seeing Nelson. You know, I never warmed up to that guy."

"I've been meaning to tell you...he's been accused of sexual harassment by a female psych resident he'd been supervising. Turns out she's not the first one to complain about him, and it looks like he's losing his faculty appointment. I was shocked. He'd supervised me and was never inappropriate."

"Maybe he was more perceptive than I was about your orientation."

"Steve, everyone was more perceptive than you were."

"Another example that love is blind."

Torman recalled Nelson's being so adamant that he should stop seeing Sandy. He was reminded of those evangelists who preach vehemently about the sin of adultery, only to have their own sexual dalliances exposed. The defense mechanism of "reaction formation" described how forbidden impulses are warded off by an insistence on the opposite of what is desired. Nelson's ethical piety now appeared to Torman as an effort to master his own sexual yearnings. "How come you referred me to him?"

"He's the only analyst in the psych department, and he was a good supervisor. He helped me understand my counter-transference reactions to a difficult patient of mine. I thought he was very insightful. I'm shocked by the recent allegations."

Torman found himself wondering about his profession and about how frequent such boundary violations were. Perhaps psychiatrists were just as likely as the rest of humanity to seize sexual opportunities, in spite of all their training. Priests, ministers, rabbis, teachers, politicians, CEO's, coaches, camp counselors, really everyone everywhere with any advantage over another experiences the temptation to screw somebody. Maybe those old Freudians were right, and we're always struggling with our sexual and aggressive drives, barely civilized creatures on the brink of running amok. He told himself he was better than Nelson, that he'd done the right thing.

Notwithstanding such thoughts, he missed Sandy and thought about her every day.

To Torman's surprise, Jerry mentioned in their session that he was thinking about doing some handyman work. He wasn't sure how to start, how to get the word out that he was available. "I don't want people to know my cell phone number, and I certainly don't want to give out my email address. That's a sure invitation to getting hacked, having all my information spread out for others to steal my identity, get me in the grip of the mafia, who are running the law enforcement in this country, who have tried to kill me more times than I can count…"

"Hold on, Jerry. Let's back up here. Maybe you could have a business email account which would be separate from your personal email." Jerry liked that idea but then questioned how he could afford to print fliers and business cards. "You smoke, don't you?"

"Yeah…what's that got to do with this?"

"How much do you spend on cigarettes?"

"Really, Doc, you don't think I'm going to quit smoking! I get so anxious at times, I'd die without a cigarette."

"There are other ways of dealing with anxiety."

"I'm not taking any fucking meds. I told you that the first time we met."

"I'm not suggesting meds. There's relaxation techniques, yoga, meditation, talk therapy with one of the counselors here."

"I don't trust anyone but you. Most of those counselors look like they haven't even reached puberty."

"What's the risk in trying?"

It was always so much easier giving advice than taking it. Probably, Torman reflected, that was his own narcissism rearing its head, his reluctance to see himself as needing help. Torman enjoyed nudging Jerry towards something healthy. Jerry's giving up smoking so he could afford to jump-start his own handyman business would be a therapeutic twofer. Perhaps too much to expect, but patients surprised Torman all the time, though not always in pleasant ways.

"What if someone wants a reference?" Jerry asked.

"You can give them my name and the number here at work." Another stretching of boundaries, yes, but Torman had no reservation about saying he did a very good job. "Eventually, Jerry, word-of-mouth will bring you business."

Later that day, before Torman left the clinic, Jerry dropped by his office to show him some preliminary ideas for a flier. At the top of the page he'd written "Handyman for Hire," beneath which he'd drawn a house surrounded by stick figures with guns, presumably poised to blow to smithereens the house and its inhabitants. Under the drawing, he'd written, "Defend your castle with the latest in technology and surveillance." Followed by, "Cops need not inquire."

"Jerry, this is a bit over the top, don't you think? Your

chances for success will increase with just a simple line or two, something like, 'Electronic surveillance, electrical work, home repairs of all kinds. References available.' To be honest, I really don't think there's much demand in Bisbee for electronic surveillance, so you might want to leave that out. And please remove the drawing and the reference to cops. How about redoing this, and I'll take another look." Jerry's face fell, so Torman added, "Overall, this is a good start. I know you can do this. We might be able to use the printer here to make a bunch of fliers. I'll look into that."

◆ ◆ ◆

Eric sent Torman an invitation to his housewarming party. Finding a gift for such an occasion is easy in Bisbee, which has a number of funky stores selling arts and crafts, "antique" items for the home, and assorted gifts. He settled on an old cattle horn mounted on wood that could be hung above a fireplace mantle or over a doorway. He wrapped it in old newspaper and stuck a bright red bow on the wrapping.

What Torman didn't anticipate was Susan's moving in with Eric. Her recent visit with Eric had clearly gone well. He felt an almost paternal pleasure in seeing the two of them together, smiling and enjoying the rush of rekindled romance as they greeted their guests at their new home. An old adobe structure, Val had salvaged the old wood beams and replaced much of the Mexican tile on the floor to create a warm, inviting interior. A spread of meats, cheeses, bread, and desserts provided nourishment, along with wine and soft drinks. The small group of invitees followed Val for a brief tour, accompanied by "before" photos displayed on her laptop.

"Val," Torman said, "are you trying to drum up business?"

"Everyone needs to understand that Steve's Bisbee shack is beyond restoration and was rejected for use as kindling," Val said, then waited for Torman's rejoinder.

"Everyone but Val is invited to my upcoming housewarming."

Anna intervened with, "Alright, you two, enough already." Torman's gaze descended to her now obviously pregnant abdomen, which triggered the memory of seeing Claire's pregnant state in the grocery store. He shook his head in an effort to erase that image. Sadness had a way of creeping up on Torman like a predator in search of its prey.

At some point in the evening he spoke with Susan, asking about her moving to Tucson and living with Eric. Smiling, she said, "Should I lie down on a couch before answering that?"

"Couch not necessary. But you don't have to answer if I'm getting too personal."

"Actually, it's really nice to see you outside the context of analysis. When I finally managed to free myself from my marriage, I wanted to avoid confining relationships. I wanted to be selfish, if that makes sense. So I pulled away from Eric, though I really liked him and appreciated his gentleness and thoughtfulness. I've pretty much done whatever I've felt like doing the last three years. I no longer feel threatened by Eric's love. And Tucson has an active art community. I feel good being here."

"Well, I'm rooting for the two of you."

As planned, he spent the night at Anna and Val's. Before going to bed, Anna asked Torman if he'd seen Sandy since their parting ways.

"I haven't seen her at all, not even from a distance, which is weird since Bisbee is such a small town."

"I can tell you miss her."

"I looked forward to her coming over every evening to walk Baba with me. We'd talk, share our pasts, sometimes just walk in silence. She was easy to be with. In a way, the lack of physical intimacy helped our friendship deepen. Now I feel as though her absence has drained all the life out of my existence."

"I know it's lonely for you, but the risk of her reacting unpredictably to a sexual relationship couldn't be ignored. You're such a good man, Steve. I know you'll find someone to share your life with." She gave Torman a hug, then wished him a good night. Torman reflected on how often he hears what a good man he is and how that hasn't helped him much with relationships. Later, lying in bed, he wondered why he hadn't run in to Sandy, wondered if she was alright. Maybe she'd experienced a manic reaction to the loss and taken off with the first man she found. Maybe she was flying around some other continent, barely sleeping, risking her life in the company of shady characters. Or maybe she'd withdrawn into a depression, unable to get out of bed, struggling with suicidal thoughts. It took half the night before he could finally silence his mind and fall asleep.

❖ ❖ ❖

Jake was standing outside a restaurant on Main St. when Torman spotted him and decided to ask how things worked out with the lawyer representing Esther's family.

"That prick finally stopped harassing us about our investigation after seeing the tape. We closed the case. You learned how to duck bullets?"

"Fortunately, none have been coming my way lately."

"I notice Jerry's driving around town trying to drum up business. You'd have to be nuts to hire that guy."

"Actually, he does really good work. He did some electrical work at my place, and I was very impressed. You know, work is good for the soul. Makes people less likely to pester police departments with frivolous matters." Torman doubted that he'd ever sway someone like Jake to change his mind about Jerry. Just as he was getting ready to say goodbye, the man who'd claimed Sandy had accused him of rape emerged from the restaurant and, seeing Jake, did an abrupt about-face. "What's that about?" Torman asked.

"That creep's name is Darren. Spent time in prison for

rape. Lives with some pathetic woman he uses as a punching bag. She refuses to press charges. Manages to get women in bed, either by force or by slipping downers in their drinks. We're just waiting to get enough evidence to go after him. Complete piece of shit. I hope he's not one of your patients."

Torman reeled with this revelation. He'd never bothered to hear Sandy's side of the story. He'd been too uneasy, too cowardly, to confront her; he'd never given her the chance to be heard. Just walked out on her, leaving her in the dark. He felt an urgent need to see Sandy but worried it was too late. Perhaps, he thought, she's better off dealing with her loss rather than having her emotions stirred up by his contacting her and confessing the real reason for ending their relationship. She's probably over her hurt by now, at least the worst of it. Let her go, let her find someone who can fully enter into a relationship with her. He's done enough damage. These thoughts and others consumed him. He couldn't stop thinking about Sandy. Nor could he stop trying to catch sight of her. He walked by her house late at night, initially feeling relief seeing a light in one of her windows, then realized she might have left a light on if she'd left town. His worrying about her escalated.

He did run into Jerry, who'd stopped to grab some coffee at the Bisbee Coffee Company. Torman knew that Jerry's vigilance about his surroundings provided him with a sense of the whereabouts of everyone. After asking Jerry how work was going, Torman mentioned he hadn't seen Sandy in some time and wondered if Jerry had seen her or knew her whereabouts.

"Haven't seen her, Doc. I've seen a light on in her house, but no sign of her. Maybe she's in trouble. I wouldn't go to the police, though. If something bad's happened, they're likely to be involved. Could put you at risk."

"I wasn't thinking of going to the police. I just thought you might have spotted her around town. I doubt she's in some kind of trouble."

"I don't know…beautiful single woman, living alone…it's a dangerous world. I could install a spy cam and keep a close eye on her place."

"Jerry, thanks, but I don't think that's necessary at this point. I think I'll just go over to her place and knock on her door."

"If you need any back-up, just call me."

"Thanks." The image of Jerry in camouflage and full battle gear providing "back-up" did make Torman smile.

On the way to work, Torman wrestled with thoughts about Sandy and what he should do, if anything. Perhaps he'd been a lifeline for her, just as she'd been one for him in the aftermath of his attack. As the day wore on, his anxiety about her mounted, becoming almost unbearable. Between patients, he repeatedly tried reaching her on her cell phone. Are you there, are you alright? The only voice he heard was her recorded one.

After seeing his last patient, Torman drove straight from the clinic to Sandy's house. He raced down the steps to the path leading to her door. Knocking produced no response. He knocked louder. With his hand he tested the door handle, which gave way with a gentle push. There was still enough daylight left to see inside the unlit home. The air smelled stale, with the hint of garbage, triggering a memory of an abandoned house he and his childhood friends used to break into and explore. A few dirty dishes littered the kitchen counter. The plants that once thrived were wilted and desiccated like those in a cemetery weeks after a holiday.

Hearing not a sound, he headed toward her bedroom door and, whispering her name, opened it. A figure lay beneath a sheet on the bed, folded up on itself, face turned away from the door. "Sandy? Sandy, are you alright?" No response, no movement. He looked closely at the sheet to see if there was movement from her breathing. He detected the rise and fall of breaths taken slowly, as if in deep sleep. Gently touching her shoulder, he shook her, saying, "It's me, Steve." Her body was warm, though she showed no sign of acknowledging his presence.

Torman looked around for any indication she'd overdosed or hurt herself. He ran into the adjoining bathroom, opening the medicine cabinet. Two pill bottles faced him, both filled to the brim. He grabbed one, looking for the doctor's name on the label. Glancing around the bathroom, he saw nothing suggesting a suicide attempt. The toilet bowl revealed dark yellow urine. Returning to her bedside, Torman pulled back the sheet. Her shrunken frame shocked him. "Sandy, wake up! Open your eyes!" He felt her pulse, which was slow and steady.

Sandy uttered what sounded like, "Leave." Or maybe she'd said his name. Her eyes remained shut. He took out his phone, googled the doctor's name from the pill bottle, and called the number. Reaching her voice mail, he left a message to call him immediately, that he was bringing Sandy to the Tucson Medical Center for an emergency admission. He bent over, reached under her body and, lifting her out of bed, carried her to his car. Breathless from the climb, he managed to get her into the back seat. Grateful for his car's navigation system, he typed in the address of the medical center. On the way to Route 80, he stopped at his house and rushed to get Baba into the car. He hoped the dog's presence would somehow help restore Sandy's survival instinct.

Within 10 minutes, Sandy's psychiatrist, Dr. Patel, returned his call. Torman explained how he'd found Sandy and his impression she was in a severely withdrawn state. He suspected she might be dehydrated as well. Dr. Patel said she would notify the emergency room of Sandy's anticipated arrival and acknowledged the importance of a medical evaluation prior to admission to psychiatry.

Glancing behind him, Torman saw Baba, seated on the floorboard behind the front seats, licking Sandy's face.

❖ ❖ ❖

Arriving at the emergency entrance, Torman parked and grabbed a wheelchair near the doors. An orderly accompanied him to his car and helped Torman lift Sandy into the chair. Careful to announce he was a physician, Torman managed to get her quickly through registration and into the treatment area. A nurse took the history he gave of Sandy's illness and recent decline. Before leaving her room, he made sure that Dr. Patel had contacted the emergency department and that a bed was waiting for Sandy on the psychiatric unit pending clearance by the medical team.

Functioning as a physician allowed Torman to feel less anxious about Sandy, but once he'd ceded control over to the emergency room and her psychiatrist, he re-experienced anxiety about Sandy's well-being. Guilt flooded him. How could he have been so callous, so thoughtless? To lead her on for weeks, then suddenly, without revealing the precipitant, tell her it was over, reeked of insensitivity, of cruelty. And the decisive moment being the encounter with some guy coming out of a bar!

He continued to beat himself up as he took Baba out for a walk around the hospital grounds. The ringing of his cell phone interrupted his self-reproach. The head nurse on the psychiatric unit informed Torman that Sandy was on the ward and that he could come up to check on her.

Entering an inpatient psychiatric unit never failed to unsettle him. There was an air of danger, of chaos about to unfold, that put him on edge and made him wary. When he worked on these units in his residency, he got used to this feeling, which diminished over time. But he rarely entered this walled-off world once he settled into his out-patient practice, so each time he crossed the threshold, he re-experienced this sense of lives out of control, of adults regressed and unpredictable. The patients walking the halls seemed to pretend to be normal, as if they knew they were viewed as unbalanced and therefore had to exaggerate normality.

Sandy's room, near the nursing station, was barren except for a bed. She was on suicide watch, so every 15 minutes someone came to check on her. A bandage covered the area where IV fluids had entered her arm to rehydrate her. She appeared just as she had when he'd entered her bedroom hours earlier: curled up on her side, facing away from the door.

"Sandy, it's Steve." He stood by her bed, hoping she might say something or turn to look up at him. She didn't speak or move her head, but he noticed her hand inch up, resting atop her hip. Torman held her hand in his and sat on the edge of the bed. He sensed she was beyond the reach of words, that she needed the safety and security of what one analyst famously called a "holding environment." Torman hoped holding Sandy's hand conveyed his reaching out to her, his effort to pull her out of the hole she'd fallen into. Perhaps it was too little, too late. He couldn't undo what he'd done. He could only hold fast.

A middle-aged woman with a tired-looking expression stood in the doorway. "Dr. Torman? I'm Dr. Patel. Can we speak?" Torman followed her to a nondescript interview room furnished with a metal desk, desk chair, and two molded plastic chairs. A wall clock, advertising Prozac, adorned one wall. The desk chair, occupied by Dr. Patel, was positioned closest to the door (in the event, he knew, that the interviewer needed to make a quick exit).

Glancing around the room, Torman said, "They never bother decorating these rooms."

Dr. Patel gave him a resigned smile. "Keeps distractions to a minimum. I need to ask, are you involved now as Sandy's psychiatrist or friend?"

"As her friend, though as you know I saw her three times at the clinic in Sierra Vista before she transferred her care to you. I realize you can't talk about Sandy with me without her approval, but I can give you what information I have."

Not betraying any reaction, she said, "Tell me what you know." Torman proceeded to describe how well she'd been doing, how she'd started online classes to get her college degree, how stable her mood had been. He told Dr. Patel about his feelings for Sandy and his ethical struggle with having any kind of non-therapeutic relationship with Sandy. Realizing it was late in the day and that he was there to provide what he knew about Sandy, he related his decision to end their relationship.

"I hadn't seen her since the evening I told her. Weeks went by, and I was aware of not catching sight of her. I began to worry and finally went over to her house today and found her in an unresponsive condition. I didn't see any evidence of a suicide attempt, her pill bottles were full, but I'm sure you're getting a drug screen. I have to tell you that I plan on being involved in Sandy's life. My decision to end our relationship was based on hearing some unfounded information about her character that, at the time, I believed to be true. That was my mistake, and I deeply regret my decision."

"My focus now is getting Sandy out of this depression. If she gives me permission to talk further with you, I will. I need to write orders in her chart. You can say goodbye to her while I'm taking care of the paperwork."

"Thanks, Dr. Patel."

"Call me Seema." She held out her hand and gave Torman a hint of a smile.

As he entered Sandy's room, a nurse was taking her vital signs. "I'm Steve, her friend," he said to the young woman dressed casually in jeans and a long-sleeve cotton T-shirt. She informed Torman that visiting hours were over, so he'd need to keep his visit short. "I understand. I'll stay just a few minutes more."

The nurse spoke to Sandy as if she were fully responsive. "Sandy, I'll be back in 15 minutes, and I hope we can talk a little at that time. Is there anything you need?" Getting no response, she continued, "Steve is going to say good night to you." This one-sided conversation seemed surreal to Torman, who thought it strange to ignore how unnatural Sandy's state of mind was. He reminded himself that he was on a psychiatric ward where strangeness was the norm.

Once the nurse departed, he sat on Sandy's bed, leaning towards her head. "Sandy, I deeply regret my decision to stop seeing you. I hope you'll forgive me. What I did was self-protective and unnecessary. I don't know how much of this you're able to absorb, but I want you to know I'll be back tomorrow and every day after, as long as you're here. I've missed you terribly." He lightly kissed her on the temple, then walked out of her room and down the hall to the exit.

The nurse in the nursing station buzzed him out the locked door. He left Sontag's kingdom of the sick and gratefully re-entered the kingdom of the well.

When Torman visited Sandy the next day, she was sitting up in a chair in the common room of the ward. She greeted him with a wan smile. He sat down next to her.

"How're you feeling?" He spoke loud enough to be heard over the TV blaring "The Price Is Right" show and a female patient shouting what she earnestly believed was the right price for a Ford F-150 pick-up truck.

"Okay."

"Baba's missed you. So have I." He noticed she barely moved. Someone must have helped her get from her room to the common area. The color hadn't returned to her face, and her arms looked skeletal in the T-shirt one of the staff must have found for her to wear. "Have you eaten?"

"A little."

"I brought you some of your clothes. I left them in your room. Is there anything else you'd like me to bring?"

She shook her head no.

Torman knew it would take time for her to pull back from the abyss. He decided to sit in silence with her. He didn't want her to feel pressured to respond to him. After a couple of minutes, he said, "Well, I'm going to go. I'll see you tomorrow."

Sandy, looking up at Torman, whispered, "Thanks."

Patients began filing into the room. Torman figured there would be some group meeting. A nurse escorted him to the locked door and let him out.

Each day he visited Sandy, she appeared a little better. She put weight back on, became more responsive verbally, and appeared to look forward to Torman's visits. Dr. Patel seemed pleased with her progress, though Torman didn't seek out her opinion on how Sandy was doing. He'd decided it was best for him to steer clear of her relationship with her psychiatrist. He didn't want to be seen as in any way functioning as a consulting psychiatrist in her care. He simply identified himself as her close friend.

Prior to Sandy's discharge, Dr. Patel gave her a day pass on a Saturday. Torman, accompanied by Baba, picked her up and drove her to Bisbee for the day. They stopped at the Bisbee Breakfast Club for brunch. Sandy ordered pancakes, bacon, and scrambled eggs, all of which she consumed before Torman had finished his bagel.

"Well," he said, "your grandmother would be pleased to see you haven't affronted God."

Smiling, Sandy asked if he planned on eating the remainder of his bagel or if he wanted to donate it to a good cause. "I'm glad to see your appetite has returned, but you're not getting my bagel. Why not order something else?"

She claimed she'd had enough. Torman noticed how at times her face clouded over, as if a disturbing thought invaded her consciousness. As they walked back to his car, he asked how she was feeling. "I'm not back to normal yet. I know that. I feel I'm getting there. I don't want to be left alone. I'm scared I could slip back into the darkness again. I can't describe how bleak things got for me. I just know I don't want to go there again."

"Does my asking how you feel upset you?"

"I don't want to be probed, but at the same time, I want you to understand what I'm going through. I don't want to fake feeling good."

"Well, maybe you can let me know when to ask and when to be quiet." She nodded her head.

"I'd like to walk up the mountain with you and Baba. We'll have to go slowly."

"Sounds good to me." Torman glanced back at Baba, whose tail thumped on the back seat as if he'd understood their conversation.

Torman picked Sandy up on the day of her discharge. He watched her say goodbye to a few of the patients and to the staff, some of whom hugged her. Patients rarely stayed longer than a week, often less than a week. Torman knew there was considerable pressure on doctors to get patients out of the hospital as soon as possible, so he was grateful that Dr. Patel managed to keep Sandy nearly two weeks to ensure she'd made sufficient improvement. As they walked off the ward, Sandy carried a bag of her clothes in one hand, her discharge medications in the other.

"How's it feel to get out?" Torman asked as they got into his car.

"It's weird...in the past, I was always eager to get released from hospitals, but this time I actually felt safe there and, to be honest, I've got mixed feelings about leaving. It still feels as though the ground I'm standing on is shifting, sort of like aftershocks following an earthquake. I'm still uneasy with the thought of being alone."

"I'd like you to stay with me. I've got the guest room. You can come and go as you please. Or, if you prefer, I could stay at your place."

"You're sure you want me in your home?"

Looking over at her, Torman said, "I'm sure. No ambivalence."

"I'm not ready to be your partner yet. It's not that I don't care about you. I do. But I need to focus on myself."

"I get that. I'm here for you...as you were for me when I was recovering from Esther's assault. That's what I want you to know."

Sandy stared out the window. She seemed to relax in her seat, though Torman sensed there was still a veil that hid a clear view of her feelings from him.

Val called with the news that Anna had developed pre-eclampsia, was in the hospital and likely to have a C-section at any moment. Sensing her anxiety, Torman said he'd come up the moment he could get away from work. He reassured Val that Anna would be fine. He then called Sandy with the news, saying he'd likely get home late that night and she shouldn't wait up for him.

By the time Torman arrived at the hospital, Anna had

undergone a C-section. The child, a boy, weighed in at 5 pounds even, with Apgar scores of 8 and 9. She was sleeping when Torman arrived, so he and Val talked in the hall outside her room. They viewed the baby in the nursery where he was being warmed by lights and swaddled tightly like a mummy. Named Aaron, he had Anna's dark hair.

"Aren't you passing out cigars?" Torman asked.

"Only to my close friends," Val said with a smile. Torman laughed, then asked how scared Val had been.

"I got really worried when Anna said she had a terrible headache. She never complains about her health. She got hold of her OB doc, who told her to go immediately to the ER. By the time we got there, her blood pressure was sky high. They whisked her up to the delivery floor. I hadn't really thought about something bad happening to Anna during the pregnancy, but seeing everyone move so fast scared the shit out of me. When the doctor came out smiling about an hour later, I was so relieved, I cried. Something I hadn't done in years."

Torman congratulated Anna when she woke up. She managed a tired smile. "How do you feel?" Anna said she felt pretty good, especially considering having her abdomen sliced open.

"Have you seen Aaron?"

"Yes," Torman said, "he's got your hair."

At that point a nurse wheeled Aaron into Anna's room for her to hold him and introduce him to her breast. Torman felt awkward, so he walked out of her room, glancing back through the window where he saw the nurse and Val hovering by Anna as she cradled her son. A forlornness enveloped Torman who saw himself once again standing outside the circle of intimacy.

In some ways life with Sandy was idyllic: they shared meals, walked together in the evenings and on weekends, talked at length, read together at night. However, there was no physical intimacy beyond the occasional hug and sitting close together on the couch. Sandy made it clear that she needed more time before taking that step and, while Torman in no way wanted to risk rushing more physical closeness, he was aware of a protective shield surrounding Sandy. He couldn't help wondering if she was having second thoughts about accepting the intimacy he was offering her. He imagined she simply couldn't trust him after his sudden and seemingly unprovoked rejection of her. What he debated in his mind was whether to broach this with her. He finally decided to ask her if she felt afraid to trust his feelings for her.

They were sitting on the couch when he asked. She hesitated, staring at him intently, then said, "That night you broke things off, I sensed something had happened that made you do that. But I couldn't think what it was. What made you decide?"

That was the very question he'd been dreading. He'd decided the best approach was to be honest with her. "Something did happen. I'm ashamed to tell you. I worry you won't be able to forgive me. I was out walking after work and this guy, Darren, whose name I learned later, approached me and warned me about you, saying you'd accused him of rape right after having sex with him. It triggered my worst fears. I never stopped to question the source. I acted out of fear. About a month later, I was talking to Detective Lawrence, and this Darren guy tried to avoid running into him, so I asked what that was about. Jake told me what a creep Darren was, how he had a history of a rape conviction, how women have complained about him. I knew then I'd made a horrible mistake. That's when I started to look for you." As Torman spoke, he watched Sandy's face and witnessed her features slacken. He fell silent.

"Steve, I've done many things I'm not proud of. Slept with some men I shouldn't have. I met Darren in a bar one night. He seemed nice enough at first. He must've put something in my drink, because I wasn't drunk but I can't remember what happened that night. I woke up in his car, my clothes were ripped, exposing me. I knew I'd been raped. I managed to get home and called the police. I was very upset. But I didn't go to the hospital and didn't press charges. They said they'd talk to him. I let it drop. I think I hated myself for getting in that situation."

Torman nodded as she spoke. After a silence, Sandy said, "You should've told me."

"Yes, I should have. I'm deeply sorry I didn't." He couldn't tell if Sandy forgave him or if she'd ever be able to. He knew his confession was likely to reverberate for some time.

Torman wanted to confide in Anna what had led to his breaking up with Sandy, how he'd learned about the circumstances of Darren's accusation, and how he'd re-connected with her. But with Anna's having a baby, it was difficult to get time alone with her. Phone calls were interrupted by the needs of Aaron, and he worried a visit to Tucson would only burden Anna, who napped or did necessary chores whenever Aaron slept or was cared for by Val. He finally decided to email her with the details of what happened. He hoped she'd be accepting of his decision to engage fully with Sandy and be comfortable with his including her in his visits with Anna and Val. He'd also asked her to share his email communication with Val.

Anna's email response was brief and mostly reassuring: "I know you've struggled with your decision for some time and have wanted to 'do the right thing.' What makes relationships work remains a mystery to me. I found Sandy very engaging and likable in my one encounter with her. Her recent hospitalization worries me; I can't deny that. My hope is that your commitment to her will provide her with stability and that the two of you will develop a trusting, enduring relationship. Val and I expect Sandy to accompany you to our get-togethers and want her to feel fully accepted by us. Love, Anna"

Torman replied with a succinct "Thanks." He wondered what sort of conversation Anna had with Val about his re-connecting with Sandy. Did Anna shake her head in dismay at his behavior? Did she analyze his decision as some form of acting out an unconscious impulse? Did she see him as a lonely, one-eyed man desperate to believe he'd found true love? He imagined Val laughing and commenting on how men are driven by their penises. What he hadn't confided in Anna was the platonic state of affairs with Sandy. Even Torman had begun to wonder about that. Perhaps Sandy was afraid of how she might react to sex with him. He didn't believe she'd cry "rape," but he wondered if she might feel disappointed or angry or used. Most of all, he suspected she was right that she needed to protect herself. He just couldn't figure out what she might need protection from.

In his mind he debated talking with her about her reluctance to engage more with him. What he couldn't get past, though, was the fear he'd come across as impatient. Nor did he want to look as though he was begging for sex. And it wasn't really sex he wanted. He hoped to recover the closeness they'd experienced before his encounter with Darren, to resume the comfortableness and openness that had slowly built up. Maybe such hope was naive, impossible. He decided to hold off questioning her, to respect her not wanting to be probed. The protective wall around Sandy needed to come down if they were to get closer, but not from his battering it with questions. He imagined she needed to feel safe. He told himself to wait. That was something he could do.

❖ ❖ ❖

Torman noticed Jerry driving a newer model truck, a shiny black Ford F-150 with a shiny aluminum tool box in the bed. Each door was emblazoned with "Delta Force Repairs," beneath which two hammers crossed each other to form a menacing-looking X, followed by a phone number. At least, thought Torman, he'd restrained himself from depicting cops being decapitated by machetes or blown apart by explosives. Jerry's suspiciousness and hypervigilance remained, yet somehow he'd managed to contain these symptoms so that he could interact with clients without alienating or scaring most of them. Perhaps his honesty and reliable workmanship allowed people to overlook some of his paranoia.

In sessions, Torman asked a lot about Jerry's work. He noticed Jerry's tendency to play down his pride and sense of accomplishment in his work. Rather than attempting to interpret this behavior, Torman focused on drawing him out, getting him to describe in detail what he did for his customers. Torman emphasized how good it felt to succeed at a task, to earn a client's appreciation. And when Jerry complained about someone not being pleased with his work, Torman took a careful look at what transpired and was usually able to convince Jerry that it wasn't his fault but rather his client's unreasonableness. Occasionally, Torman compared a client to Jerry's father falling off the ladder and needing to blame Jerry for his own failings. "Sounds like your dad on the ladder" became a helpful metaphor in their communication.

On one occasion, Torman asked Jerry if he ever got lonely and wanted a social life. "You mean, wanting a girlfriend?"

"Well, it doesn't have to be a romantic relationship. Maybe just a good friend, someone to hang out with, watch a movie with, go out to eat with..."

"I don't know, Doc. I was never popular in school. Never had many friends. Certainly no one I was really close to. Kids made fun of me. My ears stuck out, and I never had nice clothes. I wasn't good at sports. High school was the worst. I had really bad acne. My parents never got me any medical help for that. In the locker room, I was embarrassed by the zits on my shoulders and back. I used to daydream about getting revenge on all the assholes who called me names and laughed at me. That's probably why I liked the movie 'Carrie.'"

"You never had a girlfriend?"

"Not really. There were girls in school that I liked, but I kept to myself and never had a date."

"What about sex?"

"I've paid for it a few times. That was depressing. Made me feel like a real loser. I try not to think about sex. I mean, I beat off, there's lots of free porn on the internet, but I've never had a relationship with a woman I cared about. I couldn't trust a woman to love me. Why would anyone?"

"Jerry, you're no longer that kid with ears that stick out or the adolescent with acne, bad clothes, and little athletic skill. You're working now, you're basically a kind, good person. You could find a woman who'd love you. Might take some trial and error, but there's a lot of women out there."

"How come you're not married, Doc?"

"I got divorced. I didn't say relationships were easy, but I do believe they enrich our lives."

"I don't know...it seems a lot easier being alone."

Torman wondered if he was pushing his values too vigorously on Jerry. Yet he'd heard many times how Freud believed that happiness resulted from the ability to love and to work. Maybe that wasn't true for someone like Jerry. Maybe he needed to protect himself from abusive, hurtful relationships by avoiding relationships altogether. Maybe Torman was asking too much of him. Maybe he should let Jerry come to his own realization of wanting a close relationship in his life without Torman's pressing for it. Maybe this, maybe that...certainty never came easily to Torman. Sometimes he believed that was a strength of his, other times a weakness.

Torman sensed steady progress in Sandy's mood. Gradually, the darkness that filled the edges around her dissolved. Her gaiety and spontaneity returned. He felt relief seeing her restored in this way. He wanted to believe that their relationship partly accounted for this improvement. At the same time, he knew she was making a concerted effort to maintain her stability. She kept to a strict schedule of sleep, exercise, and meditation. He saw her mediset pill box in the bathroom, noticing how she never missed a dose. And, in addition to keeping monthly appointments with Dr. Patel, she'd begun seeing a therapist in Tucson, a woman who worked in Dr. Patel's office. Wanting Sandy to feel her therapy was private, he was careful not to ask about it, though he felt some anxiety about how her therapist might view Sandy's relationship with him. He imagined how a therapist might be quite vocal about issues related to boundary violations, the very issues he'd struggled with.

He told himself that he wanted her to find and maintain stability, to accomplish her goal of becoming a therapist. If he truly loved her, he would want what was best for her. So he put out of his mind the fear that she would discover that he wasn't the right person for her. He told himself he just needed to wait, that she'd come around to accept his commitment to her.

The day she left began like a usual day. Looking back, as he often did, he thought maybe she'd seemed a bit nervous, a bit distracted. But at the time, he'd left the house without any particular worry. Later, on his way home from the clinic, he found himself focused on a new patient he'd seen that day, a young woman with mental retardation and "bipolar disorder." Thoughts about her diagnosis and care preoccupied Torman during the drive.

Walking in the door, the sensation of deja vu came over him. And there it was, a note folded in half and resting like a tiny A-frame house on the kitchen table.

Dear Steve,
I think you know that I've struggled with whether to

allow myself to accept your love. But the reason may surprise you. I've come to realize I'm not stable enough to tolerate the gifts you offer. In some sense you were right to anticipate that our intimacy could bring about a dramatic response from me. It's just not the one you feared. I wouldn't have accused you of rape or reacted with rage and feelings of betrayal. I believe such closeness would most likely cause a dangerous flight into something like mania, a state of excitement and stimulation that would scare you and absolutely terrify me. What you offer is just too much, too overwhelming, for me to manage right now. Maybe at some point in the future, but not now. I need to work at keeping my precarious sense of being normal, of living in the middle ground between utter despair and extreme excitement.

Please let me go. Don't try to find me or contact me. I'm healing myself in the only way I know how. Find someone who won't be scared of all the goodness you possess. And know that leaving you is the hardest thing I've ever done.

Love, Sandy

Torman spent the evening on his couch, reading her note over and over, searching for hope, for something to hang on to. She couldn't deal with her potential reaction "...right now. Maybe at some point in the future..." That buoyed him, but her urging him to find someone else, rather than asking him to wait, deflated his hope. At some point, he began wondering what it was about him that may have led to her fleeing, something she was unaware of or wanted to spare him from knowing. He worried it wasn't simply all the goodness he possessed. Maybe she was protecting him from some painful truth about himself. After all, Claire had written how she didn't experience his unconditional love for her. Maybe Sandy felt that as well. And, in fact, he had rejected her out of fear of how she might react to sexual intimacy, a fear intensified by the accusations of a convicted rapist coming out of a bar. By the end of the evening, Torman had hammered himself to exhaustion.

Sandy had stripped her bed of its sheets, which lay neatly

folded in the guest bedroom. Torman re-made the bed with them rather than putting them in the washer. He slept in her bed for a week, wanting to be engulfed by her smell even as he derided himself for his childishness.

A week after she'd left, he walked in darkness on her street. Cloud cover masked the moon and stars. He knew she'd likely fled Bisbee, but he didn't want to risk being seen trying to spy on her against her wishes. Glancing down the stairway leading to her house, he could barely make out its outline. No lights or sign of her car. The realtor's for sale sign, near the top of the stairs, dashed any fantasies he had that she might be re-considering her decision. Where had she gone? And then the realization that the where didn't matter. She was gone.

PART THREE

ARIZONA 2016

Stuart Craven's outstretched arm preceded him through Torman's office door. A vigorous shake, then, "So, Steve, how's it going?"

"Just fine, Stuart." Torman wondered what occasioned this visit from the clinic's hand-shaking administrative director and decided to wait in silence, observing Stuart's glancing around the cramped office.

"Well, I hope you know how much we appreciate your work here, Steve. And your happiness is our primary concern. I've been wondering if you'd like a bigger office, a corner office with a good view. We're re-organizing our space here and...I thought of you."

"That's very considerate of you, Stuart, but, really, this is fine, I've gotten quite comfortable here." Hands cradling the back of his head, Torman tilted back in his chair and waited.

"Well, if you change your mind, just let me know. As I said, we want you to know how valued you are here. Anything you want, just ask me and I'll see what I can do. I wish we could offer you more money, but you know how limited our budget is."

"Thanks, I'll let you know if I come up with something."

After the goodbye handshake, as Stuart moved towards the door, he looked back at Torman, remarking he'd heard he was opening a private practice in Sierra Vista. "Hope that doesn't mean you'll be leaving us."

So, it was Stuart's fear that he would abandon the clinic like all the previous psychiatrists had. "No need to worry, Stuart. I've got no plans to leave here."

Torman was surprised that Stuart knew of his intention to open a private practice. It wasn't something he'd broadcasted, but it just shows how small a world he lived in.

In the ten minutes before his next patient, Torman looked up his initial note on Sandy. Like all his notes of first appointments, this one began with the so-called identifying data: "The patient is a 28 year old, white, single female with a diagnosis of bipolar disorder." The next section described the history of the present illness. Other sections followed. What was missing in all this was Sandy. Instead of a detailed portrait, he'd drawn a stick figure. It made him miss her all the more. There was hardly anything left of her. Her goodbye note, his memories.

He accompanied Marsha Donald to his office, unaware of the sadness lingering on his face. "Something the matter, Dr. Torman?" she asked, sitting across from him. He liked Marsha, a woman in her mid-sixties who'd presented as a disheveled, delusional, mumbling patient and had gradually transformed into a sensitive, thoughtful soul who used the little money left over from her disability check to buy the Sunday Times. They occasionally talked about articles they'd read, sharing their thoughts about them. Now she was looking directly at his face.

"Well, not really...just thinking about someone I miss."

"Girlfriend trouble?"

"Kind of..." He looked away, aware he felt like talking about Sandy but feeling, at the same time, how inappropriate that would be.

"I've never spoken of this, but many years ago, when I was in my late teens, I fell in love with a cousin. Peter was a few years older than me, already enrolled in an out-of-state college. Very handsome and kind. He had a great smile and made me laugh. At some point, I realized he was interested in me as a woman. I fell hard. I couldn't stop thinking about him. Our courtship, if you could call it that, consisted of letters we sent each other. Of course, I kept his. My mother found them and read them. She and my dad confronted me about the relationship and demanded that I stop writing him. They told me it was incest to have relations with a cousin and warned me that any child I had with him would be deformed and retarded. I was devastated. I never got over that young man. I had some relationships over the years but never felt the way I did for Peter."

"Did you confide your feelings at the time to anyone?"

"No, I was too ashamed, too fearful I'd be seen as deviant, as sick. I kept those letters, though. Hid them where no one could find them. I remember reading "The Dead" in my senior year of high school English. Do you know that story?"

"By Joyce, right?" She nodded yes, and Torman said, "It's been a long time...I remember how moving the ending was... something about snow falling all over Ireland..."

Marsha quoted the entire last paragraph. Neither spoke for a while after she stopped. Marsha was thinking about Gretta, the woman in the story who'd loved and lost the young Michael Furey, while Torman's thoughts drifted to his own sadness over Sandy's disappearance. Finally, Marsha said, "I was supposed to write an essay on the story but couldn't. I asked the teacher, Miss Engel, if I could read something else to write about and, thankfully, she allowed me to do that. I think she sensed something was going on with me, but she didn't ask and I didn't explain. Maybe I should have written a paper on "The Dead." Maybe that would have been therapeutic for me, like talking with you is."

Now Torman felt like Marsha had as a high school senior, unable to express his own sadness. He felt a closeness to Marsha at that moment, something like love. Their eyes met, and this time Torman didn't look away.

"You're a nice young man, Dr. Torman. You've got so much of your life in front of you. You get to my age, there's not much time in front of you anymore, just a lot of time gone by."

"I'm not that young, Marsha. My next birthday I'll be 40."

"Well, it's the half-way point, I guess you could say. Still a lot of living and loving left."

After Marsha left the office, Torman, stunned by their conversation, marveled at how Marsha had somehow intuited his experience of losing someone he loved and managed to empathize so fully by sharing with him the loss of her first, and deepest, romance in her life. In spite of his saying so little, a bridge of understanding connected them. Just two people a few feet apart, no longer separated by the roles of doctor and patient. He understood, for the first time, how he needed to find ways to do this not just with his patients but also with those he cared about in the rest of his life. Sandy tried telling him this, but he'd only half heard her. He recalled Sandy's observation after they'd watched the movie "Cinema Paradisio": that he kept a distance between himself and life. His session with Marsha reinforced and intensified his belief that he was ready to move closer to life, to the world and the people around him.

Losing Sandy stripped away a protective layer, leaving him easily pained but also more receptive to feeling others' pain. He'd begun to believe in his ability to be more empathic with his patients' unhappiness and better able to engage them in treatment, more willing, really, to engage them. He felt less inclined to hide behind the psychoanalytic veil of "neutrality." He had no desire to sit out of sight of patients lying supine on the couch. He planned on being in full view, eye patch and all. That's what led to his decision to open a private practice. Now his experience with Marsha revealed how moving therapeutic encounters can be and how they move not only the patient but also the therapist.

When Torman told Anna about his decision to open a therapy practice, she welcomed the news, clearly relieved to see Torman show some sign of emerging from his sadness.

Aaron, now 6 months old, was an active, bright-eyed baby who let Torman hold him for a few minutes before wanting the arms and smell and smile of his mother. Val snorted when Torman mentioned opening a private practice, saying, "What, the blind leading the blind?"

"Val, you forget. I'm the one-eyed man in the land of the blind. I'm king."

"King, my ass. One-eyed, I'll grant you."

Torman knew Val had held back teasing him after Sandy's departure, so her launching into her typical banter felt like an acknowledgement that he'd begun to return to some semblance of normal, whatever normal was for him. "You guys invited to Eric and Susan's wedding?"

"Of course. You?" Val asked.

"Yes, me. If you're nice, I'll sit with you."

Torman wasn't surprised to learn of their wedding plans. Eric and Susan's finding a way back to each other pleased him. What he tried not to feel was envy. Later, driving back to Bisbee, his thoughts turned to another couple. A few weeks ago, Jerry, near the end of a session, mentioned doing some repairs at a local halfway home for abused women. He'd described how he tried to persuade the manager of the home to invest in a good security system for the women and the children who stayed with them.

"Doc, this guy just kept repeating how they didn't have the funds, how they'd never had an incident, and I told him it just takes one maniac to inflict all kinds of injury on those women and kids. These are battered women who've escaped from really brutal men, some involved with Mexican drug cartels, with organized crime, with rogue law enforcement officials..."

Torman anticipated a long rant about the evils likely to be visited upon these poor souls and began wondering how he'd ever get the session to end. To Torman's surprise, Jerry, after pausing to take a breath, changed course. "And one of those women, a young Mexican with a 2 year old son, looked so scared, I just couldn't stand it. I started to talk with her and invited her and her son to live with me. Her boyfriend had threatened to kill her and her son if she complained to anyone about how he kicked her around. I told her she'd be safe with me. Her name's Maria."

"So, she took you up on your offer?"

"Yeah, I'm worried now you think I'm really crazy." Jerry glanced around the room as if the authorities, listening to all of this, were poised to break down the door and arrest him.

"Jerry, I don't think you're crazy. I want to hear all about your relationship with Maria and her son. This is a really big step for you to take."

"I know she's a good person. I could tell just by watching her, seeing how she handled Juan, her son. And I feel a hundred times better than I've ever felt." With that, his face lit up in a wide smile, which elicited one from Torman.

"Well, it's great to see you so happy. This gives us a lot to talk about…how about we meet sooner than usual?"

Driving home to Bisbee, Torman enjoyed the prospect of Jerry finding someone to share his life with. He'd listen carefully to Jerry's description of Maria and hope that he hadn't found one of those women who gravitate to abusive men, who was likely to return to her former boyfriend. He imagined Jerry wanting to bring Maria and her son to meet him and realized he looked forward to meeting them, to seeing how the three of them got along. At the same time, Torman didn't want to get his hopes up too high. Still, whatever the outcome, this was progress.

The wedding was at Eric's (and now Susan's) home. They'd decided on a brief ceremony conducted by an acquaintance of Eric who happened to be a licensed minister. Eric's cousins, their spouses and children, two aunts, and an uncle attended, while Susan's parents represented her family. Eric invited a few friends he'd made at the newspaper, including his editor. Susan had made a couple of friends in Tucson's art world, so they were invited. Torman, Anna and Val filled out the roster of invitees.

The ceremony was mercifully brief. Torman thought back to his own wedding, which had dragged on due to the rabbi's apparent need to put on quite a show. Neither Claire nor Torman knew much about the rabbi except for his willingness to perform the ceremony outside of a temple for two non-observant Jews. They'd speculated that his long-windedness was either an effort to bring them back to the fold or meant to torture them for their apostasy. There were no religious trappings to Eric and Susan's ceremony. Just some familiar lines about the sanctity of marriage, tucked between attempts at marital humor, followed by the usual vows accompanying the exchange of rings. However, at the ceremony's conclusion, right after the first kiss of the marriage, one of Eric's cousins managed to slip a wine glass covered in cloth near Eric's foot, which Eric dutifully crushed to the cheers of "mazel tov" from the groom's relatives. Susan laughed, while her parents looked puzzled. For some reason, Torman enjoyed this unscripted act, perhaps for its insistence that there were Jews in this room celebrating the marriage of one of their own.

After the vows, everyone sat at makeshift tables as a catering crew served food. Torman got stuck next to Jim, Susan's father, who proceeded to inform him of all his accomplishments. A good-looking man in his early 60's, he had the well-preserved look a successful executive, resembling, Torman thought, Mitt Romney. Torman listened as he spoke of his far-flung travels for work early in his career, of his rise in the company.

"We've made significant advances in the Far East market. That required a lot of strategic planning, but we paved the way for other businesses wanting to enter those markets." Torman figured "we" was meant to convey Jim's modesty. At one point, Jim leaned closer to Torman, saying, "Susan's first husband was a real catch...never understood why she left him. He's making his way at P&G."

Torman looked Jim in the eye. "I know Eric," Torman said, "and if you get to know him, you'll understand that *he's* a real catch." He wasn't sure what impact that had on Jim, but he felt it brushed him back. Meanwhile, Torman noticed Jim's wife, Marianne, steadily consuming wine at the table and maintaining a fixed smile on her face. Torman figured it was a blessing that Jim and Marianne lived so far away from their daughter and son-in-law.

After the cutting and consuming of the wedding cake, the catering staff cleared away the remnants of the meal, as well as the tables and chairs. The open space served as a dance floor, while a computer programmed with a playlist and enhanced by an amplifier provided the music. Eric and Susan took to the floor for the first dance. For the second, Susan danced with her father, while Eric tried to get Marianne off the couch but was waved away by her free hand, the other clutching her wine glass. Probably a good thing she didn't try to dance, Torman thought. Eric found a willing dance partner, the music playlist picked up the pace, and other guests merged onto the dance floor. Torman held back, never one to feel comfortable dancing, and headed to the quieter back yard patio.

Anna and Val were sitting close together under a pergola. Aaron was attached to Anna's breast, sucking on and off, eyes half-closed, a picture, in Torman's mind, of utter contentment.

Hesitant about intruding on this quiet domestic scene, Torman, audibly sighing, sat off by the side. "Steve," Anna asked, "is it hard watching Eric and Susan being so happy?"

"Well, not as hard as I'd pictured it might be. In a way, seeing them together, I feel like a proud parent."

Anna announced she was going home to get Aaron settled in bed for the night. She urged Val to stay, gave her a kiss, waved goodnight to Torman with her free hand, and drifted inside to say goodnight to the bride and groom.

Val asked Torman why he wasn't inside dancing. "You really want to know?"

"Yeah, then I'll tell you why I'm not dancing."

Torman described the first dance he attended. It was in the school gymnasium. "I was in 6th grade. Parents were present, kind of chaperoning their kids. I'd gotten up the courage to ask a girl I'd had a crush on to dance. So we danced. And danced. I was quite excited, beside myself, totally in the moment and totally unselfconscious. I don't think I said more than two words to her. Afterwards, in the car going home, my mother remarked how 'intent and sweaty' I'd looked on the dance floor. The way she said it humiliated me. Whenever I dance, I see myself through my mother's eyes, and it stops me cold. So, what's your excuse?"

"I was overweight growing up. I got teased a lot at school. In junior high, I knew I was attracted to girls. I never told anyone. At dances, girls often danced with each other, especially since the boys were so bashful. I remember dancing with a girl who was overweight like me. We were both misfits. A group of boys, lined up against the wall, began making cracks about us. "'Dancing hippos,' 'Oink, oink,' 'Feed time!' At first, I tried to ignore them. That just egged them on. The taunting got louder. I never went to another dance."

They sat for a while in silence, which Torman broke. "I think it's time we put our pasts behind us. Let's go in there and dance."

As Torman entered the house, he saw Jim dancing with one of Susan's attractive friends, while Marianne appeared passed out on the couch. Just then, the music changed to a conga line beat, with Eric and Susan taking the lead in forming a conga line. Torman, hands on Val's waist, followed her as she entered the line. Susan led them through the house and out to the back yard, where they circled around the pergola, then back into the living room. After completing a number of revolutions around the living room, all linked together in a chain, the music ended to cheers from the dancers.

After a short break, the music resumed with a Motown mix. Torman and Val danced mostly with each other, occasionally taking a different partner. Torman decided not to think but to concentrate solely on the music. Finally, late in the night, he and Val returned to the back yard.

"You dance better than you swim," Val said.

"I think we make a very attractive couple."

After a silence, Val asked, "So, you still think about Sandy?"

"Yeah, I do. I keep hoping I'll hear from her or that she'll appear at my front door some day. I wish I could go back in time and stop myself from rejecting her. Maybe she wouldn't have ended up in the hospital, and our closeness wouldn't have felt like such a threat to her stability. But I can't go back. And, anyway, I'm not sure that would have made any difference. She wrote in her goodbye note that she couldn't tolerate all the 'goodness' I represented, that she feared intimacy would propel her into a manic state. I don't know...I just wish I'd somehow tried harder, hadn't been so fearful, so caught up in my own world and worries."

"What's that line about trying, failing, trying again?"

"'Try again. Fail again. Fail better.' Somehow that falls short for me. I'm tired of failing."

The celebration was coming to an end. Goodbyes were said, hugs exchanged. Torman spoke briefly with Eric and Susan, expressing his pleasure in seeing them as a couple and saying he hoped to maintain contact with them. He hugged each of them. As he and Val walked to his car, Torman wondered what the future held for the newlyweds. That led to his wondering what the future held for him. He recalled Marsha saying he was at the half-way point. A lot of living and loving left. He hoped that was true.

"I just remembered part of a dream from this morning," Torman said. "I was going to a wedding, and I was looking through a closet to find something to wear. There were a number of suits, none of which appealed to me. In the back of the closet I discovered a sand colored suit and tried it on. I liked it but something didn't seem right, as if it weren't the right color for a wedding. Obviously the dream was triggered by anticipating today's wedding. The sand colored suit is a reference to Sandy, and my attraction to her. Also to my lingering feeling that others wouldn't find our relationship acceptable, that there could be legal dangers in pursuing a sand colored 'suit.'"

"Steve, you really put much stock in dreams?"

"I do. I'm a firm believer dreams contain truths we only half-know, or don't know at all, in our waking moments."

"I don't know...seems like a stretch to link a sand colored suit to Sandy."

"It's surprising, even amusing at times, to see how dreams work. I remember an analyst named Carrier talking about a patient of his who repeatedly dreamed of air conditioners blowing cold air. And another named Hall whose patients frequently dreamed of halls and hallways. You can laugh, but I believe such images in dreams have significance beyond their literal meanings."

"Well, I can certainly understand being drawn to Sandy. She's a real knock-out."

"She had a lot going for her. I'm certain of that. I don't believe I was simply enthralled by her attractiveness. She was smart and thoughtful. I felt more alive in her presence. And I believe she really loved me."

They arrived at Anna and Val's house. Except for an outdoor light by the entrance, the house was dark. Quietly, Val unlocked the door, and they made their way in the dark to the living room. Baba got off the couch, wagging his tail. Whispering, Torman told Val goodnight. "I'm going to take Baba for a short walk. We'll have to go dancing again." She gave him a hug.

As Torman walked Baba, images from the wedding filled his mind: Eric and Susan's wedding kiss, Susan's father awakening her mother from her alcoholic stupor with a surprising tenderness, Anna breastfeeding Aaron, his holding on to Val as they merged with the conga line. Couples joined. Torman resisted the idea that he was not whole unless connected to someone. At the same time, he knew that a career, no matter how rewarding, was not enough. Nor were friends, no matter how close. He played over in his mind his movie date with Sandy at the Bisbee Royale and their second goodnight kiss at her door, the one worthy of the movies. If only he could go back to that moment. If only. So many lives were filled with such regrets, reminding Torman of all the kissing scenes spliced from all those movies in "Cinema Paradiso."

Torman looked down at Baba and said, "Well, Baba, it's just you and me." Hearing his name, Baba glanced up at Torman, then picked up the pace as they headed back to the house.

Torman drove back to Bisbee the following afternoon. The sun lit up the front passenger seat, providing a pleasantly warm nest for Baba, who rode shotgun beside Torman. His thoughts drifted, going from the wedding to Anna and Val, to the vastness of the land he passed through, to Sandy and wondering where she was and how she was doing. He slowed down as he approached the town of Tombstone, with its tawdry tourist attractions and its desperate effort to avoid blowing away like tumbleweed into obscurity. He always wondered how people managed to survive in such moribund places. Even Bisbee lurched along, managing to survive as the county seat yet barely able to sustain its budget for necessary services. Sierra Vista would have dwindled like the other nearby towns if it didn't have the US Army base at Fort Huachuca.

Once home, Torman took Baba on a quick walk, then unpacked his overnight bag and sat down at his computer to check his email. The message from Claire grabbed his immediate attention. He'd had no communication with her since their final court hearing.

Steve, I have some very surprising news for you. Paul and I are in the process of getting divorced—a long story in itself—and he recently insisted on checking our son David's paternity. I had never questioned this and was shocked to learn that Paul is not the father. Which means, of course, that you are. I know this will be a shock to you, though I imagine not an unwelcome one. When you've absorbed this news, please call me so we can talk about how to bring you into David's life. I'm attaching a photo of him. I await your call. Claire

Torman stared at the image of his son, whose wind-swept hair, blue eyes, dimpled cheeks, and buoyant smile suggested a very happy little guy. He appeared to be balancing on a playground's teeter-totter and was holding aloft a good-sized branch. His son. Torman felt giddy. He printed the photo, making multiple copies. His hands shook as he held up the photograph.

He wanted to call Claire but held off to give himself time to think about what he'd just learned. He kept thinking how lucky he was, how much fuller—and more complicated—his life now felt. He wanted to share the news, yet told himself to let this new reality sink in before speaking to Anna, Val, and his parents.

Too excited to eat, Torman skipped dinner. He looked around the home he'd grown to love and realized he'd soon be leaving Bisbee to resettle in Cincinnati so he could be near his son. Questions without answers flooded his mind: What would he say to David? How would David feel about his sudden appearance in his life? When would he be called "Dad"? What role would Paul play in David's life? What will it be like to resume contact with Claire? He tried searching himself for feelings he'd buried towards Claire. Knowing they shared a child, at least on a biological level, made him feel a tenderness for her. Though sadness shrouded his memory of Sandy, he knew his heart still remained attached to her.

That evening, Baba needed a walk, and so did Torman. The desert air, cool in the darkness, shifted Torman's thoughts back to his immediate surroundings, to his familiar route through his neighborhood. He buttoned the top button of his shirt and gave Baba's leash a gentle tug to speed up their walk. Stars glittered in the black, cloudless sky. Looking up, he recognized the belt and sword of the hunter Orion, then found the big dipper and Polaris, the North Star. Years ago, his father taught him to use the North Star to orient himself if he got lost at night. The celestial vastness made him feel small, but not alone and not lost. He was at the halfway point. Plenty of time left. Even a one-eyed man can still see in the night. That's what he told himself as he turned back and headed home.

End

Robert Schulman

Acknowledgements

First, I want to thank the readers of my early drafts, especially those who offered comments and suggestions. You know who you are. I owe special thanks to Bea Larsen, who motivated me to start a blog and edited my early pieces. Her encouragement helped pave the way for me to take on the challenge of writing a novel. Bill Dubner provided editorial guidance, which improved the flow of the story, corrected various mistakes, and offered ideas to make for a richer tale. Lastly, I must mention again Sherry Davis, to whom I dedicated this novel. She read numerous drafts and offered honest assessments, all without complaint.

Made in the USA
Middletown, DE
24 January 2022

59522294R10163